silence is
a sense

LAYLA ALAMMAR is a writer and academic from Kuwait. She has a Masters in Creative Writing from the University of Edinburgh. Her short stories have appeared in the *Evening Standard*, *Quail Bell*, *The Red Letters St Andrew's Prose Journal*, and *Aesthetica* where she was a finalist for the Creative Writing Award 2014. She was 2018 British Council International Writer in Residence at the Small Wonder Short Story Festival. Her debut novel, *The Pact We Made*, was published in 2019 and longlisted for the Authors' Club Best First Novel Award. She has written for *The Guardian* and *ArabLit Quarterly*. She is currently pursuing a PhD on the intersection of Arab women's fiction and literary trauma theory.

@laylaalammar_author
@Layla_AlAmmar

Also by Layla AlAmmar

The Pact We Made

Praise for *The Pact We Made*:

'[A] fascinating glimpse into the complex and contradictory life of a modern Kuwaiti woman . . . full of personality and touches of humour'   *Guardian*

'So beautifully written and so important, and so cleverly crafted, it can't be a debut. But it is'   Joanna Cannon

'*The Pact We Made* deals with one woman's search for independence'   *ELLE*

'A Kuwaiti #MeToo novel of muffled suffering and a bid for freedom – absorbing, brave and compelling'   Leila Aboulela

'Brilliant book about the pressures of being a 30-year-old unmarried woman in Kuwait – the struggle for modernity amidst patriarchal tradition – and the cultural failure to acknowledge trauma. What a debut'   Pandora Sykes

'Fascinating, nuanced and understanding'   *Observer*

'Truthful and courageous, radical and lyrical. I loved it'   Hanan Al-Shaykh

'One of those books you ration so it doesn't end too soon, it's beautifully written and unbelievably powerful. I loved it'   Katie Lowe, author of *The Furies*

'Kuwaiti writer Layla AlAmmar's debut is, on the surface, the story of a woman about to turn 30 and under pressure to find a husband. But it's a layered exploration of Kuwaiti society and culture as well. And it's a look at grief, trauma and the expectations placed upon young women that will resonate with women across the world'

Sarah Shaffi, *Phoenix*

'A timely and deeply affecting debut with a voice that needs to be heard, at a time when it matters most'

Charlotte Philby, author of *Part of the Family*

'Set in contemporary Kuwait, AlAmmar asks us to reimagine the lives of modern Muslims as they struggle to reconcile the freedom of choice with the customs of their faith'   BBC Radio 3, Free Thinking

'A complex novel championing feminism in the Arab world'

The National

'*The Pact We Made* is a book about marriage, but it would be a mistake to think that it is a conventional love story. Instead, it's a book about familial and cultural expectations, the lingering effects of trauma, and healing and loving yourself again. Also resistant to easy judgement is Dahlia, who is a complex character, unsure of how to navigate a life and roles that have been thrust upon her. But it's no coincidence that she is named after a flower, something that is so easily damaged but that, with some care and attention, the right kind of light and tenderness, can be restored to something newer and stronger . . . In Dahlia and *The Pact We Made*, AlAmmar has created something strong and lasting, a book about a woman battling to exist on her own terms in a world which wants women to stay quiet. Dahlia and AlAmmar are making their voices heard, and that's a great thing'

The New Arab

silence is
a sense

Layla AlAmmar

THE BOROUGH PRESS

The Borough Press
An imprint of HarperCollins*Publishers* Ltd
1 London Bridge Street
London SE1 9GF

www.harpercollins.co.uk

HarperCollins*Publishers*
1st Floor, Watermarque Building,
Ringsend Road,
Dublin 4 Ireland

Published by HarperCollins*Publishers* 2021

1

A catalogue record for this book is available from the British Library

The quotation from Abu'l-'Ala al-Ma'arri appears in Amin Maalouf's
The Crusades Through Arab Eyes (Saqi Books 2006), and is reproduced with permission
of Westbourne Publishers Ltd through PLSclear.

The quotation from the poem 'Fifty April Years' by Khaled Mattawa is reprinted
with kind permission from the author.

HB ISBN: 978-0-00-834665-2

This novel is entirely a work of fiction.
The names, characters and incidents portrayed in it are
the work of the author's imagination. Any resemblance to
actual persons, living or dead, events or localities is
entirely coincidental.

Set in Adobe Garamond by Palimpsest Book Production Limited, Falkirk, Stirlingshire

Printed and bound in the UK by CPI Group (UK) Ltd, Croydon CR0 4YY

MIX
Paper from
responsible sources
FSC **FSC™ C007454**
www.fsc.org

'Fate smashes us as though we were made of glass,
and never are our shards put together again.'

Abu'l-'Ala al-Ma'arri

'When the soul of a man is born in this country there are nets
flung at it to hold it back from flight. You talk to me of
nationality, language, religion. I shall try to fly by those nets.'

James Joyce

'as if the world had stopped calling,
as if we had emerged
from the whirlpool of its demands
with a wild mixture of cowardice
and courage to say unto others
"I wish you did not exist."'

Khaled Mattawa

1

No-Lights-Man

East Tower, third floor, flat two hardly ever turns on the lights, especially come summer when the sun lingers in the sky and daylight is a lazy loiterer, barely giving way to night before it's back. He changes his clothes, drinks his soft drinks and ciders, and melts cheese on toast, all without the lights on. He watches the rain, watches television, labours over large and small pads of paper, masturbates beneath navy and grey sheets. He talks on the phone, puts away his crisps and Pot Noodles, does the washing-up – all in the diffuse evenings of summer.

He doesn't speak to me, has never even tried. Not when we overlap in the laundry room down the block that everyone in the estate uses, not at the corner shop, not at the café where he gets iced-coffee drinks and outrageously priced salad bowls and I salivate over the homemade ice-cream without ever buying any. He'll give a half-smile and nod from the window, shirtless or brazenly naked, scratching himself awake in the morning. But he doesn't speak, barely even looks. I like that he doesn't speak to me. It's safer that way.

He fusses around his flat for hours at a time, burning off what seems to me to be a manic kind of energy. His room isn't messy, but it is lived in, with clothes and shoes and towels strewn about and the bed hardly ever made. I never make my bed either, so I don't judge him for this. He moves things around a lot, taking a bag from one cupboard and putting it in another, moving furniture around in overlapping patterns, shifting shoe boxes from one room to the other, like he's always in the process of moving in or moving out. Unsettled, as though he can never get the shape of his world quite right. He'll line items up beside the door, only to move them back into the bedroom a few days later.

There's a box under his bed. Large and brown, he pulls it out once a day. Sitting on the floor, he drags it towards him, lifts the lid, rummages around for a bit. He pulls items out and returns them, then pushes it back in place. I don't know what's in the box. At times I amuse myself with guesses. His narrow back and bony shoulders are all I ever see, so sometimes I imagine there's makeup in there and he's doing up his face in secret. I imagine thick black liner around his eyes, and shimmery shadow on the lids, and ruby red lips and cheeks, and him admiring himself in a small handheld mirror that I can't see. Sometimes I think perhaps it contains mementoes from past relationships – cinema and concert ticket stubs, bottles of perfume left behind that he spritzes on the inside of his wrist so he can smell like her all day, or maybe a T-shirt or pair of knickers that he might sniff in the quiet of a late night. Sometimes I think maybe it's a beloved pet, stuffed and secreted in the box, so he never has to let it go. I have fun with it, but the truth is I just don't know.

I have a box too. In my head. It's where I keep the things that are too much, the things that don't make sense. Images and sounds and smells and textures languish in boxes, stuffed and secreted, stacked up in a room in my mind. They fill the corners, rise higher and higher, box over box, to the ceiling. At times, the room bulges and heaves like a belly in labour. Sharp edges poke at my mind. It's hardly ever quiet in there.

In the living room, there's an old, battered trunk he uses as a coffee table. This is where he rolls joints, pulling green fluff from a plastic bag and mixing in tobacco from a large envelope. He lines the mixture up carefully in the fold of paper, rolling and rolling, then licking to seal and pinching up the end. He smokes on the balcony. Legs dangling through the cold steel and iron bars, he watches the sky or the stars or perhaps the people in my tower and smokes. He'll chase the joints with swigs of beer and a chain of ordinary cigarettes, and sometimes I'll be lying in bed at night and all I see over there is the flick of a lighter or an orange tip burning against the darkness, and I don't feel so alone.

He turns the lights on when he has a girl over. Girls get nervous if you keep them in the dark for too long. When he's entertaining one, the flat's lit up like Christmas – bright overheads, soft lamps on side tables, those little fake candles that are popular with restaurants and cafés because it means they can charge you another pound or two for your pasta or mixed salad.

I imagine those are the kinds of restaurants he takes his girls to, places with flattering lighting and house wine so good she wouldn't think him cheap for ordering it, and names like *Piccola Cucina* and *Cucina Vittoria* where he can impress her by saying *Cucina* means "kitchen" in Italian, and that means the place is rustic.

2

The Dad

South Tower A, second floor, flat three. The Dad always forgets his card like he's nostalgic for a time when doors were opened with actual keys and he can't acclimatize to this new reality he's found himself in. My building doesn't work that way – it's older, not part of the renovated ones springing up around the area – but still it's the one thing about him that I can relate to. He'll call the kids, usually on the phone, or just using his voice if it's a Friday night and he's pissed. 'Matt! Chloe!!' he'll shout, trying one name then the other until one of them slides open the balcony door. Their buzzer must not work because he tells them to throw their card down. Usually it's the boy, Matt, who does it. A gangly blond thing who doesn't look at all like his father, he leans over, whips his arm once, twice, and once more before releasing.

The card flits and drifts down. Sometimes it lands right at his feet so that the Dad raises a thumbs-up into the air before bending to retrieve it. Sometimes it flutters around his head and he grabs for it like a child chasing butterflies. Sometimes it lands in the thick hedges that line the courtyard, and he lets out a string of swear words trying to get it out.

There are times, when he's down there swearing, so his shits and fucks rise up into the air, that No-Lights-Man will be on his balcony smoking and he'll roll his eyes at me before either going back inside and sliding the door shut or turning his record player up louder to drown it out. The Dad swears for a long time. Even when he gets up to the flat, his voice travels out of their window and into mine, with him yelling about this fucking building and how he doesn't want to add the card to his wallet with his bank and ID cards because that's not where a key belongs, Helen, and why did you insist on this fucking place that's got its head up its own arse.

The kids' mum is, by contrast, quiet and little. I don't know that I've ever heard her voice. Perhaps she's like me. She's a mouse of a woman, small and unassuming, with thin brown hair and big blue cartoon eyes. She keeps her head down when she walks, shoulders slightly curved as though frozen in the act of hugging herself. She scurries places – quick steps to the corner shop or across the road, shifting restlessly at the lifts or pedestrian crossings like she's late for an appointment or like someone's watching her.

Sometimes there are handprints on her, purple finger marks around her arm or a thumbprint at her collarbone, and if she catches me looking, she pulls the neck of her jumper tighter or pushes the sleeves down over her hands, and I pretend not to see and try to convince myself it's okay that I do.

He, the Dad, hates that I watch from the windows. When our eyes meet, when he's at his own window or on the sofa or pulling shirts from the wire tree rack in their living room, he'll shake his head and make a sort of 'What?' gesture, hairy chin jerking forwards in defiance. It's like he owns the whole bloody estate. There's a holiday let in their building, on the third floor, flat two. Hardly anyone rents it, and I don't know if it's because the owner has stopped putting it up, or if it's because the place is shit. From my window I see exposed wires dangling from the ceiling and stains on the pale blue armchair and lines of grimy booze bottles against the window that shimmer when the sun hits them a certain way. A few months ago a couple did stay there though, two Americans, weighed down with hiking packs and duffel bags and a large suitcase with a tag that read KTM. They had the door propped open as they were moving their stuff in, and the Dad was stuck outside while they pushed and pulled at all their crap. He just stood there, a fierce scowl on his ugly face, nose bright red. He didn't hold open the door or offer to help or say hello. He just stood there, hands on hips, grumbling and scowling until they made way for him.

He's the sort who will take your still-damp clothes out of the dryer and dump them on the floor because he thinks his load's more important.

3

The Old Couple

West Tower, fourth floor, flat four. My neighbours are an old couple whose last name I've not bothered to learn. It's Eastern European, I think; maybe Jewish. He, Tom, looks like he was sturdy once, but now lists sideways when he shuffles down the hall. He's always meticulously dressed, in crisp white or beige button-down shirts and heavy blazers with straight-pressed trousers and shiny brown shoes. With him I get the sense that his impeccable presentation, the fact that he's always so clean, is a kind of defence mechanism, a guard against people who might tell him he doesn't belong, to go back to where he came from. It brings to mind the way a homeless man, should he manage to wrangle change for the bus, will then behave faultlessly so as not to be removed. There is a dark spot on Tom's large nose that never goes away, and the middle finger of his right hand stops at the second knuckle.

He was in a war, but I'm not sure which one. That doesn't really make him special; point to any man his age, and it's a fair bet he's been in a war. It's the younger ones you can never tell with – the guy in the shop holding himself a little too rigidly as he looks over the bread shelves; the young mother whose eyes are constantly scanning the street as she waits for the bus; the little girl who startles too easily or the boy with no expression on his face.

My neighbours keep their windows open most of the time – strange for old people, even in the summer. Back home, my grandmother was in a perpetual state of near-freezing. Even in the sweltering days of July, she would be wrapped in thick shawls and woollen cardigans. In January, she sat practically *in* the furnace we used for heating tea and milk. Baba would shout at her to move away like she was his sixth child rather than his mother, shaking his head when she refused and muttering about the stubbornness of the elderly.

Tom is quiet, but she yells a lot, whether it's at people on the phone, or him, or the television. She likes game shows, and I'll hear her call out, '*The Witching Hour*', or 'It's *South of the Border*, Yutzi!' The television's on all the time, the volume up high. It fills the space where conversation used to go, I suppose. I don't hear them talk much; mostly it's just ads for life insurance or cleaning products.

Day in and day out, their life, like mine, is unchanging. The sounds of tea and toast in the morning, the greeting of the television switching on to the news, grumbling from Tom about the weather – or at least that's what I imagine old men grumble about. By noon, she's wondering whether they should go to the shop, but they never actually leave before two or so. Then, hours and hours of game shows. Dinner is the banging of saucers and pots that jangles my nerves so that I have to put on headphones to combat it. If it's a very bad night, the earplugs go in, and I toss, sweating and trembling, beneath the covers or abandon my flat entirely and go down to the courtyard to sit in the cold evening air. Eventually, the night is gone, and it starts all over again.

She's a frail one – Ruth, his wife. Like a bird, with arms like twigs and twitchy eyes that miss nothing. I don't like her. She seems always to be judging things. When we're in the lift she looks me up and down as though searching for anomalies, something that's different to how it was the day before. It makes me nervous, this scrutiny of hers. I can't think what she's looking for, or in what way she finds me wanting. She mumbles to Tom about it – when I'm next to them at the mailboxes or passing in the aisle at Hasan's in between their complaints about their aching joints or the weather or how the cut grass in the courtyard irritates them. She'll say things like, 'There's the strange one,' and he'll reply with, 'Why is she strange?' and she'll say, 'Well, even her kind should have friends.'

The thing is, when you can't speak, people assume you can't hear either.

———————

I have terrible allergies, but I didn't discover them until I'd left. There's something about home that can inoculate you against such things. Your eyes don't tear up with the changing of the seasons, your nose doesn't betray you when the wind shifts and the pollen count ratchets up, your skin doesn't react to the scratching of summer dust or the suffocating seals of its humidity.

It was when I was hiking through Hungary or camping out by train tracks in Greece that my body began attacking itself. It felt like ants were picking at my eyes, crawling into my throat and up my nose. My nostrils plugged themselves up in defence as though there were in fact insects attempting to burrow their way into my head and chew at my mind. There *were* insects enough there, worms and ants and spiders and beetles and flying things that buzzed around my ears, and in my dreams they did get in, everywhere. But in protecting themselves from these would-be invaders, my nostrils also waged war on oxygen, so that breathing became a chore and my chest tightened up in protest. The ache in my head was constant, and for all the things my nose refused to let in, there was no limit to what it was prepared to release. A T-shirt was relegated to the job of oversized handkerchief. I tried to keep it clean, but resources were scarce, and all I could manage was dipping it in the dirty river every few days and wrapping it around my head – tight, the way my grandmother used to do when her head ached – to dry.

My allergies persisted as we slipped through country after country and on through to France where for twenty-six days and nights I scratched my eyes so much, they did bleed. So dire was the situation that on day twenty-four or twenty-five, while little crabs scurried across the beach at Dunkirk, I briefly considered going back. Could I survive in England with my body at war with itself? Would my nose and eyes and throat eventually grow used to the new conditions I hoped they would find themselves in? How different could the climate there be, across that churning, frothy sea?

I would never go back, but I began to wonder if there was anywhere in the world that I belonged.

This city, here in the middle of this country, has made a liar of my history. It is as though I was born here, so complete has been my immune system's acceptance of the air and greenery and blossoms and bees. Those months of itches I couldn't reach and nosebleeds and impenetrable nostrils seem like a minor irritation and that night in Dunkirk has faded into the recesses of my mind along with all the other evenings when mad thoughts filled my head.

4

The Juicer

East Tower, fourth floor, flat three, right opposite me. The man there is a honeycomb, pale with yellow hair and eyebrows. In certain lights though, he could be Spanish or Italian; his face is cut like that: aquiline nose, high cheekbones. People look more alike than some would have us believe.

He's a health nut. Always juicing things – bloody beets, tangy bright lemons and massive grapefruits, long thick carrots and cucumbers. Sometimes he'll pop in a pear or apple but not often. And lots of kale and spinach, mounds of it. It's a wonder he isn't sweating green by now. I call him the Juicer. Not a very inventive name, but then I'm not an inventive person. Apart from the juice, which is breakfast every day, he grills various things for dinner – thick chicken breasts that he spends ages pounding down, or plump prawns he spends far too much time prepping. He has salmon at least three times a week, carefully folding thick strips of foil around the fish and lemon slices and dill.

His flat is sparsely decorated: a small sofa, hard and uninviting; a squat square coffee table; a thin white desk in the corner. He seems uneasy with comfort. My living room faces his bedroom. He sleeps on a firm-looking mattress, though he doesn't jump onto it every night like I still do mine, so it's anyone's guess how hard it is. There are no clothes lying about his room, no books stacked haphazardly in a corner, no shoes (or boxes) half under the bed. It is all order and precision. If I stand at a certain point at the window in my room, I can see straight through into his bathroom. It's only happened once, when he first moved in. Perfect timing that I was there at the moment he turned to reach for a bar of soap in the shower, before the water'd had a chance to steam everything up, and I saw all of him.

He has an extremely large member.

The Juicer goes to the fancy organic shop up the street. He wrinkles his nose when he passes Hasan's – the corner shop the rest of us go to at least once a day. The shop is actually called Maqbool. It means 'acceptable' in my language, which I find to be a rather defeatist sentiment, so in my head I call it by the proprietor's name.

It's a full-fat shop, stocking jars of thick, gloopy oils and tins of pure *ghee*, syrupy pre-packaged *baklava* and plump dates stuffed with nuts. The aisles overflow with imported crisps and packets of powdered soup and condensed milk and tea stamped in Turkish or Arabic or Urdu. The fridges to one side of the shop are stacked with bottles of juice and whole milk, creamy cheese spread like we had back home and sweaty, individually packed slices of American cheese. No goods fresh from the bakery for Hasan – only massive *naans* and paper-thin *saj* and heavy, sugary loaves and puff pastry creations that disintegrate the moment you touch them, all wrapped up in plastic.

Hasan is a small man who looks like he was tall once. Everything about him gleams, from his thick nose to his high forehead to the black hair lying in shiny strings across his crown. Mrs Old-Lady-From-Next-Door, Ruth, says that's how all Pakis are. I heard her explaining it to Tom as they looked over the jars of pickled things one day. 'They can't help it, dear,' she said in response to his grumble. 'He could bathe three or four times a day and be just as greasy. It's how their kind is made,' she added. Her husband seemed unconvinced, and whenever Hasan rings them up, Tom grips and pulls at his handkerchief as though fighting the urge to reach across the counter and wipe the man's face.

The Juicer's life is regimented. Up by five, he does his routine with the exercise set-up in the living room. Then juice – sometimes blood red, sometimes deep green, often brown. The big gym bag on his shoulder and out of the door by six. He's not back for twelve hours, then steamed salmon for dinner. I never see him drink, not even wine or a beer with dinner. I never see him smoke up like No-Lights-Man does either.

He doesn't have many vices. Though I believe he's bisexual, if that can be termed a vice. He has women, many women. He's fucked them all over the flat – on the hard, uninviting sofa; on the pale, hardwood floors; up against the walls or the exercise machine. I've seen heads thrown back in ecstasy, mouths open to the ceiling. I've seen them bent over the dining-room table where they don't need to mask their discomfort. I've seen blurry bodies in the shower, reaching and grasping.

But occasionally, not often, he'll have a man over. Never the same man twice, but they're all as fit as he is. If they ever stayed overnight, I imagine they'd happily share his juice breakfast. But they never stay. I don't see what happens with the men. The Juicer pulls the blinds closed. One time he looked directly at me, a grin on his arresting face as he jerked them shut.

I can only imagine he's on the bottom of such couplings. Like I said, his member is extremely large.

5

The Deceit of Memory

These are not the sort of observations my editor is interested in. Well, she's not my editor yet, Josie from the news magazine with the big name, but she says she might be if things go well. I sent her what I now know the industry terms a 'spec' piece, about the city through the eyes of a new immigrant. In her emails she assures me that such articles are always topical, and it's all people are wanting to read about given the state of the world, and could I tweak this and that before she publishes it. She's promised a very modest payment for what she calls my 'insider accounts', and I imagine it must be some sort of outreach or corporate social responsibility initiative for the magazine. I'll take it though; benefits only stretch so far and work opportunities are scarce when you can't (or *don't*, as Dr Thompson insisted) speak. She wants my views on things like 'assimilation', a term I didn't think they used, a concept I didn't think they expected, outside of America. She asks if I wear the *hijab* – as though that signifies something – and whether all my family made it out and how bad the fighting is. It feels like a test, as though the answers to such questions enhance my credibility, as though they might confirm that I am what I am and not some leftist, liberal populist in a mask. I don't answer such queries, or I answer them selectively, the way I'm selective with what observations do and don't go into the pieces I send her.

In a way it is about privacy. When you come from a place where the walls have ears and you spend your life hiding and fabricating, trying to learn the rules to games you have no hope of ever winning and searching for cracks from which to scurry out, your instinct is to hold certain matters close to the chest.

It's about self-preservation, that most basic of human instincts.

Everybody here wants a story: doctors looking over bruises and scrapes and boils that don't heal; officers asking to see papers, proof that you are authorized to be here; strangers on the street who think they recognize something in your face from home. They all want stories – how did you get here? How long did it take? How easy was it to process your papers? Do you know someone at the office they could speak to about their cousin or aunt? They want to hear about the hardship and the struggles and the people who died along the way. Josie wants it all. She doesn't come out and say it, but I know she means the harsher, the better. She wants a nice little packet of memories she can serialize for her readers. Even better would be memories tied up with those observations she's so fond of.

I don't know how to explain to her that I am cornered by memories, caged in by recollections. I feel persecuted by the things I remember and by what my mind chooses to hide from me.

Josie quoted de Maupassant to me in her last email, *'Our memory is a more perfect world than the universe: it gives back life to those who no longer exist.'* She can't have known what it would mean to me or how I would take it or maybe even how carefully one should choose their words when corresponding with a writer, but I doubt that when de Maupassant arrived at this pithiness he was thinking of a world such as the one I'd left behind. If he had, he would not have made a claim of perfection, either in the world or in the memories that supposedly preserved it.

The human need for stories is itself an obstacle to memory. Like our dreams, we are not content with images or scenes or fragments of sensory stimuli – the hint of melon dew we smell, or the blood pouring from our eyes and ears and mouths like river water trickling over smooth stone, or the pale horse with a mane like a greasy cloud streaking across a blue sky. We try to construct narratives – what happened before the blood came? What happened after I saw the horse? What does it *mean*? We try to place these elements within a structure that makes sense, wading back through fragments, trying to stitch it all together into a coherent pattern – a beginning, a middle, and an end. Something to cleave to, something to reassure us that everything is okay in that head of ours and that the monsters and ghouls and *jinn* that visit us in the night ARE NOT REAL.

My dreams are harsh forests, dark and eerie with hideousness: hands grab at my ankles, trying to pull me down into the earth where the dirt can fill me up with another kind of silence; things unseen rain down on me, sticky and metallic on the tongue; it is either very hot or very cold, nothing in between. I don't speak in dreams either, but I scream. A lot. Waking drenched in sweat and piss, I claw at my chest like there's something plastered there with hooks sunk into my ribs. It never leaves, just slithers under my bed waiting for another night to come.

But I was talking about memories, not dreams, though there are more than enough of those and the latter have a nasty habit of muddying the former.

There is a kind of deceit to memories, where you're never entirely sure something happened the way you remember. I read a book on forgetting, and it said most people can trace their first memory to the third or fourth year of their lives (Dostoevsky thinks you can remember things from when you're two), but I don't see how it's possible. I mean, you can say you remember something from then, but can you be absolutely sure it's your memory and not one you've claimed from stories you heard? I know many stories from my child-hood: my eldest brother, Firas, running away from home when he was sixteen and I was eight (the instinct to run away is deep in my family, I think). I believe I recall Mama's tears and Baba's fury and shame, but the story had been recounted in whispers so many times by relatives and neighbours and even strangers in cafés by the citadel that I can't be sure. There are memories born of repetition of certain acts: *Eid* rituals, the slaughtering of sheep and the hoarding of paltry sums of money that we thought were fortunes; breaking the fast and the neighbours who always sent over the most pungent stews; the hours at the public baths.

That's my first true memory, I think, though even that is not a true first, but an amalgamation of memories, the way I have a hard time believing Noah's flood happened as told, that the story isn't simply a compounding of countless, smaller floods that coalesced into an all-consuming myth designed to teach us something about hubris and submission.

Mama would take me and my siblings down to the *hammam* once or twice a month, lining us all up on a bench with orders not to move. She'd hand out sandwiches – pitta breads rolled up around creamy white cheese and drizzled in honey – to keep us occupied, then call us over one by one. She'd scrub us down with this harsh, rough bar of soap, scrubbing until our skin was red and threatened to split, hissing that we weren't clean enough yet when we protested. She'd trap us between her knees (Mama had the strongest knees in the world) and scrub our heads with her soaped-up hands until we were faint and entirely compliant. Only then would she declare us done, sending us outside with a towel and calling over the next one. This happened every couple of weeks, so I don't think I could pick out the first time she took me.

How much have I forgotten simply because it happened so often?

If you go to the baths often enough, you're not going to recall each trip. If you run off with your siblings every few months, you're not going to remember every smack and pinch you got for it. If bombs go off each day, you're not going to remember each one and who it killed.

It seems to me that complicit in the very idea of memory is the act of forgetting.

6

At Night My Mind Folds in on Itself,
Like Origami

It is a hot day. Scorching. Too hot for the season, too hot for this part of the country, but such things are out of our hands.

We're in the park. The great park, with its rolling grounds and thick trees, the one that curves down the south side of the city like the staff of Moses just before it's transformed into a snake. The grass beneath our feet is young and prickly. The expanse above is a blank white space. You could scrawl every lament you've ever had up there, unhindered. There is nothing in the sky, but I keep checking.

The smell of burning hits me, and in a moment I recognize it as *kebab* and vegetables and garlic potato cubes and maybe a whole fish stuffed with spices. I can't see the cooking, but I can smell it and saliva pools heavy in my cheeks. My whole family smells it, and we move like a pack of wolves scenting blood: Firas, the hunter, darting between the trees; Mama, nose pushing forward, Baby Lama tucked up against her milky breast; Nada runs with her children, but she is the same age as them, three five-year-olds with light brown hair and white legs sprinting through the grass; Baba is high up in a tree, but he crouches there on a branch that looks like it shouldn't be able to hold him, gripping his skull in fingers that are sharp like talons. He refuses to look at us. I cannot see Ahmed.

Firas says the cooking is happening by the river, pointing down the hill to where the thin ribbon of water winds through the grounds. The others switch direction like a school of fish sensing a predator, heads turning as one towards the sound of rushing water. The river should not be that loud, but none of them take notice. Or if they do, they are untroubled by it.

Khalid is there, beneath a canopy of trees, a blindingly white *keffiyeh* wrapped around his head. It's cleaner than any I ever saw him wear, hard and shiny as a helmet. Strong enough to deflect whatever falls from the sky. I take a step forward, even though he is altogether uninviting. Arms folded, eyes hard, his lips move in that same old recitation of Darwish he gave to me hundreds of times, so that though he doesn't speak, I hear the words as clearly as when he murmured them down the line on lonely nights in Damascus.

A poem about identity, he said it was inscribed in the breast of every Arab – whether they were, like him, rooted in Palestine or not. Those roots, stretching back before the invention of time, before the blossoming of eras. Those lines, I could see them, blood red, as though Khalid were scratching them onto the wall of my mind or pressing them into the chambers of my heart.

I shove at my family, blocking their path. I don't want them down by the river. There's nothing there, I shout, only filthy water. Red, muddy water. No, Firas says, there's food, so much meat, juicy and ours for the taking. I pull at Mama's arm, dislodging Baby Lama so that she squalls in alarm and Mama's loose breast goes flapping in the wind like the end of a scarf. I grip Firas around the chest, but he's stronger than me and pulls us both down the hill. I turn and try to run away, leaving them to whatever waits at the water's edge, but they will not let me go. One hand from each of them takes hold – Firas on my left arm, Mama on my scalp beneath my hair; Nada and her children cling to my legs. Even Baby Lama paws at my shoulder.

Khalid's voice grows louder in my head, full of anguish and disappointment. I was never brave enough for him. He recites commands, admonishments, and warnings upon warnings upon warnings. About dignity, about land. Names and titles. He speaks of unrelenting hunger, of dining on the flesh of usurpers.

I slide down the mud and mulchy grass, screaming, and Baba wails, like an old woman in the throes of some inconsolable grief, from his perch in the tree. I don't want to see the river. Anything but the river. They won't let me go, pushing and pulling and shoving. They push until gravity takes hold and forces me down the incline. Dirty fingers, caked in dried flakes of blood, pry my eyes open when I squeeze them shut.

But the river is blue and calm, burbling over brown and white stones like a lullaby from long ago. Birds chirp in the trees, hopping from branch to branch, free and at peace. The water looks cold and my siblings rush into it, splashing and kicking and laughing. They lie down on hard stones that must dig into their spines and throw their heads back to take long, deep gulps. Mama sits at the river's edge; the baby latches back on to a nipple and she smiles down at her, trickling water on Lama's forehead, like a priest at a baptism. I look behind me, but Khalid is gone, and I feel the mourning rise up in me again.

Nothing is cooking. The smell of meat and burning is strong in the air, but nothing is cooking, and I'm the only one who's still hungry.

7

When the Rain Comes

. . . The notion of 'us' versus 'them' is hardwired into every religion. If you don't believe what I believe, leave your foreskin on to prove it or drink this wine and believe it's the blood of the Lord or turn your face away from Jerusalem when you pray. The Buddha said, Islam *itself* says, that there is only one truth out there, only one message that's sent down over and over. Just the one message, one truth, one well from which everyone drinks. And yet somehow the message gets twisted and corrupted and adulterated by our own clumsy attempts to humanize it, to create systems from the ineffable.

The Voiceless, *The New Press*, 10 May 2017

Hasan has an advert for Quran CDs up in the window. Free Quran CDs, translations in Mandarin and Urdu and Malay and a host of other languages. The announcement is written up in small, small type, a script so tiny that you have to press your nose nearly to the glass to read it. There's a lengthy disclaimer beneath saying that it's not about proselytizing but about making the word of Allah accessible to anyone who wants to hear it, and I think that the font is so small, it obviously can't be an effort to convert anyone. Although it also occurs to me that some people might think Hasan's very presence in this quiet English city is somehow, in itself, an act of proselytizing.

Something about the sign rubs me up the wrong way. Perhaps it's the presumption, how it assumes that there are people who desire this translation and would not otherwise have been able to obtain it, that they have been waiting for Hasan to offer it, like the special syrup he imports ahead of Ramadan or the packets of sugar rocks he keeps in the back and which you have to ask for. It's as though they can't find such translations online or ask their local imam to supply them with one. It feels like Hasan is overstepping his bounds as a grocer, dipping his toe where it doesn't belong. He doesn't even sell prayer rugs. I am uncomfortable with this blatant display of religious affiliation. Is it too much to ask that my local shop be free of it?

I've communicated some of my thoughts on religion to Josie, usually as PSs at the bottom of emails or comments in the margins of the pieces I send her. She's published one so far. I didn't want to use my real name – I haven't even told her my real name – and so at the bottom of the article is a short bio that reads, 'The Voiceless is a young immigrant from the Middle East studying for a degree in Political Science.' It's an online degree, but she doesn't need to know that. Josie says the reception has been good, but no comments have appeared beneath the article on the website, so I don't know who she's talking about. She encourages me to write more, to be fearless – a directive I can't help but snort at. She's asked me to expound on thoughts of religion, to re-tool entire articles so they come from that angle: *Did the war make you hate religion? Has all that death and destruction and pain made you abandon God? Do you have an uneasy relationship with all religions, or is it only Islam?*

We don't wrestle with the Problem of Pain, so at least there's that. Ours is an Old Testament god, one who does not shy away from conflict, who doesn't hesitate to mete out punishments, who is unafraid to show creation how utterly unfair life can be and that your one measly existence DOES NOT MATTER in the grander scheme of things. This is not to say that we don't also console ourselves with the hope that God cares about the suffering of each and every one of us, but there is a Job-ian acceptance of earthly woes, an acceptance predicated on the certainty that all accounts will be settled in the afterlife and however you laboured or hurt or were wronged here will be nullified in paradise.

I don't share that certainty of cosmic justice. As I see it, the hubris of the atheist is matched only by that of the ardent believer.

The bell above the shop door jingles and No-Lights-Man comes in with a willowy blonde. She's so tall, I think if she raised her arms she could hug the moon. He guides her forward with a hand low on her back where shirt and leggings fail to meet. She looks around, nose wrinkling and thin lips pressing down tight as though she's strolling through a fish market. He walks her around, pointing things out while she scowls.

Hasan ignores them both. He ignores most of his patrons. It's what I like about him.

It's not so difficult to know what people want. At the root of it we all want the same things: freedom, happiness, safety. I want to write what I want to write without the fear of a knock at the door and an interrogation room. I want to love who I want to love without the fear of death or corrective rape. I want to wear what I want to wear without the worry that men will see my skirt or the buttons on my shirt as an invitation. That's it. The freedom to live how we want to live.

Back home, religious differences run so deep and go so far back that no one bothers to talk about it any more. People think the war is about religious freedom, about black flags and opposition to a secular government, but it's not. The media seized on this idea, putting up side banners and trying to explain to viewers the difference between Sunni and Shiite, Kurds and Arabs, pie charts showing how a country has divided itself up. I get it. Religious conflict is sexy. It's easy to sell, the way it fits into the simple, dichotomous way people prefer to view the world. It's easy for news producers and politicians to frame it in terms of a cosmic war being waged in a land far, far away. But it isn't real. This isn't a religious conflict – or if it is now, it certainly didn't start out that way. Initially, in those private salons all across Damascus, with that Statement of 99, that intellectual fount of all Springs, it was about freedom. It was about the right to live with dignity, the right to think without fear, the right to exist *outside* of a state of emergency. It was about rising unemployment rates among a restless youth and free-market policies that benefited the few rather than the many. It was about the rains that never came, the migration and the cities straining under the weight of all the people they held but could do nothing with.

The tall girl's nasal voice shakes me from my thoughts. She's complaining that there's nothing healthy to buy, just 'processed' junk, says she doesn't put garbage in her body because her body is a temple or some such rubbish. She's not wearing a bra, nipples standing to attention beneath a pale pink skinny tee with the words 'nama-slay' across the chest, and No-Lights-Man has problems looking her in the eye when she's speaking.

'Come on, babe, it's not that bad.' He looks around as though seeing the shop for the first time. 'All you were wanting was some coconut oil and he has it here.' He moves down my aisle, nicotine-stained fingers running over the jars and bottles as he scans the labels.

'This place is disgusting,' she sniffs, taking mincing steps after him, long legs fluid in their leggings. She might be a dancer. 'Do you really buy food here?'

'Nah, babe, I don't put anything bad in my body.' He catches me watching and winks like we're co-conspirators in his effort to pull this girl.

'Let's go to the other place,' she whines, pulling on the hem of his hoodie.

'The other place is closed.' His big hands grip her waist, pulling her close, and I think if she can't tell by how he looks what a liar he is, then she deserves whatever venereal disease he might give her.

———————

The rain is coming sideways this evening. There's a thunderstorm in the forecast, but it hasn't shown itself yet. The sun is out, and I scan the sky for a rainbow. Leaning out as far as I can over the railing of my narrow balcony, I let the raindrops pitter patter on my face like tiny fingers. Sometimes the rain and the wind are the only things that touch me for days. If I'm careful, watching how I hand over bills to Hasan or how I position my palm for him to drop change into, if I angle my shoulders when I pass people on the street or keep three feet of space between myself and others in a line, I can go months without contact.

When I came here that was the hardest thing to get used to, this reality where everyone is in your personal space all the time. Get on a bus and there's someone jostling you so they can get off. Walk down the street and people are shouldering past you. Sit down in a park or on a bench and whoever's next to you will decide they want to have a chat. Never mind that I don't talk, still they tell me their life story, about the kids they're on their way to pick up or the doctor they can't get in to see or the bus that's never on time.

It isn't like that where I'm from. There, you have your boundary and I have mine and if the lines are crossed, it means that a fucking disaster has occurred. It means there was a bomb and people are running and they don't care who they touch and knock along the way. It means a woman was at a protest alone and men have circled her and hands are reaching under her robe and fingers are pressing into her. It means gunfire has erupted and someone is shoving you under a table until it fades away.

Seagulls squawk overhead, startling me so my hands grip the rail of the balcony. Shadows and reflections move against the towers' walls and windows. I track a bird, its wings spread, as it soars overhead, across the courtyard, past the Juicer's window and on down the block. I don't know the names of any of the birds here.

And then the rain is gone, and the clouds go back to white. I will never have enough of this weather, with its friction and changeability, its demands for submission. I will never have enough of four seasons in a day and taking an umbrella even though the sky is empty and blue. I love how the city is transformed by it, buildings going dark and streaky, cobblestones overflowing with bright moss and squishy with mulch, the park grass glistening and wet and dotted with muddy puddles.

The limit does not exist here. I can go where I like – some combination of bus and train and I can be in a whole other country in a few hours. A late-night walk down the block, though not really recommended for women anywhere, is at least not a guarantee of attack. The Juicer can fuck a man without fear. Hasan could stand in the park shouting about God and the Prophet. I could leave the house in a sundress, bare arms and legs shiny in the sun, hair playing in the wind as Gibran intended.

In that other place, my other life, there were limits everywhere. One wrong word could land someone in jail, though more often than not they were just gone. Walking down the road, you were a target. Going to the shop was an ordeal, full of logistics and mathematics, and the strong possibility that you might not return. There was no option of taking a bus, and the first time I did, at dawn, leaving everything I'd ever known, I was too petrified to enjoy it.

There was peril, tremendous peril, everywhere.

And when I first arrived, I couldn't assimilate – there's that word for you, Josie – I couldn't reconcile myself to the notion that I was free to go anywhere. So I set invisible borders that I abided by for a good, long while. The park to the south I wouldn't go beyond – where the rolling green meadows stopped, so did I. To the north, it was York Crescent on one end and the record shop on Albert Street on the other. East and west boundaries had their own end points as well: a graveyard at one, and a train station at the other. I caged myself into this three-square-kilometre area, learning it inside out, every alley and street, all the mews and yards, every shop and pub and church and cemetery, until nothing about it surprised me, until I felt safe.

The day I moved beyond my boundaries involved another tenant in the towers. One of the holiday-let flats was taken by a British family from somewhere down the coast, one of the 'mouths – Portsmouth or Bournemouth, I think I heard them say. The mum was always in the laundry room, invariably chatting with anyone she found there. It was mum and dad and two boys, one about ten, the other just two or so.

Mum would have the little one underfoot as she folded laundry or went to Hasan's while the father had the older boy. I'd see them kicking a ball around the courtyard or watching the man who juggled balls in the park for coins. In the early morning or afternoon, they ventured out as a unit, the dad with the little one on his shoulders, mum holding hands with the other. They went for pizza and to the playground and rented bikes. I believe they had a happy holiday, though you never know what really goes on in a family, even if you can see through their windows.

I was walking in the park. It was a grey day, another day with the threat of rain that hadn't come down yet. The sky was heavy and flat like the pavement. There were dogs out, their owners tossing balls and calling them back when they ran a bit too far. A trumpeter played a mournful tune at a crossroad of paths. A group of young men stood around a bench, smoking and taking swigs from cans. Matt was with them, the son of the Dad from South Tower A, second floor, flat three who shouts all the time. He was trying to look bigger than he is, in a hoodie at least three sizes too large and jeans that bagged and billowed around his thin legs. His blond hair was shaved down to the skull and his eyes looked hard as a rat's. The boys were loud, and I moved in the opposite direction.

That's when I saw him. Ben, that was his name, the older boy. He was a few paces ahead of me, digging into the wet earth with a stick. He'd already scratched his name into the ground – how young does it start, this male inclination to claim things? – and was now busy with a hole. I stopped and looked around, but I couldn't see his parents anywhere. Panic flared, bright and cold, at the back of my head, but it wasn't my own. It was remembered from when Mama had lost sight of my little brother at the market. I had only been ten at the time, but I'd felt her fear like it was my own, and like all children, when she cried, I did as well. She was pregnant again, and I remember standing by the wilting lettuce while her huge stomach led her up and down the aisles as she screamed his name. I wonder now if she wished she could just keep us all inside her, if she could have just been perpetually pregnant, loving us and caring for us when we were completely safe, in her belly where nothing bad could happen.

Ben wasn't safe in his mother's belly. He was out in the park where so many bad things could happen. I looked around again, wondering at his careless parents and how unlike them it seemed to let him wander off. He turned and saw me, his little face breaking into a smile.

'Hiya,' he said. 'You're the lady from the window.'

I flushed in shame, turning my face away, though I shouldn't have done. I *was* the creepy lady who spied on her neighbours from the window; I might as well embrace it.

'Look at this,' he added, holding up his hand. All I could see was mud and mulch. 'Oh, no.'

I looked closer, only just making out what appeared to be a squashed worm between his thumb and index finger. He looked up at me, green eyes shiny and bright, like the grass after the rain. 'It's dead.'

I pulled at a thread in the pocket of my jacket and shuffled my feet, looking around again for his parents. I was not and am not equipped for comforting people, least of all a little boy. I wanted to tell him it was okay, that it was only a worm, that it was nowhere near a tragedy in the grander scheme of things. I wanted to ask where his parents were and if he wanted me to walk him back to the towers. But I didn't say anything, I couldn't say anything. The silence in me, gripping me by the tongue, filled me up and wouldn't let me speak.

'Ooh, it's all right, I found another one,' he exclaimed, pulling a wriggling brown thing from the earth. He showed it to me, cradling it in his palm. I nodded and felt a rusty smile stretch my face. 'I want to show it to Charlie,' he added, getting to his feet.

He moved off across the grass, doing a walk-skip, and I kept up easily, staying three or four steps behind. He was going the wrong way, opposite the towers, towards the southern border of the park. I picked up my pace and reached out, tapping his shoulder until he stopped and turned. I pointed behind us, back to the flats.

He shook his head and pointed the way he'd been going. I shook my own head and repeated the action, so that we were both shaking our heads and pointing in opposite directions.

'Mum and Dad are there,' he said, holding his free hand up over his head and pointing at his chest as though to indicate adults belonging to him. I nodded and jerked my chin for him to go on.

He returned to his skipping, moving away from me, but as I couldn't see his parents from where we were, I started following him again. I kept a pace or two behind and when he noticed, he began chattering to me and to the worm about whether his mum would let him keep it in a jar or something. I imagined the conversation would not go very well, could see his mum screaming about it even as dad laughed. Ahmed had done stuff like that – aside from running away every time Mama took him out in public, he was always catching creepy-crawlies and sticking them in boxes or dusty drinks bottles he'd found on the road. He'd come home with crickets and lizards, spiders and beetles. Once there was a cockroach in the box, one so big that it made Mama scream, and she pinched him black and blue for it.

We reached the southern border of the park, *my* southern border, and I stopped even as Ben skipped across the bicycle path without pause and without bothering to look left or right, his bright blond head shining in the sun. I winced, my head whipping in both directions, but the way was clear. I stood on tiptoe, trying to see over the hillock ahead of us, trying to spot his family. I still couldn't see them, and he was moving up the incline, and I had to make a decision.

I took one step and then another and another, and then I was on the other side, my heart pounding in my chest and my footsteps weak like I expected the ground to give way beneath me. I looked ahead, but I couldn't see Ben any more. With a jolt, I hurried up the hill, the wet earth sending me sliding back until I found my footing. There was rain then, little drops of it splattering my head, cold and hard.

When I came over the top of the incline, I paused and swallowed a gasp. There was a garden there, a community garden of some sort. Flowers in bloom, colours popping like candy – baby blues and yellows and bright, bright reds and oranges. Poppies and white daisies and hydrangeas and long rows of purple lavender. There were winding stone paths and chalk signs naming all the flowers and plants. There were little hand-painted windmills and birdhouses up in tree branches. In the distance was a larger playground with slides that gleamed and children propelling themselves high on swings, screaming out their laughter. And beyond that was the rest of the city, church spires and buildings new and old and shops and other parks, that I hadn't explored.

I saw Ben, his red jumper amid the flowers as he barrelled through the garden, only just staying on the path. I watched him run past it, out onto the open grass, and keep running. Running and running until he'd crossed over to the playground, to where his mum and dad sat by a sandpit, watching the little one, Charlie, pack sand into a bucket. Ben reached them, proudly holding out his palm. Mum screamed at the sight of the worm, then broke into a laugh, pushing Ben towards his dad who reached careful fingers into the cradle of his son's hands and pulled out the worm, holding it up for inspection. There were no tears, no screaming about where he'd gone to, no panicked pinching and twisting of the arm or ear. It was fine. Ben was fine.

He pointed behind him, at me, but I was already turning to head back down to my park, wondering what it must be like to live in such a safe world.

8

Hollow Shells

Mama would be in the kitchen. Our kitchen was old, outdated. Large white tiles and cheap blue cabinets with a white trim. An old cooker with four burners. Never enough for all the people she needed to feed. The stove was also white because Mama thought that anything white looked more expensive, but she was wrong. There was always a film of grease on the countertops that no amount of scrubbing would do away with, and a beige fan whirred against the ceiling all year. Along one wall was the table we never ate at. It was made of a heavy wood, nearly black, something Baba had inherited from someone and refused to part with or sand down and paint white. It had come with eight chairs, more than enough for us, even if one had been, for years, a permanent receptacle for shopping bags and sacks of flour or rice that Mama hadn't put away or cases of water bottles or old radios and clocks Baba said he would fix but never got round to.

We didn't use the table. Baba thought we would, said it was a modern thing to do, but at mealtimes Mama would hand me the roll of plastic sheet to lay out on the floor of the living room. *Who needs a table when the floor is more comfortable?* I think she just hated looking at that chair, Firas's chair, with its heaps of stuff on it. At least on the floor there was no assigned seating. We all just plopped

33

down wherever we happened to find ourselves when we were ready to plop down. Laughing and talking over each other, hot sauce and *hummus* and bread and pickled things passing back and forth over plates piled high with food – tart *fattoush* and *fatteh dajaj*, *muhammara* that lit your tongue on fire, *kebab karaz* and crunchy *kebbeh* with a cool, minty yoghurt and cucumber sauce.

In the dream, I'm always at that table.

Twenty *kousa* are arranged before me in sterile rows, like medical instruments, cleaned and prepped with their tops sliced off. There's a pot of garlic and onion and olive oil that Mama is stirring. In my hand is the sharp-tipped peeler, and in my other palm is one of the twenty *kousa*. I stab it with the peeler, scooping and pulling at its innards with methodical, second-nature movements until I have a hollow shell in hand. I've done this since I was ten, and I make quick work of it. Cleaning up the walls, I scrape and scrape away at the flesh until there's nothing left. Baba hates courgettes; he only tolerates them for the stuffing Mama will fill them with – the ground beef and rice and onion and spices that she has set out in neat bowls and cups on the counter, all pre-measured and apportioned like she's hosting a cooking show.

'. . . to study in Damascus. It's much too far for a young girl on her own. And with no family there. What will people think?' she calls out, dropping bay leaves into the tomato broth simmering in a big pot over the open flame.

'I'm right here, Mama, no need to shout,' I reply, stabbing at another *kousa*. It makes a foreign sound, wet and harsh. Not what I would expect, and I look closer to see if the vegetable's gone bad, but it's as hard and shiny as the others. 'There must be lodging for single female students in the city. And how can you say there's no family when Amer goes there? And Donya will be joining as well soon.'

34

Through the dusty windows I see a blue sky and chickpea-coloured buildings. Across the way our neighbour – an older woman my siblings and I long ago dubbed Tante Shunta because she never went anywhere without her handbag – is draping a broad, white sheet over her washing line to dry. There's the bag, black leather rubbed grey, hanging from the crook of her elbow, swinging into the wall or out over the expanse between her flat and the ground as she twists and struggles with the sheet. It's too big and she labours under its damp weight, but there's no one to help and she will have to manage somehow. The street outside is too quiet.

But far away a series of cracks snap the air. *Pop pop pop*, like fireworks.

There is courgette flesh in my hair, white and pale bits stuck between the dark locks like when plaster rains down from the ceiling. The flesh is soft when I press it between my fingers; a redness oozes out until it's tinged pink. Panic nips at my breast and I flick the flesh off in jerky movements. Shaking my head down at the table, I say, 'Baba approves, doesn't he?'

'So different now. These girls wanting such odd things.' Mama tosses fresh parsley into a pot, and I wonder where she found it. There have not been fresh herbs for a while now.

'I'm an adult,' I reply, moving on to another vegetable.

'She's ruining herself,' Nada says, coming into the kitchen with a baby on her hip. I don't recognize the baby. It must be one of hers, but I don't recognize it. The panic crawls up my throat, expands there, as she picks at some rice as though to test its firmness then pushes it between the baby's full lips.

Tante Shunta has the sheet up, suspended and stretched on the line, and she's gone back inside to where I can no longer see her. The sheet is not as clean as what Mama would have achieved. There are yellow stains in the corner, pale and ignored; I don't want to guess at their origins, but the sight of them fills me with a squirming shame I cannot account for. At the centre, I see a small red dot, the diameter of a coin, dark and saturated. No, Mama would never tolerate something so unclean.

'I know, but they don't listen to me, do they? He says people won't talk about someone who's all the way down there, as though Damascus were a different country.'

'Maybe they won't,' I say, turning back to the table, trying to swallow down the sensations seeping like acid through my chest. I press trembling fingers into the newspaper spread out beneath the wet clumps of courgette.

'He is so stupid sometimes.' Nada shakes her head and puts a dummy in the baby's mouth when it begins to whimper, its little eyes lifting to the ceiling.

'You and Mama are the ones living in a different world.' I grab another vegetable as the popping sounds outside grow louder, closer. 'Things are changing. A woman doesn't have to be married with children by the time she's twenty to be considered successful.'

'I know, and that's what I told him. I said, you don't think like everyone else, so you don't know how vicious people can be, but he only says, I know best.' Mama shakes her head and pinches some salt and pepper into the broth. 'I thought we had finished with you all running away.'

'Why aren't you listening to me?' I shout, throwing down a hollow shell and starting on another.

'It's on his head, Mama,' Nada says. 'You've done what you can. He is the one who will have to answer to Allah for whatever she does down there.'

'Or whatever is done to her,' Mama murmurs with another shake of her head.

'Always ignoring me. Everyone in this house is always ignoring me, but I suppose that's just another consequence of having so many children, eh, Mama?' I scoff, throwing down the peeler.

'Nada, see to the vegetables, will you?' she asks.

I stand and toss my head back, feeling bits of flesh fly off and hit the tiled floor in wet plops. 'Yes, see to the vegetables,' I say, gesturing to the table, 'as though I've been no help at—'

On the table, laid out in rows, are twenty *kousa*, their heads neatly sliced off. They are whole, innards untouched and shiny and waiting to be pulled out by the clean, sharp-tipped peeler lying on its side. The popping sounds are above my head now – it sounds like the world outside is crumbling – and I look up as dust and plaster begin to snow down around me. I'm alone in the kitchen, the room filled with nothing but screams, though my mouth is wired shut. I taste metal on the inside of my lips. My eyes turn to the window; the red dot has expanded and bled, a live wound creeping across the white face of the sheet.

9

An Incandescent Fear

There's a mosque on one side of the park. It's a big building, the only proper mosque in this quiet, English city. Its walls are shades of beige and sienna, as though it were purposely importing the colours of home, some tiny gesture to say, 'We haven't forgotten you or the way the desert and the dust dominate no matter how high into the sky you build.' Its minaret is not very tall, but it is thick and robust. It's purely for show, though – no calls are issued from its high window, no *muezzin* drawing the faithful into its folds multiple times a day. The names of Allah are worked into the facade in blocky Arabic script, strong and substantial; there's none of the flowering calligraphy you would see in Turkey or Iran.

The mosque is governed by a man called Imam Abdulrahman. His name means Slave of the Merciful, the Merciful being one of Allah's ninety-nine names. I've heard people speak of him in Hasan's or on the street as they exit or enter the shop. From what I hear he's a good man, a compassionate man, one interested in building bridges rather than walls, as the saying goes.

Ramadan is coming in a week or so. I realize it when I pass by the mosque and see that they're holding a final feast in celebration. Theirs must be some new brand of hip imam. Islam is not a celebratory religion, but there they are with 'Welcome' banners up and

38

tables set around the courtyard in an inviting crescent shape. More crescent moons and sharp-edged stars, cut from multicoloured and glittering paper, are threaded through the gates, along with small, twinkling lights in pale yellow and blue and green and red. The tables are covered in a patchwork of fabric: intricately woven patterns from Bangladesh and Iran and Pakistan and Egypt and Iraq and the Levant. Suspended over the tables are thick Bedouin woollen tents, strung up between lamp posts and the iron gate and tacked to the walls of neighbouring buildings. I've never seen such tents here, and I wonder how Imam Abdulrahman managed to get them. He's allowed the younger men to bring in speakers hooked up to devices I doubt he knows how to work. They play Pakistani pop and Iranian psychedelic and Arabic love ballads from the fifties, and already some of the men are jumping around in wild, feverish dancing and making eyes at the girls who stand against the walls and giggle into their palms. A few of the girls try moving their arms or shoulders or hips before subsiding under the glare of a parent or brother or uncle of a cousin twice removed. Old aunties in their *salwar kameez* and *saris*, too old for modesty to matter, jerk their shoulders and bop their heads in time with the beat as they stir stews and flip *naan* on huge hot griddles.

The sign outside the mosque gates calls it a Unity Feast, where people can celebrate their heritage and share their culture. The sign boasts that more than ten countries are represented here today and that anyone should feel free to join the festivities. I see handwritten signs propped up around booths or hanging above them – signs in Arabic and Urdu and Punjabi and Bengali, the English names seeming incidental at best.

The imam's there, in the courtyard, directing his flock to and fro as they set up mounds and mounds of goods: there are fresh samosas and pakoras; jars of chutney and *ma'booch* and pickled vegetables;

huge pans of long basmati rice steeped in bay leaves and cardamom and saffron; big pots of curries and thick, chunky stews. I see long-spouted pots of tea being passed around and steaming cups of spiced milk. Families run around trying to set things up while children nick sticky *jalebis* off tables and evade the swatting hands of the old ladies manning the booths. Older children sit at tables meticulously filling out price cards to prop up by the food, their traditional shawls and shirts fluttering in the breeze.

In curious twos and confident threes and fours, the white people come. It's unfair to call them white people, I suppose, since they could have any multitude of heritages, so let's call them non-Muslims, though even that might be a misnomer since most of us don't walk around with our religions stamped on our foreheads. They come, these people, eager to find out what's going on or perhaps hoping it's a free meal. They come and Imam Abdulrahman welcomes them with open arms and smiles and flat palms that gesture to the mounds of food. In filling their bellies, I suppose he hopes they'll fill their minds too. I watch them mingle and chat and hear them laugh and call out to one another across the courtyard, and I wonder whether this, here, isn't the answer. Not interfaith dialogue, but just dialogue, and I wonder if I can slip that into a piece for Josie without it coming out trite. There are mums and dads with kids in tow, older couples under umbrellas, packs of friends coming up from the park, students from the university campus further down the road.

The Holiday-Goers are here. An Asian family, they moved into South Tower B, second floor, flat one last week. It's a holiday let, quite nice. A three-seater, beige leather sofa with its back to the floor-to-ceiling windows – not what I would've done. A low, light wood coffee table sits in the centre of the living room with a short plant and some books arranged on it – the kind of books not meant for reading, I imagine. The kitchen there is smaller than mine, and so is the bedroom I can see; a double bed takes up nearly all the floor space so the teenage daughter has to jump over it to get to the bright orange suitcase she has up against the window. The Holiday-Goers always prop their suitcases up against the windows, even though all the flats have access to storage. I suppose they're not unpacking entirely, so it's good to have them to hand. Mum Holiday-Goer had one open in the living room for several hours out of which she pulled clothes and shoes and boxes of biscuits and tinned food. It reminded me of holidays when I was very little and Mama used to pack bread and huge jars of spreads and olives and pickles like we weren't going somewhere with a grocer on every corner, as though we'd starve without fava beans for breakfast.

The father and mother huddle under an umbrella while their daughter tags along behind. Mum and Dad are conservative in lavender and pale blue windcheaters and beige trousers and heavy hiking boots, while the girl wears white knee socks and patent-leather Mary Jane platforms and a short black skirt with a blue and white sailor-type shirt tucked into it. Her black hair is up in pigtails and she's got on this bubblegum pink lipstick that makes her mouth look enormous. She looks like a caricature of herself, or one of those Harajuku girls that were popular at one time. She seems like an alien following along behind these boring parents.

We walk into the courtyard together, me slipping in behind the Holiday-Goers, and then I take the place of their daughter because she has immediately split off to the other side of the courtyard while I trail behind her parents. They stop at booths and ask for samples of things in broken English and awkward gestures, murmuring to each other in what sounds like Japanese when the patrons tell them there's no tasting and that they must buy.

The imam's eyes scan the crowd, a benign smile on his face. Every so often, his eyes fix on me, following as I move from stand to stand.

Dark eyes tracking me, but when I look at him, they dart away to watch the rest of the courtyard. Moving past the crowd, they settle on the street beyond, and I follow his gaze to see what has his thick brows suddenly so furrowed.

Five men pace back and forth outside the mosque. At their head is a large man with a hard-looking gut and broad shoulders. He smokes his cigarettes and casts angry glances at the people beyond the black iron gate. His friends stand around, mimicking his glares and scowls and passing a plastic bag of beer cans between them. They're not of the curious, I can see that straight away, and I can see that Imam Abdulrahman sees it too. Members of his congregation, young men with fire in their veins, come up to tap his shoulder. They whisper in his ear and incline their heads towards the men at the gate, but the imam just nods and claps them on the back and urges them to return to the party. Turning his back, he moves through the crowd, calming the men who look like they want a confrontation and reassuring aunties and mothers and fathers that there's nothing to worry about.

If he's calm, I can be calm. I purchase a paper cup of cardamom chai, followed by a pair of plump samosas with mint sauce. I gorge myself on buttery garlic *naan* and hot, creamy butter chicken in styrofoam bowls and crispy *poppadoms* and a chicken *shwarma*. I wash it all down with more hot tea, feeling warmer than I have in weeks despite the rapidly cooling temperature as night falls. At each booth, I stop for a dessert – gooey *gaimat* and chunks of coconut-y *besboosa* and teardrop-shaped rice dumplings.

There's a Syrian table tucked away in a corner. I've never seen the family manning it – the mother with the white veil on her head and tightly pursed lips, the father with his thick moustache and large, bulging eyes, the children running around and under the table. I've never seen them, but their faces carry a familiar look. It says they've seen things, experienced them, and come through to a place they don't recognize and don't quite know what to do with. I avoid them. Even though my belly aches for the taste of home, I cannot endure the inquisition that would follow if they saw something we share in my face.

Turning abruptly, I see Anime Girl over by the door to the mosque, chatting to a group of young men. They stand in a semi-defensive circle, as though they're afraid of this munchkin of a girl. I move to see her face and realize what has them so nervous.

She's a vixen, a little minx. She stands there with her hip cocked to one side, legs akimbo in a stance that makes her look like a broken doll, neck weak so her head lolls to one side. Her eyes are bright and shiny with rapid blinks, lips pushed out, and she twirls a thick pigtail around the fingers of one hand. She is a Lolita, cunning and bold, a Hooria of paradise, and the men are right to be wary. They are young, the men, but nowhere near young enough for her attention.

There's murmuring and pointing going around the booths now, rapid fire, the way a rumour spreads, and Mum and Dad – I see them over by the teas and coffees – feel the change in atmosphere and turn this way and that in search of their daughter. Dad catches sight of her, and then he's skipping up the steps to the mosque, yanking her roughly by the elbow so that she lets out a little squeak of protest. He drags her back down and straight out of the courtyard, berating her in rapid-fire Japanese that sounds like bullets going off, the mum hurrying behind them.

I snort in amusement and suck sugar water off my fingers.

'Dirty Pakis!'

The music is loud, but the imam and I, at opposite ends of the gate, hear it. We turn to the men beyond the courtyard as another insult is lobbed over the iron gate like a grenade: 'Fuckin' ragheads!' The slurs land on the other side like duds, drowned out by the thumping beats and the chatter and laughter. I feel the tension though, in my gut. A vibration against my diaphragm telling me to go home, but I stay and watch, like someone who thinks they might serve as a reliable witness and so sticks around after an emergency to talk to the authorities.

The imam ignores them, back erect and proud as he walks down the wall of the courtyard and comes to a stop in front of me.

'*Salam*,' he says, putting a hand on his heart and inclining his head. The dome of his head is bald and shiny in the fairy lights hanging over us, only a few grey wisps remaining on the side, above his ears. His brows are peppered with grey as well and so is his beard, which is not too long, but long enough to announce his piety. His eyes are dark chocolate, almost black, and lined with thick lashes, and they sit deep in his face, suspended above the soft pouches of his lower eyelids. His cheeks are gaunt, lips thin and firm, but he has a pleasant countenance, and it is smiling at me.

I nod back, my eyes darting away from him to watch the men. A nervous energy radiates off them, like a sweaty odour. I don't see how the imam can be so complacent.

'I've seen you in the streets and the shop, but you have never joined us here,' he says. His voice is strong but unintimidating. It is a voice of authority that doesn't need to impose itself or showcase its strength, and I imagine his sermons must be relaxing to hear. Back home the Friday sermons were litanies of abuse, the imams shouting across rooftops as though in competition with or opposition to each other. They'd scream about the evils of modernity, the immorality of women, the dangers of idleness. On and on and on until you wondered if they said anything at all during the week, or if they just saved it all up for the Friday explosion.

I shake my head, and he inclines his again, eyes narrowing like I'm a specimen he's studying. I don't like to be studied, and I turn away, nervously wiping my hands on a tissue I fish out of the pocket of my jacket. He waves his hand in front of my face and when I look his way, he gestures to his ear in the way I've become accustomed to people doing.

It seems easiest just to nod.

His eyes turn down at the corners, features rearranging themselves into an expression of sympathy. He points to his lips and I nod again reluctantly.

'You are welcome to the Friday sermon. The women prefer to sit off to one side, but I can make you a space in front of me, so you can follow along.'

It's terribly presumptuous. I frown down at the cobblestone pavement beneath my feet, wondering what it is about me that screams Muslim. I look up across the courtyard, seeing the mums and dads and couples and kids and wonder if he approached them all as well. I am fair-skinned with dark hair that I have not covered since the day I left home. I dress in jeans and jumpers and the same damn clothes everyone else here wears. I've assimilated, Josie, so why does this imam automatically assume I'm a Muslim in need of his spiritual guidance? Is it my constant patronage of Hasan's? Or is it that I've been consuming the food here in such a way that makes him think I am desperate for something anywhere near resembling home?

It's not tattooed on my face or plastered on a badge pinned to my lapel, this thing I am, but he sees it. It's written on me somewhere, perhaps in a language only people like him can read. A despair maybe, or a longing that I cannot seem to quell. I hate that he sees me, hate the idea that I am, in this particular way, so transparent. I hate that he is looking at me, talking to me, wanting to stand next to me as though there could possibly be anyone in the world I can rely on.

Does he think he can fix me, this imam in this little city where all I want is to be invisible? Does he think he can cure me with religion, tell me everything is going to be okay, that this is all part of Allah's grand design? Does he think anything he says will be something I don't already know, or that he might say something that could actually make me feel better? My experiences are far beyond him, and if he does in fact know or has guessed what I am, he can't possibly have a frame of reference for it.

There's a shout, and then the men storm the gate. Led by Mr Big Man, they push through the throng, milling around the front, and start indiscriminately shouting at people to go home. The imam turns and steps away from me, carefully shifting people so he can move past them.

'You go home!' one of the young men of the mosque counters. 'This is a private party.'

'This is my fuckin' country, raghead!' Mr Big Man shouts, his face an ugly mask.

The hypocrisy is too much for the fathers to stand, and fists rise into the air and shouts grow louder, for how can the subcontinent be British without the UK being subcontinental? Someone knocks over the speakers or they disconnect and the music is silenced, the shouting taking on its own rhythm and beats. Imam Abdulrahman intercedes, pushing back the fathers and uncles and young men filled with fervour, and attempts to rationalize with the intruders.

This is his first error, an error more naïve than I would expect of him. It's one you see repeated on the news, in op-eds, in document-aries, in social media posts. There's this idea that if only you bombard bigots with enough facts and data and statistics, you can cure them. This notion that their hatred comes from a place of ignorance is one people have a hard time shaking. It's not a lack of education, and Mr Big Man over there doesn't care that it's a peaceful party or that the imam has no plans to convert him or anyone else. It's fear; fear of the unknown, the Other, fear that things are changing in ways he can't predict or control. Fear doesn't waver in the face of facts. The chances of a bomb going off in this little city are next to none, but it doesn't stop me from breaking out in a cold sweat every time I hear fireworks.

'Shut your gob,' Mr Big Man says, a pudgy finger rising to wag in the imam's face. 'If you don't like it, fuck off back to India!'

The crowd gets well and truly riled at this, the congregation pushing against him, wanting to bodily remove these men from their court-yard. Because now it is *their* courtyard. The welcome banners don't apply to these men and now some of them aren't sure they want any non-Muslims there. Those curious people – a few of them have gone, slipping out unobtrusively at the first sign of trouble, others have stayed to try and rebuke Mr Big Man, as though their arguments are more rational, or perhaps that they might carry more weight than Imam Abdulrahman's.

There's shoving and arms reared back to threaten punches and Mr Big Man and his friends are purple in the face, their rage an incandescent thing that has assumed independence, an identity all its own. This is escalation. This is lack of control. This is how calamity strikes.

The iron gate swings – open or shut, I can't tell which – and the resounding clang breaks through the air sharp and loud, and it punctures my mind so that I squeeze out of the courtyard and run all the way home.

––––––

Bile coats the back of the throat, saliva a sticky web between trembling fingers. Tears leak from two black eyes, but they aren't on account of sadness or anger or despair (real despair produces no tears at all). The wetness on the face is a purely physiological response to repeated provocation of the gag reflex.

The face in the mirror is cracked. An angry line – a lightning bolt, a jagged scar, a shattered bullet casing – cuts through the reflection. Seven years of bad luck hardly seems fair, but rules are rules. There is blood on the glass, smeared there, so it appears as a diagonal line contouring one cheek.

She looks like me, only not. A shadow, a mirror image, or a pale imitation. But look hard enough, and I can pick out my mother's brow, coarse and unapologetic, my father's nose, strong and straight, my grandfather's bearing, weary with scooped shoulders and the grief of generations.

I can see mud ancestors from a time before time.

The face, for all its lineage, lacks expression, a reflex from a survival technique learned long ago. Eyes, mouth, cheeks – all clean, a canvas for you to throw your paint at. I am a girl with no name, a girl with no face. I can be whatever you see. Arab. University student. Writer. Fatty. Muslim. Whore.

On the journey here many things were said about me, in fields where our fingers snagged on wire fences, in camps with sagging tents and loose shit in the street, on trains with too many bodies and boats that were not boats at all, on dirt roads and rocking buses and growling trucks. They called me a bad seed, a blight on the family honour, a brave one, a deviant held fast by *jinn*, the one who never smiles, a whore who sleeps with men for protection, good with the children, the strongest woman they had ever seen, the weakest, that my head is empty or my father cut out my tongue before I ran away, that I'm from this city, no, that city, from Syria, from Iraq, from Afghanistan.

I am all these things at once. I am none of them. Perhaps the result is the same.

There are silver shears on the sink, a tool that can be used for so much. They're heavy to hold, substantial and full of purpose, and when they slice into my hair, it is with a sharp, well-defined sound. *Snip. Snip. Snip.* Years of hair fall away, thick black waves floating to the cold floor tiles. Hair that was twisted into elaborate plaits by a mother's hands and pierced through with bright, fragrant jasmine blossoms for wedding parties. *Snip. Snip.* Hair whose thirst was quenched by the olive oil of Ebla. Hair that was yanked in anger, tugged at playfully, caressed and looped around gentle fingers. *Snip.* Hair washed in the waters of the Aegean, the Danube, the Balaton, the shores of the English Channel.

It all falls away, twisting and coiling like little black snakes at my feet.

10

The People in the Windows

In South Tower A, fourth floor, flat three there lives an old man. Very old, with white candy floss hair and dark spots on his scalp and a back that will no longer hold him upright. He trembles all the time, hands shaking as he carries a plate of chocolate biscuits to his armchair, arms beset with tremors when he reaches for a book as old and battered as he is, teacups rattling when he sips from them, so the liquid dribbles down a chin he doesn't bother to wipe.

He lives alone in that flat. Or perhaps it would be more accurate to say he is in the process of dying alone in that flat.

No one visits, and he visits no one. All of his days are the same, and I imagine he can only tell that they are passing by the delivery people knocking on his door. Once every two or three weeks, a man will come with two bags of groceries – milk, biscuits, bread, butter and jam, porridge and bananas and cans of soup. These are the things the old man consumes, an identical rotation of meals at the same time every day. He takes only a few bites, then seems to forget it's there, so the porridge will grow crusty in bowls and toast will go dry and hard until a cleaner clears it away. A service comes every few weeks, never the same woman, but always with a bucket and mop and dusters and supplies. The women move him around the flat like they do the furniture, to the armchair when they're doing the bedroom, to his bed when they're hoovering the living room. They don't talk to him, just lift him up with hands hooked in his armpits and transfer him to a different place. Occasionally, he'll order a chunky stew or rice dish, trembling with joy, I think, when the buzzer sounds and he lets the delivery man in. Those meals he spends a great deal of time on, intent on finishing them, so that I imagine the stew or rice is cold by the time he reaches the bottom of the bowl.

Ruth starts up with her pots and pans next door. A slam here, a clang there. A booming racket. It's like she's a one-woman band, and I know all of her hits. Right now, she's playing a long-drawn-out number called 'Dinner'. I'd heard nothing through the walls earlier and had hoped they'd ordered in or gone out – occasionally they'll go to a Russian place down the block. But there it is, the nightly slamming and banging that I cannot stand. I wish she would turn up the television.

Across the way, in the East Tower, third floor, flat two, No-Lights-Man is looking in his box again. The lights are off, as usual, and a record spins on the player in the living room, the sleeve propped up against the wall in a way that looks precarious, like it might go sliding to the floor any minute. He sits cross-legged, head down, with things I can't see in his lap.

How alone is that old man? Is he the last living soul in his family, like I might be? It seems unlikely. He looks like a native of this place, if such things can be discerned through a window. He doesn't look like me or the old couple next door, not like he might be from a country that was systematically killing its people, or a place where it is not out of the realm of possibility that your entire family might perish.

I flinch, pushing my palms against the glass to settle myself, whether against unbidden memories that bob up from muddy rivers, or dreams that last far beyond waking, or Ruth's incessant noise, I can't tell. She is yelling at Tom now. I think he's losing his hearing, but the way she shouts, you'd think he'd gone deaf already. She yells in whatever language it is they speak. In public, at Hasan's or in the street or the laundry room, they use English, but at home, through the walls, it's this foreign, angry tongue that I hear most often. I don't know what she's yelling, but I imagine it's something like, 'Do you want crackers in your soup?' or 'Of course I'll make tea, how long have we been married?'

In South Tower B, Anime Girl is at the window. She wears a white vest, a black bra visible beneath it, and pale pink knickers. She's brushing her long hair over one shoulder, her hand moving from crown to tip, hips swaying to a tune only she can hear. Every so often her head tilts towards the window but never her body. She kicks a thin leg out, twirls a foot, stretches her pale neck and lets it sway.

Putting the brush down, she snakes equally thin arms up under the hem of the vest, unhooks the bra and pulls it out slowly, letting it drop to the floor at her feet. Turning, she keeps her face down, shuffling from side to side, sweeping her hair so it fans out behind her, thrusting her little chest so her nipples push against the vest like mosquito bites. Turning again, so her back faces the window, she bunches up the hem of the vest and pulls it over her head, letting it too fall to the floor.

She's putting on a show. For whose benefit, I can't tell. There is no one watching from South Tower A. I don't think anyone in the East Tower has a view of the Holiday-Goers flat, so I think it must be someone in my own building. I chuckle at the thought of Tom next door to me, right now, salivating over her taut, young flesh, but it is not a serious thought. I cannot imagine him being intrigued by such a thing at his age. Perhaps it's the father on the second floor, the one with the four children who visit him every other weekend. Or maybe it's the university student who lugs a heavy backpack in and out of the building at all hours of the day and night and who seems in a constant state of despair, as though he's having recurring first encounters with some especially cryptic philosopher. Or maybe it's the tween son of the single mother on the first floor.

Her chest is bared now, for anyone looking at the window to see. When she hooks her little fingers into the waistband of her knickers, I turn away, just as Ruth slams something into the sink.

I grab my jacket and flee to the courtyard.

11

Revolt

We would meet on Fridays. When the week's classes were over and the day of rest had begun, Ossama, Khalid, my cousins Amer and Donya, Sama, and I would meet at Ossama's flat. This was back when the Fridays had no names, when they weren't dubbed Friday of Dignity or Friday of Patience and Steadfastness or Friday of Your Silence is Killing Us, when Friday was just . . . Friday. Ossama lived off-campus, blocks away from the university, in a single bedroom in a tower in one of the commercial districts. We would all cram into his tiny living room for a late lunch or an early dinner or just to hang out when we didn't want to be around the school any longer.

We watched the events in Egypt unfold in that cramped room. Not on TV but through our mobile screens. On Twitter, on Facebook, via messages whipping back and forth, invisibly, through air and space, we watched Egypt unravel. We saw the thousands in Tahrir Square, the square of freedom, where the impossible became inevitable. We passed shaky videos of chanting and protests between ourselves and heard about those who were missing and those who were gone. We watched as the Fridays acquired monikers – the Day of Revolt and the Friday of Anger and the Friday of Departure.

And we waited.

'It will come here,' Ossama said, knobbly knees jiggling as he tapped at his phone. 'It's only a matter of time.'

'Yes, yes,' Amer concurred with a little shake of his shoulders, like a dancer warming up for a show. 'The doctor is next.' Khalid looked up from the book he held, dark eyes flitting around the room as though we weren't alone. He was always watching doors, anticipating knocks and shouts and the men who take you away. There are eyes everywhere. All the time. When he'd bought a laptop for school, the first thing he did was tape over the camera. We laughed and called him paranoid, but he just put another layer on.

Sama shook her head, leaning back against the sofa and crossing her arms. 'He's too strong.'

'Nothing will come of it,' Khalid agreed, long fingers turning the pages of the short story collection in his lap. I could tell he was agitated and unable to concentrate, that he was only pretending to be unaffected by the updates Ossama and Amer and Donya kept announcing with such inappropriate glee. I longed to move closer to him, to loop an arm around his neck and rub his earlobe in that way I knew soothed him, but he was too proper for me to announce our relationship like that, even to close friends.

Soon there came a call for our own Day of Rage, a call to gather in early February, a show of discontent, but it was ignored, and our chains did not rattle. Not then, anyway. A week later, photos went around of the dim underside of a bridge in the city, the words *Now it's your turn, Dr* splashed across the stone in drippy black paint.

We didn't speak of it.

There were hardly any protests in Damascus during those initial months of revolution. No, revolution is the wrong word for what happened. It is a word that needles me still; the inherent wrongness pricks my mind. If you chase down its meaning, there is a circular notion embedded within it, a return to a starting point, a return to where you don't want to be. That's what the prefix is for; it means 'again'. I was studying English at university, linguistics, so I knew all about prefixes and suffixes and word roots. The origin of revolution, the base hidden there, is revolute. It means to roll backwards, to roll downwards, like a leaf curling in on itself.

That is not what we envisaged for our country.

Much better that it had been called a revolt. That they had all been called revolts, as though a great illness were convulsing across the region. Here, too, is that annoying prefix, with its pulling back into a rotation, its circling of an axis. But at least this word, along with the notion of rising against and casting off and breaking away, brings with it a sense of abhorrence, of utter disgust and nausea that is a good deal more fitting to the subject matter.

Sama withdrew from school and fled home to Jordan. Mama told me to come home, that she found the distance between us unbearable. Khalid's mother was saying the same. *What if you should need us or we you?* she asked, her voice tinny on the line as Khalid rolled his eyes at me. *It would take at least five or six hours to get here.*

Amer and Ossama were impatient with Damascus anyway, with the silence we were all choking on. There were rumblings in Aleppo, particularly from students at the university there, and they were eager to join.

Already Mama was thinking of how to leave, planning it, contacting distant relatives in Latakia and Beirut and Alexandria, looking for a safe haven, even while Baba counselled patience. *The north remains loyal*, he said in a phone call, but he sounded weary and I didn't think his heart was behind the sentiment.

He said things were bound to settle down, that everything would return to normal.

12

Residues

'I said, it's nearly as exciting as home when we were coming up.'

Ruth is on her balcony, bundled up in so many layers she looks like a giant snowball the colour of dirty dishwater. Her grey and white hair is pulled back in a severe bun that shaves years off her face. I can almost imagine what she looked like when she was young: strong nose announcing her brazenness to the world; small, shiny eyes that could penetrate the darkest of hiding places; a mouth I can almost see pursing coquettishly as she ensnared whatever man she'd chosen. She clutches the phone, pressing it against her ear. Her left hand is all age: wrinkled and thickly knotted with big knuckles, like she's spent her whole life kneading bread.

'The police came again,' she continues in a voice loud and sharp with authority. 'Oh, yes, the police went to the mosque. I told you how those people over there were making a ruckus? It carried on for ages and more and more of them kept coming. All these men, Mila.' She shakes her head and ducks back inside. When next she emerges, she has a rag which she uses to wipe down the railing even though it looks like more rain is coming. The morning sky is grey and hangs low. She doesn't see me crouched on my balcony, my back to the cold brick behind me.

'It's too much. That leader over there, at the mosque, he's wanting to turn the whole neighbourhood. Tom says I am silly, but it's true. Every month doing something like this, luring stupid people into that place so he can whisper his magic into their ears. It is magic, Mila! Sorcery! You remember how they were, the wife of the spice man with her pouches and herbs and coffee cups she read the future in? She predicted Nev's death, down to the hour, you know she did.' She slaps the damp rag against the metal, so it makes a high-pitched sound that whistles into the wind. 'Anyway, there were too many of them and then some neighbours made complaints. Not me, I don't want trouble. But it brings attention. We have the Muslim shop. Tom and I, we buy milk and tea there, what do we need a Muslim priest preaching for? What? Yes, yes, one of those . . . So, the police came and they shooed the people away. I heard in the shop, they were saying some men came to attack the mosque, but I think they lie. They want sympathy, you know? Anyway, maybe things will be quiet now. Tom and I go to temple and pray with others, but we don't shout about it in the street. "Look at me, look at my God . . ." It's disrespectful, but you know how they are.'

Later, after the rain has come and gone, I venture outside. The sky is still formless and dismal, like lead. I scrutinize it as I walk, trusting my feet to move me around this city on their own. I still have trouble believing this is the same sky that hovers over home, that this barely-there haze of sun is the same one that shines there, that we are all blanketed by the same dome. But I mustn't think of it as home. It's not home. This is. This small city with its two-hundred-year-old buildings – almost no history at all, really – and its church spires and sprawling parks. This is home now. The flat back there, in that other place, has been blown to bits, the building reduced to ash and rubble. There's nothing to return to.

My feet take me to Hasan's where a steady stream of customers file in and out of the shop, carrying their fruit and veg, their packets of flatbread, their jugs of cooking oil. I don't go in, passing the door and walking further down the block. I hurry past the mosque, only taking a glance sideways into the courtyard as I pass the gate. The space is quiet: tables and chairs have been folded up and stacked against one wall, like the imam doesn't believe anyone in this city would steal from him; there are bulging black bin bags piled up on the street outside; the 'Welcome' banners have been pulled down and are slumped up against the building, words of welcome turned to face the wall. The place is deserted. I check my watch, but I don't know when the prayer times are, and so I don't know if this is a reaction to last night or just a normal lull in the day.

I walk further down the road, skipping over puddles and racing across junctions before the lights change. I pass the bar with its sign advertising a secret beer garden in the back where men with rolled-up sleeves and women in short skirts will grip bright cocktails and pretend they have things to talk about. There's the old church with its notice-board full of service times and music nights, and the estate agent whose windows I stop to look in at homes and flats I'll never be able to afford. The streets are full of people, but I hardly notice them – mums and dads clasping the hands of children or pushing them in prams, harried students carting books with laptop bags hung carelessly on their shoulders, men in suits with their heads bent over their phones while they wait for the bus . . . They seem like mannequins to me, or a trick of light and atmosphere, and if I were less careful and bumped into someone, I'd just go right through them.

I turn down a street where there's a bookshop with a bright red door. Under the awning the owner puts out boxes of books that he sells for 50p but that he's equally fine with people just taking. I know this because on the day I discovered the bookshop, not long after I moved here, I was looking through the boxes, piling books high into my arms because I thought they were free; that he'd put them outside, unwatched, so that people would take them off his hands. The books were in a terrible state, their covers faded and torn, water-stained with broken spines and ripped pages, but I still wanted them. When I was done and turning to leave, he came out of the shop, arms full of more tattered books, and looked me up and down as I reshuffled my finds between my hands and walked away. I've been in the shop countless times since, and he's never mentioned it.

He's at the folk and fairy tales section when I come in, and his large head turns at the sound of the bell. No smile, just a nod, before he faces the shelves again. He's a big man, but not like the man who stormed the mosque. The bookshop owner has the appearance of a gentle giant, tall and broad with dark ginger hair and pale freckles dusting his face. His eyes are small and deep and brown, and his hands are big enough to hold ten books at once with little trouble.

The bookshop owner is not friendly; I've heard him bark at customers who ask stupid questions (*All these books for sale, then?*) and I've seen him scowl at people asking for terrible books that he nevertheless has in stock and which he hands over with an expression that implies he's smelled something awful. He can't be much more than forty, but he's exceedingly prickly. Far too prickly for someone his age, but there's no telling what a person has been through.

I move to the opposite end of the shop, scanning shelves full of titles – hardbacks and paperbacks, with bent covers or in pristine condition, bundled together as volumes in a set or sitting on their own. I'm still agitated by the incident at the mosque. I feel it in the numbness in my fingertips and the ants crawling across my scalp and nibbling at my upper lip. It strikes me as odd that such a small thing should affect me like this. Humans are meant to adapt, to grow desensitized by repeated exposure, but that doesn't always work.

There's a fireplace against one wall, dormant, for obvious reasons.

But within the hollowed-out space is a computer monitor depicting the moving, dancing flames of a blazing hearth. There's even sound to go along with the image; little speakers pushed back behind the screen emit slight crackling noises. It gives the feel of some old-time drawing room, like something from Austen or Dickens. An atmosphere. A veneer of sorts. If you don't stand too close, if you don't scrutinize, it would almost fool you. It's ineffectual, but so pretty to look at.

The owner comes up behind me, and I turn and stare up at him. Wordlessly, he drops a book into my hand and walks back to the other side of the shop. This is how we communicate; he hands over books he thinks I'll like or pushes them across the counter when I go to pay, and I occasionally leave one-line reviews in books I've read, which he will then amend or add to as he sees fit. There's a copy of *The Da Vinci Code* pushed deep into a shelf with several pieces of paper tucked into it on which we had a long, drawn-out argument about the role of pop culture in sparking deeper, theological discussions. Today's recommendation is a book of essays by Ursula Le Guin – a writer I've never heard of. Within the opening pages is a note that says 'The original anarchist'. I can't help but chuckle at the idea of anarchy being a product of words alone, as though they don't need accompanying action to be of any sort of use.

Movement outside the window catches my eye. Matt, the son of the Dad in South Tower A, second floor, flat three, is running across the road to intercept Old Ruth. She's still in her faded grey cardigan, hair still pulled back impossibly tight, and she's hobbling up the street with her arms full of bright Sainsbury's bags. It's the first time I've seen her with them, and I wonder if she's taken her business there today, a good fifteen minutes out of her way, just to punish Hasan and the Muslims of the mosque for what happened last night. Or perhaps it just made her nervous and she thinks some sort of attack is imminent, and so she's chosen to avoid the entire street.

Matt stops her, and they share a few words. He tries to take the bags off her hands, and she resists – three times by my count, just like Arabs do – before finally relenting with a smile. She hands over the shopping and gives him an affectionate pat on his pale, spotty cheek before leading him down the road towards the estate.

I turn back to the shelves. Pausing at that fake fire, I hold out my hands; I imagine warmth wrapping around my permanently chilly palms and brushing against my face. I try not to think of other fires I've stood in front of, fires that dot the dark European landscape like stars in the night sky, beautiful and alive and desperate.

13

Echoes

The news is full of refugee pieces. They're on every channel and all sorts of websites – video diaries, insights brought to you by pseudo-celebs, in-depth interviews. It's as though the more fresh-faced, young women they can find with hoodies raised up as they gaze across borders back at their homeland or logged on to wifi while huddled in a tent at the Greece–Macedonia border, the more likely they are to convince the public there's nothing to fear here, that a refugee will not kill you. There is no horde of barbarians at the gates. In point of fact, these people are escaping the barbarians.

At a time when access to data is quite literally limitless, ignorance cannot be anything other than a choice, and I wonder how many of the people those BBC and *Guardian* and *Independent* pieces are targeting actually watch/read/follow them?

It's an algorithm. You will have heard of it. Thought up by some hi-tech brain in some town in California where we'd all love to live. As you click on links or heart various articles or follow certain organizations, the algorithm goes to work streamlining your feed, so that when you log on, you are steered towards content you like and views you already hold. They call it an echo chamber, but it seems to me it's more of a cage, limiting your views and experiences to the extent that nothing unexpected or unsolicited ever crosses your path. And what other outcome can a device like that have but reduced tolerance?

The question then becomes one of how people might break out of it. Or, perhaps more accurately, how do we break them out of it? Because it seems the onus is on us. As though we should all walk around like modern-day prophets urging others to come out from the darkness and into the light. I'm not sure I believe that, or that it's a responsibility I am morally bound to take on. Is it my job, as a Muslim, to try to convince you not to be afraid of me? That my people are not hardwired to hate you, to want to blow you up on a tube or ram you with a van?

They said globalization would make the world better, but instead the word has become some hysterical shorthand for anything that threatens the status quo. They said the internet would bring us all closer together, that it would turn the world into a little village, but it hasn't. Instead we have splintered, split off into islands drifting further and further apart.

After all, the internet that elected the first black US president and set the Arab Spring ablaze is also the internet which ripped the UK from Europe and elected Dr Strangelove over in America.

I'm not so sure about this one, Josie says in her latest email, attached to which is my draft article with tracked changes and comments I've only glanced at. *It lacks the coherence and direction of your previous pieces. Why don't you give us some of your memories instead? I'm particularly interested in your experiences in making your way here or even what things were like back home before you left. Could you focus on that? Try to draw those memories out rather than focusing on purely rational analysis of the state the world finds itself in, viz. media and facts. There are more than enough talking heads going on about that. I think your personal narrative would make for highly readable pieces. Sit on this for a few days and get back to me?*

Yeah, but who knows where we'll be in a few days, Josie.

There is an obsession here with memory, its preservation and dissemination and accuracy. The obsession is typified in the language itself. Memory, recollection, recall, retention, remembrance, reminiscence, impression – who needs that many words for one concept? It's as though more and more synonyms were thought up in reaction to the porous quality of memories, their ability to morph and be stained and leave you and haunt you, as though if we had more words for them, they would be more inclined towards permanency or, at the very least, clarity.

In my language, we have one word for it, and we make do, and memories are painful things we have no inclination to solidify.

Let it go, Dr Thompson had said, which I took to mean 'forget'. *It's the only way forward now.*

Are memories ever true in their entirety? Josie asks me for them, but I feel like I'm lying if I say something happened fully in this one way. How much can I trust my mind with my own story?

Why don't you give us some of your memories instead? She asks it so easily, as though it were as simple as No-Lights-Man pulling his box out from under the bed, as though it were not in fact a matter of pulling corpses from the ground, their foetid breath washing over you as they speak of all the things they've seen. She wants me to flay myself, to dig deep, to mine all that I have swallowed. Perhaps even drag Little Ahmed up, muddy water dripping from pale brow . . .

No.

I move to the wardrobe and pull out the big black suitcase I keep my documents in. It is full of official paperwork, hospital records, school transcripts, my passport and birth certificate. All the papers that prove I'm a real person. There's also a battered Arabic–English dictionary and notebooks full of daily logs and journals that contain quite a few of those memories she wants but that I have, until now, resisted dipping into.

What dark things lie here, I'm not sure. Much of it is gone from my waking mind, held only in my nervous system – the beating of my heart, numbness in my extremities, feelings of impending doom. Dreams, dreams, dreams. But still, I pull out the papers and notebooks and start to go through them one by one.

'faces like gargoyles crying in the dark cold hands dry and rough like cardboard. its been three days with one flatbread'

'sandwiches snatched out of outstretched hands, there was a man leading prayers down by a muddy river. i didnt join in, um hasan glared at me later and wouldn't let the girls show me the bunny they found'

'Patient is a young female, 24 years of age, Caucasian and of Arab descent. Referral documents indicate that she has received treatment for gastrointestinal parasites, anaemia, severe dehydration, tuberculosis, and chronic bacterial skin infection.'

'i don't cry any more. my body has better use for the moisture'

'there were potatoes in the mud today full of little black things that didnt look like ants to me. it reminded me of a film baba used to let us watch with a boy in a concentration camp or something and they give them these ugly potatoes and he says the bugs are good to eat because at least its protein'

'Neuroimaging results show no abnormalities in physi-
ology. The mesencephalic region appears unremarkable
with no sign of lesions. Frontal lobe and basal ganglia
are also unremarkable. White matter appears normal
with no sign of SMA impairment. Consequently, a diag-
nosis of akinetic mutism (AM) was ruled out. After a
thorough psychological evaluation (detailed below and
in the accompanying documents), the patient was placed
on Sertraline, 25 mg/day with a planned increase as
per the schedule below. Patient will also undergo
Cognitive Processing Therapy.'

*'screaming today, pop pop pop of gunfire and the scent of scorched
earth. Bombs in the clouds that you can hear but cant see Hanging.
a nice volunteer on the macedonian border gave us water to clean
our eyes. it was cold.'*

*'The river is dirty here full of shit i dont want to go in who will
smell me anyways maybe it'll keep them away'*

"سجل!
أنا عربــــــــي
أنا اسم بلا لقب"

'On admittance to the ward the patient presented
with intermittent outstanding catatonic symptoms.
Patient, though fully conscious, was unresponsive,
immobile and mute. For three days, there was a marked
reduction of nearly all motor function, including
facial expressions and gestures. Such a presentation
prompted this clinician to order a second round of
diagnostic tests. These results were also negative
for any abnormalities.'

'Tear gas rocks smoke on the tongue guards snap their teeth like wild hungry dogs'

'On the fourth day, the patient exhibited a hysterical mutism characterized by what this clinician has determined is an obstinate and voluntary silence unaccompanied by abnormalities in the muscles of articulation. Patient was able to cough normally and facial expressions returned in the form of glaring and scowling as well as intermittent expressions of confusion and/or shock. Psychiatric evaluation commenced by administering an online Minnesota Multiphasic Personality Inventory (MMPI) test. The patient was also allowed to provide written responses to the Rorschach and Thematic Apperception Test. A sentence-completion test was also administered.'

'where is human rights?
just tell me where it? Ali X'

أهلاً وسهلاً

'You have to be a real person even in the most impossible of conditions'

'The patient exhibited prolonged latency in responding to questions. This, in addition to the time required to write responses rather than submitting them orally, resulted in the tests being administered over three days.

Overall results indicate that the patient's personality has deteriorated, with abundant signs that
the ego is unable to mitigate the effects of
post-traumatic stress and/or to mediate reality.
Basic affective controls are barely intact, and
patient relies on a variety of defence mechanisms
to contain the underlying failed psychotic process,
including intellectualization, compartmentalization
and repression. In particular the patient exhibits
severe detachment from physical and emotional experience, with at least one recorded episode of
psychogenic amnesia.'

*later the boys found pipes and pretended they were guns and the
girls went looking for more flowers before the rain i wonder if it
snows here and if he'll come to me again*'

get in the boat he said. it'll be all right he said'

'Patient responses show a preoccupation with sex
and anatomy with some evidence of repression of
sexual and/or physical trauma. Intellectually, the
patient registers at the high average/superior level,
writing far above the normal range. Visual-spatial
reasoning and perceptual-organizational skills are
highly developed, though functionality appears some-
what diminished at the present time. Working memory
was found to be below average.'

'DONT.GET CAUGHT! GET CAUGHT AND <u>IT IS OVER!</u>'

'it seems i'll never leave this beach. but at least i've avoided the jungle down that way. Because we're animals, right? bad things are happening there and they say it'll be closed or ruined or set fire to. There are crabs everywhere and little Black Flying things. Scratching is bad but i can't help myself. they say a man from Tategem will take us to uk but they've been saying this for a long while and i'm thinking maybe it's all been for nothing'

'The Thematic Apperception Test indicates a fatalistic view of the world, characterized by high pessimism markers. To her mind, the world is full of doom with humankind utterly lacking in redeeming qualities. These results are corroborated by the Rorschach record which indicates that the patient devotes a considerable amount of energy to staying alert to her surroundings. This excessive concern indicates a feeling of constant peril, as though a situation could become life-threatening if the patient fails to closely monitor it. Patient shows a distinct lack of trust in others, imagining all persons she comes into contact with to have malicious intent. Physical examination and medical history indicate that this is not an entirely irrational response.'

14

لاجئ

There's shouting in South Tower A, second floor, flat three. Terrible shouting that rebounds up the balconies and into every open window like a volley of sharp arrows. The Dad is in a rage, and for once I don't shut my window against it, don't try to drown it out with music or earplugs or a pillow over my head. I sit on my balcony, with my back against the wall, and I listen.

The Dad stalks around the living room like a tiger that's been moved to a smaller cage, and he shouts at Helen. I can't see her, but I imagine she's cowering in a corner. 'I told you not to question me! If I want to get pissed after work, I will! I work hard, don't I? I keep you in this fucking flat you're so happy with. I keep your kids in food and clothes and do I get a thanks from you? No, it's just more fucking complaints and questions and murmurs. I'm so sick of your fucking murmuring, Helen!'

She does murmur, and I can see how it would annoy him.

In his ranting rage he knocks things over – a tall glass from the coffee table rolls off onto the carpet below, a picture frame drops and cracks against the floor when he pounds a fist against the wall, a lamp standing by the sofa topples over when he moves past it. It all looks accidental, every time he knocks something over, but I know it isn't. He means it, the way he means to stomp over to the corner I can't see, but where I know she is, like a boxer feints in a fight. It's meant to frighten her, and how could it not? The Dad is a big man; he could've been a boxer himself in another life, or maybe he was at some point in this one. He's tall, with broad shoulders and arms and legs like massive tree trunks, and from across the way, his clenched fists look like white tennis balls hurtling through the air.

Movement catches my eye and I look up. Off to the side I see No-Lights-Man on his balcony. Gripping the rails, he leans over and cranes his neck this way and that to find where the commotion is coming from. The way the towers are aligned, he can't see that side of South Tower A. He must recognize the Dad's voice, but he can't seem to place it tonight. I think he must be high because he's only there for a moment before turning around and shuffling back into his flat, sliding the window shut and locking it behind him.

If Helen responds to the Dad's ire (and I hope she doesn't), I don't hear it. I do see him grip her arm and yank her from her corner, flinging her around so she lands on the sofa, her left ribs connecting with the hard armrest in a way that makes me wince. She cries out, a squeaking shriek like an injured bird, and I turn my face away as he lunges at her.

There's a flickering light in the dark room next door. The daughter, Chloe, is on the bed, massive headphones covering her ears, eyes glued to the computer screen before her. She's small like her mother, drowning in an oversized jumper and loose sweatpants and the duvet piled around her. I don't see Matt anywhere, but I suppose they must have another room and he might be there, or he might be out with his friends. I see him sometimes, drinking and smoking in the car park behind a cheap hotel down the way or moving in a pack of boys down the block to and from school. He's hardly ever home any more, or if he is, I don't see him from my window.

73

She's on the floor now, the Dad looming over her, his massive hands around her throat, throttling her. I am shaking and there is a salty wetness on my lips. I grip my mobile so hard my knuckles look pale and bloodless. It's only for the internet and emails and such, but I unlock it now, my trembling fingers punching in the code, opening the phone function and typing out 999. My thumb hovers over the green 'Call' sign, my brain screaming at me to just do it, to make the call, that someone is going to die because I can't get my tongue and lips and vocal cords to function. A tinny voice answers, 'This is Emergency, how can I help?' I stare at the phone in my lap. There is a boulder in my throat, I open my mouth, try to push a word out, a syllable even, but there is nothing but a guttural sound, like choking. 'Can I help?' the voice asks again. Yes, you can fucking help. Trace this call and come and help. All those conspiracy theories about how Big Brother is watching and screening and listening in on our phone calls and monitoring us through our laptop cameras, fucking find where my call is coming from and send the police. Helen is screaming now, a shrill wail that fills the sky, and I think he must not be throttling her after all if she has enough air to make that sound. Looking over the edge, I see him straddling her; she's on her stomach and he's trying to turn her back around and she's trying to crawl away and Chloe is still watching her computer instead of using her clear bell of a voice to call for help and what is this war being waged in their home and why is no one on Helen's side in it?

The door to my right opens, Ruth nearly falling out onto their balcony. A phone is stuck to her ear and she's shouting the address into it and yelling at them to hurry up. She leans over the railing, and I suck in a breath because she's so small, the wind might lift her up and over it, and she yells across the way, 'Let her go, you coward! I'm calling the police, I am, and they are going to put you away! You can't do that! You can't!'

He can and he has and we all know this isn't the first time and it probably won't be the last. Ruth sees me in her periphery, turns her pinched face my way, sees me sitting there trembling, with snot and tears streaking my cheeks and mouth. Her lip curls and her nostrils flare in distaste, and she turns back to watch the attack until the police arrive with their competing sirens and wails and flashing lights.

———

That night I dream of Serbia.

We're out of Sombor, finally. They kept us there for hours, me and the runaway families I attached myself to – the Alis from Homs and the Husseins from Iraq who pretend they're from Aleppo and the AlKhalafs from Raqqa, whose patriarch cries long into the night about the bombing of the mosque and the sacrilege and injustice and humiliation of it all. I camp beside these families. I don't have a tent, but some NGO-er gave me a tarpaulin, and I string it across some branches.

You don't sleep with the children tonight, says Um Hasan from the Alis. On bad nights, nights when the terror is too close and fresh in the mind, her tent is a womb she shelters her family in. Ten or fifteen of them all piled one on top of the other so that it reminds me of the raft to Lesbos. I sleep on the ground under the open sky and fuck it all if some man decides it's an invitation.

Young men shouting into the dying light of every dying day. When the struggles are done – the search for food, for water, for a place to sleep, for a smuggler and a truck to carry their families the rest of the way – they subside into their tents and give in to rage. VOILÀ LA RAGE QUI EFFRAIE LA SOCIÉTÉ CIVILISÉE! Yelling at their children for straying too far away in their games,

75

at teenage daughters who venture out of the tents or wander along border fences and smile at guards, at old aunts and mothers and grandmothers for being stupid and burdensome and useless. Rough slapping of hands against skin. A vengeful fuck. A fist to an abdomen. A plea to Allah.

There's a woman here, older than time, shrivelled as a fig in the sun. Flat face, empty eyes in hollow sockets, arms like matchsticks. She's made of paper, and her family is blowing her across a continent. She doesn't eat; her daughter or daughter-in-law or someone she must be related to in some way shoves spoonfuls of broth between her cracked lips every so often, but most of it drips down her chin to her chest and lap. She prays all the time. More than five times a day, like she thinks the original fifty is the actual revelation. Outside their tent, by the bright wood huts, down by the muddy river, on railway tracks so her family has to shove her out of the way of train cars coming from a long way off, when we're huddled up in groups waiting to cross a border or board a train or be given aid, on long walks through dense forests, when you can't tell where in the sky the sun is, she drops her bag, folds her arms across the crease of her mid-section and starts *al-fatiha*.

Memories, or fevered imaginings. They sear me, bright white and hot. *How many months is it?* he asks. *My husband is just over there,* I lie, even as I know the opening of my legs will be required to get out of this. Scurrying by rivers and forests and marshes, begging for food and hoarding any cash I can save or steal or manage somehow to earn. Across Turkey and those terrible Grecian waters. Vomiting until my insides feel like they're twisting up and out of my throat like vines. Clinging in furious waters to a raft that is more of a balloon. The stinking heat of Macedonia, bleeding blisters and insect bites, and Kosovo with nothing but a small hip sack and every document I have about who I am.

76

My family finds me here, if only in dreams.

Here where it's the dead of winter and toes are falling off, where the people in the fields are breaking frozen leaves from trees to suck on while others find icicles on the poles and the tin sheets that hold up their tents and walk around with them in hand like lollipops.

The sun shines. Every day, but it's just for show.

No heat.

               Nothing thaws.

                             Nothing melts.

I walk, dragging them all behind me, and when I can walk no more, Mama lines us up around the dead fire pit, eldest to youngest. She places us between her knees, clamping down on our hips, and scrubs us with black soot and ash.

It burns, Mama.

        She scrubs down pale chests. Armpits until they bleed.

                It burns. Scalps until we are faint.

Have they made it to Alexandria? Are Mama and Baba and Nada and all the little ones sitting around a big plate of steaming saffron rice and fragrant cuts of lamb? Are they drinking cardamom tea and full-fat camel's milk? Do they sleep on feathers, wrapped in the weighty comfort of a winter *bisht*?

'Egypt is not more stable, Baba! What is happening here will happen there! Where's the law? Look at the news!'

'Ammu Ghaith is there and your tantes and my friends from university. You will be safe there. They share our language, our religion. We will be safe and you can be married and have a happy life.'

I ran because I would not trade one oppression for another.

We are in Serbia.

Tomorrow or the next day is Hungary.

This is where the real struggle begins, he says. Sweat drips wet and metallic onto my face, into my mouth.

How can it possibly get any worse?

It will never happen. I will never reach the end. My life is here, in the ebb and flow of humans pushing and being shoved back across borders, shuttled from detention centre to filthy campground to open fields and rocky beaches. This is to be my life.

Wake up now, the sweaty man says, pushing harder. *You're no fun.*

لاجئ

Ref.u.gee

/ ˌrefyoo'jē/

Noun: a person forced to leave their country in order to escape
     war, persecution, or natural disaster.

Synonyms: fugitive, exile, displaced person, asylum seeker, boat
     people

So many words. Why do you need so many words? What will I say if, when, someone asks? What will I tell them I am? I lash out at border officials, at men who push me too far, at women in village centres who spit at me in their foreign tongues. I use my words on them all, abusing them in Arabic and English and all the other languages I've picked up along the way – Kurdish and Turkish and French and a smattering of Greek.

Fugitive and *exile* sound like I've done something wrong. *You do many wrong things,* he says, finishing up and rolling away. Yes, maybe, but fleeing across these European borders is not one of them.

Displaced person sounds too much like *mis*placed person, and though I am lost much of the time, I am not that.

Boat people is Aegean waters, and I will not claim it.
Asylum seeker
Yes: here, at last, is some truth. Asylum.

Ref.uge
/ ˌrefyo͞oj/
from the Latin *re- fugere*, *re-* 'back' and *fugere* 'flee'.
Noun: a condition of being safe or sheltered from pursuit, danger,
  or trouble.

The synonyms here are more innocuous. They carry no judgment
– shelter, protection, safety, security, sanctuary.
Consider the prefix, he says as he walks away.
Ah yes, prefixes. Those pesky English devils that gnaw at the heels
and push bile up the throat.
No such problem with the Arabic. No prefix there. Just the long
la, as though you were about to break into a lamentation. Then the
sharp jerking nod of the *ji'*, the *hamza* stopping you from venturing
any further into the grief that lies there, ensnared and entangled, in
such little letters.
I am a refugee. Here, in Serbia, by the waters of the Danube,
which sometimes are still mirrors for white fluffy clouds and sometimes are muddy with froth and blood and raindrops and sometimes
carry big green lily pads down through Romania, I run my finger
over the word again and again.
If *recall* and *recollect* mean to 'call' and 'collect' again, does *refugee*
contain within it, hidden and folded in a dead language, the notion
of perpetual fleeing?

15

The Last of Her Kind

In the morning I cradle my mug of coffee and wander up and down Hasan's aisles. He sees me from his spot at the till and makes some sort of gesture that looks like a warning not to spill in his shop. I nod in his direction and hold the mug closer to my chest; the heat of the ceramic against my skin centres me somehow.

I did not sleep well, and the pink hours of dawn were spent on the floor of the shower while stings of water pelted my head and shoulders and back. I was cold and hot, trembling and flushed, bloated and acidic, and I rocked there for hours, straining to get a word past my lips. When I subsided into tears, I was still quiet. I shaved my legs, but it was just a ruse, an excuse to hold the blade at the wrong angle, to take careless swipes at my ankles or the skin behind my knees, to release my breath at the sting of pain, the distraction of thin, pale lines of blood. I wondered if, at that moment, my family's blood was spilling elsewhere – in Cairo or the waters of Queiq or some other place I didn't know them to be.

Pain is a good distraction. A nick of a razor blade, a lighter too close to the thumb, a stapler to the soft pad of an index finger, a tattoo where the skin is thin and the bone too near the surface.

I stand at the till. My arms are full of honey and cheese that I will pull apart into long strips to lay down on large pitta bread. The

80

empty coffee mug dangles from a finger, and I see Chloe in the queue ahead of me. She looks as well rested as I am. Still in the oversized hoodie and sweatpants she was wearing the night before, her hair is oily and limp on her shoulders and there are dark circles under her eyes.

'I live right round the corner,' she says, her voice holding a distinctly teenage whine. 'I'll bring the money for it later, I swear!'

Hasan shakes his head and pulls the bottles of grape drink closer. 'Bring the money now.'

'I can't go there now,' she fumes. She has big blue eyes like her mother and they're rapidly filling with tears. Hasan is immune, shaking his head and gesturing for her to move along with a flick of his hand.

He doesn't like them; I've seen the evidence when they come into the shop. The whole family irritates him: the Dad is a prick who never says please or thank you, just drops coins and notes on the counter for his purchases, as though he wouldn't deign to touch Hasan; Helen scurries here and there around the shop, picking things up and putting them back because she can never decide what to get; Chloe and her friends turn up their noses at his offerings or complain loudly about the smell of spice; Matt and his friends just stalk up and down, knocking items off the shelves and kicking at big sacks of rice until Hasan chases them out with a string of Punjabi words. He lets some of us do what she's asking. Sometimes I take things, holding them up as I walk out of the door, and I forget about it until he presents me with a tab at the end of the month.

He won't offer Chloe such privileges so I lean across and put my food on the counter, drawing her bottles over and sliding my crumpled notes across to Hasan who accepts them without so much as a pause. He hands over the change, and I pile my things back up into my arms and walk out.

Chloe stops me with a hand to my shoulder before I even cross the road. When I turn, she says, 'Thank you,' to which I nod before making to turn around again, but she stops me.

'That old nan in your building,' she says, over-enunciating every word, 'she pointed at your window last night, when she were talking to the police, and she said, "The deaf girl saw everything too." Can you read lips?'

I nod.

'Did the police come and talk to you?' she asks, eyes wide with worry. She's a miniature of her mother: same build, same mousy hair, same eyes and face. I imagine a long, matrilineal Russian doll of identical women going back through time, that with Chloe and her mother, we are reaching the tiniest incarnations. I wonder if somewhere in their line are women who were giants, stomping across the moors and peaks with red and gold and brown forests for hair, eyes the size of lochs, cheeks cut like the cliffs of Dover.

I shake my head at her question, and she breathes out a long sigh of relief, her eyes quick and darting as they scan the road back to the towers. 'I hope they don't. That old lady told them more than enough. Nosy old slag.'

I frown, though I don't disagree with her assessment.

'Are you going home?'

I press my lips together and nod, indicating the items in my arms. Her two bottles of grape drink dangle from each hand.

'Can I come?'

I shake my head; hard, vigorous shakes, so that my short black uneven waves whoosh back and forth across my face. No one comes to my flat. Ever. It's my place, my sanctuary, my hiding hole. It is the only place, in the entire world, where I feel halfway safe. So no, she cannot come; no one can come there.

'Please,' she says, taking a step closer to me, eyes looking like they take up the whole of her face. 'I saw you last night, on the balcony. I've seen you there before, watching and scowling at him. You care, I know you do.'

My mind retorts that *she* clearly doesn't, or she would have tried to intervene with her parents or phoned the police herself rather than wait for the neighbours to do it.

'I can't go home, not right now.' She shakes her head, wisps of hair trailing over her shoulders. 'She's gone to get him.' Her eyes meet mine, hard and wet. 'She's gone to the station to get him out, and she's going to bring him back, and I can't be there when she does. Please.'

In my flat, Chloe is respectful. She doesn't say any of the things I sometimes entertain myself by imagining someone might say if they were to enter my flat. She says nothing about the mess of books and papers and laptop strewn about the floor like an offering to some pagan god of letters. She makes no comment about the half-eaten stale bread on the counter or the dishes piled in the sink. She doesn't patronize me by saying it's a nice flat or how she admires the fact that I don't have a television because you can watch everything online now anyway.

She moves carefully and quietly through the space, stepping over the cracked-open spines of books and discarded pens, over to the desk where she perches on the red desk chair with the loose screws. It teeters precariously, and she grips the desk, but even that wobbles at her touch. Finally, she's steady, keeping her balance in the seat, and holds out a grape drink.

It tastes rank, hard and sour, but I swallow it anyway. I put my groceries away while she scans my bookshelves. Her eyes move over books by Orwell and Koestler, Fisk and Darwish and Said, fingers following to trail over the Steinems and Didions and Byatts. She

83

pulls out a short story collection by Ghada al-Samman, and I grip my bottle tighter as I join her in the living room. She runs her fingers over the glossy white finish and screws up her face; I can't tell if it's the Arabic script that has her befuddled or the unnerving cover, with its watchful owls and dark skies and jagged landscape. There's a story in there with a woman who insists it's better to die by the heat of falling bombs than the chill of silent indignity. Chloe flips through the book, eyes scanning the foreign words and the foreign experiences they attest to, experiences of displacement and exile and pain that she can't even fathom.

I wonder if she has any idea of the knowledge that is right there, literally at her fingertips. What do they teach them at school in this country? What do they teach them these days? I feel a desperate urge to stuff a tote full of books for her to take home and read instead of frying her brain on whatever show she's streaming, the show that flickers off the screen in the darkness of her room.

It's too quiet, but there's nothing I can do about it. To play music off the laptop would alert her to the fact that I can hear, and that's not a conversation I'm about to have with anyone. So I sit there, against the wall, and drink the disgusting juice.

'She's weak,' Chloe says, flipping the pages of another book. This one is a ripped and battered copy of Milton's *Paradise Lost* that I rescued from the boxes outside the Ginger Giant's bookshop. I haven't read it yet, but it's a story everyone knows. 'I hate how weak she is.' I don't say anything, obviously, and she just carries on. 'I don't know how she can let him treat her like that. She just sits there and cries. She doesn't fight or get back at him or anything.' She shakes her head down at the stained and torn pages, and I realize she's doing that thing strangers do around me, saying what they want to say because they think I can't hear them.

I play along, turning to look out of the window. The Juicer is in his flat, going through his Saturday routine. He's punching and kicking at the air, a series of reps, followed by skipping followed by sit-ups and push-ups. His shirt is off, exercise shorts hanging low on his abdomen so that the cutting lines of his hips are visible over the waistband. Sweat glistens on his skin. The light is hitting him well. He could be a model for a sports brand or an energy drink.

'Sometimes I think she deserves it,' Chloe mumbles, much in the same way I've heard her mum do in the shop or the laundry room. 'I hear him hitting her and I think, just fight back, just do something. Maybe she likes it. Maybe it gets her off. I mean, it must, since she's gone down to the station to get him out, to bring him back to us.' She comes towards me, crouching down so I look at her lips. 'Do you think it's possible she likes it?'

I meet her eyes and shake my head. She doesn't move, like she wants me to elaborate. Sighing, I grab a pen and notebook from the floor beside me.

No one likes being a punchbag.

Chloe reads the piece of paper then looks at me again. 'Have you been hit before?'

She shouldn't be asking questions about me, my history, my story. It's not her business. She's nothing to me, just like I'm nothing to her. But she's looking at me in earnest, desperate for an answer, and I can't think why it would reassure her, or what she hopes to learn, but her eyes won't let me go and I end up nodding in response.

She nods as well, and it makes her look older than her years. I wonder what she's been through and if she's been through things that would make her an adult at fourteen or fifteen or however old she is. Has he hit her too? Is she hiding purple marks?

I turn towards the window again, and she does as well, a puff of breath escaping her when she sees the Juicer. He's doing pull-ups on a bar stretched across the doorway; knees up, ankles crossed, his abdomen crunches over and over, biceps curl and uncurl, all that muscle moving and bulging and twisting. The very picture of the perfect male.

Chloe lowers herself to the floor, crossing her legs, and we watch.

16

The People in the Windows

In East Tower, fourth floor, flat three, the Juicer is watching TV. It's a fancy one, big screen curved and looming from the wall like an officer in an interrogation room. He's playing the defendant, cowering, it seems to me, on the hard, uninviting sofa in black trainers and black exercise shorts and a white T-shirt too clean to be believed. He has a sliver of a laptop open while he watches what looks to be a documentary of some sort. I can't see it that well, but there is an animation of what I think might be rows and rows of cows. Then, there's footage of a chicken coop and pigs and butchers and a milking line. There's a big, colourful food pyramid with levels crossed out and a man talking passionately about something, and every so often the Juicer will pause it and start typing like mad with a horrified look on his beautiful face.

In South Tower A, second floor, flat three Matt is in Chloe's room. She isn't there; there's no one else in the flat as far as I can tell. Still he pauses at the door, head tilted towards the hallway behind him as though he's heard a sound, but their door hasn't opened and he's alone. He moves quickly, crouching beside her bed, his too-big jeans dragging and pooling at his feet. One long, gangly arm reaches under the frame and pulls out a plastic bag. He opens it, peering inside as though to check its contents, and takes out a can of spray paint with a bright red cap. There are other cans in there, but I can't see what colour they are.

No-Lights-Man has a new girl over in East Tower, third floor, flat two. It's not the ballerina with the long arms he had with him in Hasan's, but his flat is lit up all the same. They're on the balcony smoking, both in ratty jeans and dirty trainers. Neither looks like they've showered in the last couple of days, hair falling about their faces in oily-looking strings, and it seems to me they wear their dishevelment with pride, like it says for them, *we have more important things to worry about than squeaky-clean hair.* This lack of hygiene is a luxury for them. She's writing furiously on a notepad, trying to keep up with the flow of words coming from No-Lights-Man's mouth. He gesticulates, the hand holding the cigarette flying this way and that as he makes some point or another, pausing every so often to take a swig from the can between his legs, or maybe just to let her catch up.

Not a conquest, I think.

In Aleppo, after our mothers made us abandon university and come home, we would gather at Amer's place. His father had sent his mother and sisters off to safety, and by that point he rarely left the back room. When we were there, we'd hear the Quran blasting from the radio, and I could imagine him, my mother's cousin, sitting on the bed, arms crossed, rocking back and forth while the world outside shattered and burned. Amer had taken over the living room, converted it into a kind of command centre. It was a bare space: a two-seater black sofa against one wall; an aluminium desk against the opposite one and another desk off to the side that sometimes served as a dining-room table. (*Mama and Auntie took the good furniture,* he said with a wink when I asked about their beautiful oak coffee table and entertainment cabinet with its shelves of books and records and photo albums. All gone.) There were two chairs that went

along with the desks and which we would drag over near the sofa to
sit on while watching black and white films on the old TV set in the
corner; there were pallets and large pillows to sit on and two tall
fluted *narghiles* beneath the grimy window. In the centre of one wall
hung a large portrait of the president, his icy eyes boring into the
room. The first time we came over, Ossama nearly jumped out of
his skin when he glimpsed it over his shoulder, sending me into a
fit of giggles. Khalid scowled and raised his eyebrows at Amer, who
shrugged and said, *Just in case*. And every time we were in the flat,
Khalid would glance uneasily at the portrait, as though anticipating
red dots of surveillance to appear in its corners or for the eyes to
track him around the room.

This was where Amer and Ossama would draw and paint their
posters. The rest of us gave suggestions – symbols to include, large
black boots or olive green guns or red red birds. Khalid would suggest
slogans – ones used in other Springs, ones used when we'd all been
here in the past, ones he'd made up. Amer or Ossama would do a
rough sketch on a loose scrap of paper, altering and fiddling with it
until we were all happy before committing the design to a poster or
banner. Khalid doubted whether it was worth our time; he wanted
to be out in the streets, among the crowds doing something, and he
was always the first to volunteer to take the posters and banners out,
to affix them to walls and stick them to windows in the dead of
night, when, maybe, no one would see.

They see everything.

I shake myself, watching as Matt drops the spray paint back in
the bag before rising and loping out of the room with it. It reminds
me of Ahmed and memories flood my mind faster than I can banish
them. He was always taking things and hiding them – toys, the
remote control for the television, Baba's portable radio. He never had
a reason for it, only that it amused him. He would secrete things

round the house, but he'd go around moving them from one hiding place to another, so that if the radio was under the boys' bed one day, it was under the girls' mattress the next, or shoved deep in the back of a wardrobe, or buried in a load of laundry. It annoyed Mama no end, and she was constantly telling him off and twisting his ear for it, but he just carried on for as long as he could.

I draw invisible letters on the glass, stand-alone Arabic letters, like if I disconnect them from words, they won't mean anything. No-Lights-Man thinks I'm signalling him or something because he tilts his head at me, shaking it as though to ask what I'm doing. Dropping my hand, I clasp it in the other behind my back and shake my own head. His face breaks into an easy smile, eyes locking on mine for a moment before he turns his attention back to the girl.

What do they see, the people in the windows, when they look into mine? I try to project myself, release this body and all the things that weigh it down, soar over concrete, and inhabit some space over there. I imagine looking out, seeing through the eyes of another. What is it they see in West Tower, fourth floor, flat three?

She lives alone. All her furniture is red or black – red swivel chair at a big black desk, black bookshelves crammed and overflowing, a red coffee table with dings and chips marring its surface. There's no sofa, so she sits on the floor and writes in an endless line-up of notebooks – red ones, black ones, ones with patterns, hard covers and soft, massive ones that take up her whole lap or tiny ones that fit in the palm of her hand. When she finishes with one, she moves on to the next, or abandons pen and paper entirely to tap at the ancient laptop on the desk.

Heavyset, naked she looks like a Rubens, with rolls and folds and thick thighs. There is a quill tattooed on her left shoulder, the black feathers wrapping up so the tip curves over towards her neck. From Hasan's she buys thick cheese spreads and pre-packaged pittas and the biggest jars of instant coffee he sells. She sits on the hardwood floor and reads her books, turning the pages with just the tips of her fingers while smearing large chunks of white cheese on open pittas and laying down strips of salami before rolling them up to eat in large, careless bites. She washes it all down with litres of orange energy drink. Just like home, only subbing in Fanta or Tang.

Her flat overflows with books. Novels, short story and essay collections, books on history, philosophy and religion. There are texts on anthropology and archaeology and mythology and any other -ology she can find. In some of the books the text goes from left to right, others right to left. Leaning towers of them line the walls, jagged piles that from across the way look like the city's medieval skyline. There are always a few lying about on the floor where she writes, set out around her like some miniature Stonehenge or fairy circle. They're stacked up on the desk, in big piles that occasionally topple over when she tries to pull one out from the bottom.

The Juicer leers at her from across the way when he thinks she isn't looking.

A beep from my laptop; I turn from the window.

My lungs are never full.

An email from Josie, more notes on the article she doesn't like.

What am I doing?

I sit down to read.

17

The Eye

The room is dim because the windows are dirty. So streaky with grime and black specks and bad omens, you can hardly see through the glass. The sun tries, but it's weak at this time of year and only a hazy light manages to penetrate.

It falls on an equally dirty floor of plain white tiles, mottled with grey. There are scuff marks from shoes and black grease and dirt carried in from the street and discarded sweet wrappers and loose paper that no one has bothered to throw in the bin. A red plastic cup is kicked back and forth across the floor whenever anyone moves – perhaps it's a game, or just a series of accidents.

Outside, *malak almawt* hovers over the streets of Aleppo, the Angel of Death flapping his mighty wings like a shroud caught in a strong wind. He touches down often, so that death, instead of rain, falls from the sky. Death stains every household, every soul. Each arrest, each detainment, each rape, each death is the snuffing out of a candle. The land is going dark, and soon there will be nothing here at all.

But today the sun's rays fall on two desks. They rattle, all loose screws and ill-fitting drawers. The chairs squeak when Ossama and Amer shift and move between their workstations to see what the other is doing. The backs are ripped and bright yellow sponge pushes through the cracks. Sometimes, when we leave, bits and pieces of it will be stuck to the backs of their T-shirts, and I or Donya will pick at them like gorillas grooming their mates.

High in the corner of the ceiling, where the light cannot reach, is an eyeball. Large and white with red veins, and a bright iris with a fully dilated pupil, it moves with us. Scanning back and forth, back and forth, from one wall to the other, from window to door, it misses nothing. It sees the plastic cup roll across the floor. It sees the wobbling desks with their loose screws. It sees me trying to wash the windows without falling four floors to the street below. It sees Ossama and Amer labouring over their length of fabric, huddled over it so the Eye can't see what they're drawing.

The white cotton is pulled taut between the two desks, anchored at various points with things we've found on the street or brought from home – a rock, a can filled with sand, a Quran, a broken radio, a black boot. Ossama and Amer spread their free hands across the fabric, pulling it even tighter as they bring the markers down, moving the colour across the cotton in firm strokes. Knotted guns, heavy boots on heads and cracked waterwheels blossom on the banner like spring flowers, unfurling in delicate lines and intricate curves. Slogans, in precise Arabic lettering, take up all available space – 'One, one, one: we are one', 'Death before humiliation', 'Your bullets kill nothing but our fear'.

Khalid stands against the wall, arms crossed, his dark gaze flitting between the Eye and the huddle. He's in a white T-shirt and dirty faded jeans, a black and white *keffiyeh* draped over his bony shoulders. There's a look of disapproval on my love's face, in the set of his thin lips, but it is not that disapproval born of fear. Long cow lashes shutter over his eyes and he shakes his head and mutters, 'This isn't going to work.'

We ignore him. I wash the windows, Ossama and Amer continue to draw, and Donya joins their huddle, pulling it in tighter.

There's noise now outside the window. People are shouting, whether with joy or rage or impatience is never clear. Chants rise and fall, gunfire pops like fireworks only it sounds less real, children scream slogans drilled into them for years at school, *Yasqut, yasqut, yasqut!* and *Who created you?* Where have they come from? How do you teach a child to hate? Do they know what it is they shout? A deep buzzing sound passes over the building. A warplane, and we, all of us – in the room and in the street and in the heavens and all the hiding holes of the earth – hold our breath until it passes.

'The light is much better now,' Ossama murmurs, and I move away, grinning at my now-spotless window.

The noise picks up again, shouts of *Show us! Show us!* rise up and through the windows into the room. Amer stands, cracking his back with a loud sound, and drops the pen into a dirty glass with a ping. 'It's done.' Ossama straightens up too. His marker goes behind his ear, but he concurs with a nod. Starting at the bottom, Donya helps roll the banner up into a scroll.

I move to Khalid. He doesn't look pleased. My sour, serious man. I pull the *keffiyeh* off his shoulders and wrap it over the lower half of my face, securing it behind my head, over my *hijab*. He shakes his head but tugs here and there to make sure my features are covered.

We move to the window, all of us. I take one edge and Ossama, face covered in his own *keffiyeh*, takes the other. 'Three, two, one!' We unfurl the banner in one thrust, the fabric rippling down in white waves. We expect cheers, more celebratory gunfire, but there is only silence.

We lean out of the window. The people are gone. Or were never there. And the banner, the banner is empty, a blank canvas, like cloudless days of the past when we didn't need to constantly lift our gaze to the heavens.

Pulling back into the room we turn, as one, to the Eye.

18

The Voiceless Apostate

. . . At the end of the day, anyone who says he's a Muslim is a Muslim. What follows is if they say their actions are motivated by religion, then we should probably take their word for it. Cries of 'That's not Islam!' or 'They aren't real Muslims' or 'They're not us' are not only unhelpful but fundamentally flawed.

There is no cult of orthodoxy in Islam, no pope, no keeper of the faith. There is no higher authority to judge your piety, no intermediary between you and God, no gatekeeper to salvation. Perhaps if there were, these attacks would not happen. The truth is that Islam is a religion of self-governance, a *true* democracy where consensus forms around individual imams and religious scholars. There are brands of Islam with wildly different tenets: one says tattooing your body is fine, another says it's *haram*; one says anal sex is only distasteful while another says it annuls your marriage in the eyes of God; one says self-flagellation is an important act of commemoration, another says it is an affront to Allah.

Like most things in life, there are pros and cons to this. On the one hand, it means free will and self-determination are built into Islam – 'There shall be no compulsion in the religion.' On the other hand, there's no one around to tell fundamentalists to knock it off.

The Voiceless, *The New Press*, 31 May 2017

The first pieces Josie published flew under the radar, but this – an op-ed in reaction to the concert bombing in Manchester – has lit the touchpaper online. It isn't as though I've said anything new; people have been saying the same thing for years. These thoughts have been repeated in books and on news shows and lecture series. Perhaps those people are also being roasted online for their completely correct thoughts. I take what I think, what I know, what I learn and hear, and I package them into little one-to-two-page articles. It is exactly what Josie wants, and she could not be more pleased with me. In her last email, she even said, 'There could be a series of essays here, or even a book at some point.' Imagine that, me with a book on the shelves of your local bookshop.

It's a dream from childhood, one I gave up on almost before realizing I had it. Baba valued education – he was the one who pushed me to study literature at university, sighing long and loud when I settled on linguistics instead – and he always said the only way to truly be set free was to read. In those days my country was a haven for intellectuals, and there were books everywhere. Baba would bring stacks home to me, most of them in English and only a few in Arabic because Mama feared the politics of Arab literature. We would go through them over the weekends and at night before Mama tucked me into bed. *The Secret Garden*, *Oliver Twist*, 'Rip Van Winkle', books filled with Aesop's fables or cautionary tales from the Orient like the one where a boy wades far out onto an exposed beach in search of seashells, only to be swept away by the incoming tsunami. When I was little and first read that story for myself, I thought all disasters happened like that, as though they were all preceded by a period of nakedness and exposure before the chaos swallowed you up.

It's not true. Sometimes disaster comes out of nowhere.

I sift through the dregs of humanity, those people with nothing better to do than post comments online. Living their nice, pumpkin-spiced lives, thinking the world conforms to their limited understanding of it, they're shocked by the things I say. Left-wing, bleeding-heart liberals who are unable to see that some people are just terrible come at me with their apologies and explanations and extenuating circumstances. They accuse me, *me*, of painting with a wide brush, of not understanding my own culture and religion, that I'm no better than once-upon-a-time Muslims who leave the faith only to immediately begin attacking it.

@SkyRider: I'm a Muslim and I can tell you they AREN'T real Muslims.

@BrewMan: What exactly are this person's qualifications again?

@TheLionOfGod: The Voiceless doesn't understand the relationship between creator and creation. This is the problem with their opinion of Islam.

@Mattbow199: has the Voiceless ever heard of protestants?

@theSavageLiberal: The majority of my friends are Muslims & not one of them agrees with this horseshit.

Well, okay then. theSavageLiberal has spoken – we can all go home now.

He and his ilk miss the point entirely. I see so many responses like this, so many comments at the bottom of the article (I keep asking Josie to disable them, but she says the goal is to encourage discussion, not shut it down), that I go through the whole piece again, rereading it with more care than I know those commenters did the first time, and I cannot see what they see. Josie assures me that my writing is clear, and that such comments are to be expected – *You want intelligent discourse from a comments section?* – a rite of passage, a good sign even, but it still leaves me confused and off balance.

There are others as well. Others who might share something of my background – young activists from Cairo, exiles from Palestine, professors of Arab history from Jordan or Lebanon. Some acknowledge the validity of what I say, others hedge and soften it with 'maybes' and 'some'.

There are still others who tell me to burn in hell, that I am blaspheming somehow with my opinions. They tell me the fundamentalists are upholders of the 'true faith', whatever that is. They say these people are fighting the oppressors, the Western devil, the insidious ideologies of freedom of thought and action. They compare me to Salman Rushdie and Ayaan Hirsi Ali as though I have gone anywhere near that far with my words. I imagine it's like punching a timecard for these people. Log on in the morning and think, *where shall I spew my vitriol today?* I wonder where they find the time, what they hope to gain from it, whether they are in any position to comment on the things I say.

One man calls me the Voiceless Apostate, which I have to admit has a nice ring to it.

———

Dear Voiceless,

I really wish you would tell me your name. Firstly because I feel rather silly to always be referring to you as the Voiceless, but more because I feel like we're friends. I want to be a friend to you, and I'm willing to help you in any way I can.

Please do not be discouraged by the comments and responses online this morning. I promise you there is nothing but support from the team here. The chief is especially pleased with the pieces you've been sending. The people writing these comments are nothing but hateful trolls, and anyone who listens to them is just as ignorant.

So let me know how you're feeling and when I can hope to see another piece.

All the best,

Josie

The morning is beautiful. Sun bright and warm, a mild breeze – harbinger of a proper summer. I consider a walk in the park, maybe a foray further out, pushing against those invisible bounds that still sometimes tighten around me. I could take a book to the park, lie on the grass, under a blue sky where no bombs have a chance of falling. I could walk up and down the cemetery, reading the words etched into those forever stones. Back home, they wrap you in a shroud and put you in the ground without a marker (the ground must be so filled up now). I could go to the cemetery, marvel at the impossibly old dates, the names that don't carry emotions any more, and revisit the epitaphs I like best.

But I log on to the computer while I sip my coffee. I stand at the desk, reading one comment, then another, then another.

@IAGA: this guy knows what's up.

@NickPick: Sad to see someone who should know better spouting this shit.

TheShahmansays: YOU are the problem! The prophet (PBUH) and the Quran said that if you kill one person, it's as though you've killed all of humanity. The logical conclusion from this is that these terrorists DO NOT REPRESENT ISLAM. Why is this such a hard concept to get into your head?

Before I know it, hours have passed and the weather has turned. It is slate grey outside, full of gloom and darkness. Raindrops are fat splatters against my window. The wind is blowing, a harsh and ill wind by the looks of it, one that could sicken you. It is nothing like the winds that blew me across Europe, though. Those winds could kill.

In the laundry room, I find Ruth and Helen. The fluorescent light that dangles from the ceiling is blinking out a Morse code no one can read. Helen sits on a hard plastic chair, trembling, face splotchy with tears, while Ruth rubs her back in brisk swipes, like she's sweeping

99

breadcrumbs off a table or beating dust from a rug. It doesn't look comforting – it looks like she's hitting, worsening, bruises that already exist – and it doesn't reduce the sound of Helen's weeping.

They barely look up when I enter, although Helen flinches and tries to pull herself together, yanking the sleeves of her jumper down over her hands and pressing the material to her purple-ringed eyes.

'Don't mind her, dear,' Ruth says with another hard pat against her back. 'She can't hear us.'

'It's all right, I'm fine,' Helen replies, sniffing and holding herself up straight, though the posture looks painful. 'I know what I need to do.'

'You need to leave that man,' Ruth says, putting a finger in Helen's face, which causes her to flinch again. 'I don't want to keep calling the police here.'

'I know. I know. I'm sorry.'

I move to one of the machines, filling it with sweatpants and T-shirts and pants.

'I want to leave,' Helen whispers. 'I do. I want to take the kids and go, but I can't. I'll take Chloe up north for the summer, but I can't make Matt do anything. He's so much like Sean.' She shakes her head, eyes locked on the spotless white trainers on her feet. 'I can't believe how alike they are.'

'This is why you should take the boy too,' Ruth argues, turning my way, but I just keep fiddling with my clothes.

'I can't,' Helen says, shaking her head again. 'He's impossible. He won't go, and I can't make him.'

Ruth is shaking her head too now. 'No good for him to stay with that man. He will learn bad things.'

He's already learned them, I think.

19

Immersion Therapy

I'm deep into Poe at the moment, and I think Josie is catching on. I've started peppering my emails with words like *damnable* and *vengeance* and *a thousand injuries*. In my pieces there are allusions to the *'spirit of perverseness'* and the *'subterrene waters'* that thrash and rush beneath our waking minds. Josie places question marks next to these occurrences; sometimes she types *'word choice?'* but usually it's just a question mark, like she thinks our correspondence has progressed to a point where words are occasionally unnecessary, which I suppose it has. Most of the time I am successful in keeping my words as they are, and it has resulted in people online accusing me of faking my refugee status. They call me one of the elite, charge me with intellectual snobbery, say that I am no more a voice for the voiceless than an MP would be for the average citizen.

What they don't realize is that some of us come from a life that was just as privileged as theirs.

Khalid and I used to argue about Poe. Though I was studying linguistics, I continued to read those novels that took me out of my home and allowed me to venture beyond – to Brontë's moors, to Forster or Kipling's India, to Twain's American South, or Poe's bleak tableaus. Khalid could never understand it. He could never relate to those stories that took place in such alien worlds. He said that to enjoy a piece of writing, he needed a way in, something familiar – if not necessarily comforting – to cling to. He said our literature was a fabric. Like Damask itself, a rich brocade, a tapestry stitched with all our many tragedies and triumphs. Our own culture, our history, our language, all across the region, from the cedars of Lebanon to the Atlas Mountains, were so replete with wonders that he thought it very near treason to abandon it for the stories of colonizers and imperialists.

No time for them, he spoke instead of the silence in the literature of home – our Kingdom of Silence. He spoke of the impossibility of producing anything at all in such a place. He spoke of how much more creative our poets and writers had to be, of the unending search for more obscure, more impenetrable metaphors with which to vaporize the unbearable truths around us, rendering them a hazy mist, released to float and drift between stark, black lines. The silences were there, he said, in every poem and story. Zakariya Tamer, Kabbani and al-Maghut, Ulfat Idilbi. Gaps and lacunae in which the writer had tucked the sardonic and absurd, the uncanny and belligerent, the chillingly futile.

He had little patience for my justifications, shaking his head when I said I found Poe's brand of darkness appealing – the admissions of human frailty, the pulling apart of the sticky, gossamer threads that tether us to one another, the acknowledgments of how the mind can come undone and rattle about the skull like a billiard ball. His eyes would narrow when I told him how those writings all felt terribly intimate, like Poe was whispering the words in my ear, for my benefit alone. Whether it was Montresor speaking to his not-so-fortunate friend, or William Wilson and his paranoia, or all those unnamed narrators with their melancholia and murderous rage, I feel a kinship with them. They are speaking to me, about me, consoling and bolstering me. It is a confirmation that no matter how long it's been since someone has touched me or looked me in the eye, I am not alone. There is someone out there who has been gripped by fear and loathing as I have.

There's a short piece, a fable called 'Silence'. I've read it so many times, I'm well on my way to committing it to memory. Amassing Poe collections, I have vintage editions from the 80s and 90s with red and black covers depicting skulls and bloody knives, versions with plain green or black covers, editions with illustrations by Harry Clarke or Rackham or Doré. I pick them up at weekend markets or online auctions or the Ginger Giant's shop. I read them all. Walking around my flat or lying in bed, I read and reread the stories, marking them with a ballpoint pen when I find inconsistencies and typos in the text.

I imagine myself as his editor, imagine him there, scowling, on the floor of my living room, his back against the wall, legs stretched out and crossed at the ankles. His arms are also crossed; of course they are – who likes watching someone read what they wrote?

'If you insist on reading my words,' he says, 'you might do me the courtesy of reading them aloud. They are like the plays of Shakespeare, meant to be heard rather than read.'

I don't comment on the hubris of this but think that if any writer in history could warrant such a comparison, it would be him. I ignore the directive, though, and continue to pace in front of his black leather boots as I start 'Silence' from the top. I can almost feel his Demon (in my mind, he's tall and thin and blue-pale as the moon) place his hands upon my head as he starts to describe that saffron river on that oozy Libyan shore. Grey clouds churn in the sky and the towers – East, South A and B, my Western one – rock and crash against each other with the sound of bombs. Barrels of death fall from the sky. Blood drops from the sky. It pearls on the skin like dew and gathers on the lashes so that everything is hazed in red.

Poe has no patience for me, grabs the book from my hands, and now I'm the one writhing. 'You must shout the words to the heavens!' he cries, arms outstretched, pale face shining up at the ceiling. 'Your voice must ring out each syllable and every beat of cadence. Otherwise, what is the damn point?' My legs twist on the bed, throat clamped shut like always. My mind wrings itself into pleas for forgiveness. His disappointment is a knife, a sharp blade skinning me as I jerk and convulse. I want to tell him I love the taste of his words, how they feel rolling around the tongue of my mind's voice, how they slither down my chest and hum into the caverns of my heart, how they sometimes slide further down and pluck between my legs, where I can no longer distinguish pain from pleasure.

He can't hear the screaming in my head, or he doesn't care. He reads the fable himself, his voice strong and smooth and animated as it bounces off the walls. Standing tall at the foot of my bed, he squares his shoulders in the style of some Roman god and twists up his features – dark brows and heavy eyes and droopy lips – until it gives an impression of loftiness of thought or wildness of care or whatever effect Poe has imagined for his man.

'*I read the fables of sorrow, and weariness, and disgust for mankind, and a longing after solitude . . .*'

My heart pounds to the rhythm of his cadence, the tattoo of it tripping up on his phrasing and intonation.

I am sweltering, suffocating, tearing at my shirt and kicking off my shorts. I grip the headboard, pulling my arms taut so that the sweat pooling in my armpits can cool. The blood spatters harder outside, bullets rapping against the windows. I see it, but the only sound is Poe and his agitated reading. Back and forth in my unlit room, his frock coat billows around him as he stalks into the recesses and wades into his wilderness of poisonous lilies. He roars, like the trumpeting call of an elephant, like the hoarse cry of a hippo. He shrieks and curses and becomes livid with violence, and I tremble and shudder and grow weak and wan.

And then, as abruptly as he began, he is finished. Silent, illimitable, he stands at the foot of my bed, white cravat loose and limp around his neck, and stares me in the face. Eyes like two miniature black stones, like marbles, like hard little pebbles of apathy. Khalid's face is there, suspended above the cravat, then it's Poe with a sullen look under a white helmet, then Khalid again. They flicker back and forth like a light switch, toying with me, tearing at the fabric of my mind. There is no sound; it feels as if my heart has stilled, ceased trying to pound its way out of my ribs. The towers stop crashing against each other, the rain stops, the world stops. There is nothing, and still I say nothing.

Khalid/Poe laughs. A loud, barking cackle. Falling back against the wall, sliding to the floor, he grips his belly and laughs and laughs and laughs. He laughs until tears glisten around his eyes and his mouth screws up like he's in pain. The jarring sound pierces my brain. I clap flat palms over my ears and turn away onto my side.

Across the way, No-Lights-Man is on his balcony. He's watching me. The tip of his cigarette burns orange and beneath his boxers he is erect and heavy.

20

Horse Latitudes

In the light of the new day, he speaks to me. I knew he would, through the fog in my mind with the knowledge that he'd seen my feverish strokes and convulsions, he would speak to me. When I woke in the morning, and the melancholy men had gone, and my mind was my own again, my first thoughts were of him and what he might have to say about what he'd seen.

He's in the laundry room down the street. Slouching in one of the uncomfortable plastic chairs in the corner, legs stretched out in front of him like he's hoping to trip someone, he moves a pencil across a notepad. From the angle and the nature of the movement, I see he's sketching, not writing, and my first instinct is to turn and head back to my flat. But those rooms are too quiet, too reminiscent of the night before. My terror is still too fresh, and I cannot be there any longer.

He greets me with a 'Hey' as I walk past, but I pretend not to hear, moving to one of the farther machines with my laundry basket held in front of me like a shield. He snorts, but it doesn't sound unkind or particularly dangerous. When you stop speaking, you become a very good listener. I was never much of a talker to begin with, but the things I hear now that I don't speak would shock anyone. People let their guard down, speak as though a stranger is not present. Or perhaps it's just that they don't see me. I've heard late-night bus drivers fantasize about murdering their bosses and women in aisles at the shop laugh about the best way to poison their husbands. Once at the train station, a man began to speak, in the crudest terms, of all the things he would like to do to me. I've learned to decode sighs and mutterings, to read danger in scoffs and chuckles. I understand hums and haws as though they were entirely spelled out. I hear everything.

I hear No-Lights-Man move, the creak of the chair as he unfolds himself from it. Stuffing my sweat-soaked clothes and bedsheets in, I punch out the settings on the machine. I turn and startle as though I haven't heard his approach. He holds up his hands and turns the notepad to me.

The old woman is telling everyone you're deaf

I read it and return my eyes to his with a shrug. It is the closest I've ever been to him, and I can almost see what all those girls who come up to his lit-up flat see. There is a roguish charm about him: his eyes are dark and set deep in their sockets; his lips are full and seem on the verge of finding something to smile about, as they do now while he moves the pen across the paper again; his cheeks are rough with a day or two of stubble; and his hair is tousled and reaches to his shoulder in wavy, thick strands, like a black-haired Jesus.

Ahmed's face superimposes itself so perfectly onto his features with a suddenness, a violent suddenness, that shakes me. Ahmed with blood in his eyes. Ahmed with arms twisted in a way they shouldn't be. Ahmed crying but unable to produce tears. Ahmed floating, face down, in a river he shouldn't have been anywhere near. They are violent images, carrying that ethereal quality of half-remembrance and half-dream and horrid imaginings that fill the gaps memories and dreams leave behind. I swallow down the panic but my heart is a small, angry bird fluttering in my chest.

He turns the pad to me again, eyes locked on my face.

I don't think you are + I think you can talk.

My face shows nothing of the panic that threatens to consume me. The only one who could've told him that is the Juicer, and I've never seen them interact. I would have seen it, I'm sure. They are diametrically opposed beings – the Juicer is all about order and control and power while No-Lights-Man is loose and free and unconcerned. What could they ever have to speak about? When would they have spoken? I look at him again, trying to decide if he is one of the men the Juicer would have over late at night, someone he would close his curtains for, but I don't see it. There's grime under the fingernails at the edge of the notepad, his clothes are wrinkled, jeans stained, trainers faded and scuffed. No, it's not possible for him to have attracted the Juicer's attention.

No one would believe you had either, a voice in my head whispers. I shake myself, to dispel both the voice and the scenes that flash behind my eyes in rapid succession. It's like a slideshow from one of those old projectors we used to have at school, and the teacher would come out with a box of slides and push them into the machine one by one to show us birds and monkeys and insects. I blink and he has me against the wall by the door to his flat, lips pressed into the hollow of my neck. I blink again and he has me on his dining-room table, my shirt unbuttoned so that my breasts threaten to spill out of my bra and my soft stomach is uncomfortably visible. Blink again and he's pushed me onto my back, saying he doesn't care, pulling my jeans down my legs and telling me he loves a round woman with thick thighs every now and again, like I'm an indulgence, a guilty pleasure, like the red meat he allows himself once a month or the mini chocolate bar I've seen him eat twice in the time we've lived across from each other. He had me on his dining-room table, then against the window like he wanted me to see my dark, empty flat across the way, then again on the hard, uncomfortable sofa. The third time was when I finally made a sound. Quiet throughout, we'd communicated in gestures and eyes and hands and fingers. But that final time, when I felt electrified, as though I was about to die, I screamed. One long, loud cry as my body convulsed beneath him. He looked down at me, face and neck and shoulders damp with sweat, with triumph, and his honey-coloured eyes went wide, thin lips twisting into a smirk. I still didn't say a word. Pushing him off, I put my clothes on and left.

'I don't care,' No-Lights-Man says. 'I find it curious, but I won't tell anyone.' I lift my eyes to his again. He's smiling, not smirking. 'I'm Adam.'

I nod, my head still reeling with images, body vibrating with residual anxiety. He smiles wider, and I realize he wants reciprocation. I hold out my hand and he gives me the notepad and pencil, and I'm careful not to touch him in the hand-over. Already this feels too close, like I'm crossing too many lines, but I take them all the same. On the notepad is his sketch, the words he'd written for me scrawled around it, but I am only now of the mind to really take it in.

The drawing is intricate. He's drawn an Asian woman; a girl, really. She's wearing a school uniform, short-sleeved shirt and dark skirt and ankle socks and Mary Janes. Her back is to the viewer, head turned like she's looking at something at her far right or is about to look over her shoulder. Her hair is long and dark and straight, a thick fringe almost obscuring heavy-lidded eyes. He's captured hard eyes and a sly mouth. The girl in the sketch has a secret. There's a thin wheel at her back, like she's some kind of wind-up doll, and flowers bloom around her bare thighs, leaves and vines twisting up around her arms. It's beautiful and delicate and not at all what I would have expected of him.

I scrawl a compliment along the bottom – even though I know

what he wants is a name – something about the lines and shadowing, and hand it back.

'You see this thing in the Middle East?' he asks as we climb the stairs to his flat.

There's always a 'thing' in the Middle East, I think, and my only response is a frown that he doesn't see because he's facing the other way. A constant stream of breaking news, our gift to the world . . . along with the oil and fundamentalist ideology, of course. You're welcome, and we'll see you when the cosmic checks come in. It used to be a pretty sweet deal for Western nations – take our oil, grant us some democracy and condescension, and everyone goes away feeling a little bit better about themselves. The world isn't like that any more. It's smaller, easier to get places, to make more compact bombs, more innovative solutions to the problem of the infidels. If they think attacks like Westminster and Nice and vans ramming crowds will bring an end to Western interference, they're just as stupid as Americans who call the last twenty years 'The Birth Pangs of Democracy'.

Democracy is not, nor should it be, the ultimate goal of all modern nations. Democracy rarely works as it should and most often does not work at all. For a democracy to function, you need an informed electorate. In order to get one, you need a free and fair and *responsible* press. Not even America, the freest nation on earth, has that. How is Egypt supposed to? How is Iraq? How are any of the others?

I don't think Adam is looking for this sort of discussion, and in any case, I would need multiple notebooks to have it, if indeed it is a discussion at all that Adam is looking for. He asked me to come up and 'hang' for a while. It's been my experience that 'hang' could mean any number of things, but based on what I've seen through the window, I'm hoping it's music and a cigarette or two.

In his flat, I step over the mess of clothes and shoes lined up at the entrance. Through an open door I see the duvet and lumpy pillows piled up on his small bed. A frisson of excitement rushes through me. The box is there, just under the bed, with its stash of whatever it is No-Lights-Man sifts through every day. I wonder if I could sneak a peek at it. Maybe he'll go to the loo or down to the shop for a drink he will now realize he doesn't have on hand to offer. Maybe he'll leave me alone here, and I can snoop.

'Have a seat,' he says, gesturing to the sofa. I would rather be on the floor, but I sink into it anyway. It's soft, the leather buttery and worn, and I imagine all the other people he's had here – friends, family, colleagues, all the people who surround you when you're normal and alive and well.

His view is so different from mine. He can see into my flat, almost level. I see the red of my desk chair and the edge of a black bookcase through the iron rail of my balcony. Ruth and Tom are pottering around their flat. No-Lights-Man, Adam, has a good view of them too. Tom is in a dark brown armchair in front of the television, a cup of tea and a plate of biscuits on a table beside him. Ruth moves around in the kitchen, and I imagine the cacophony of the pots and pans I would certainly be hearing if I were home.

'Do you mind if I put a record on?' Adam asks.

Shaking my head, I take the can of cider he's offering. I don't see Little Ahmed in him now – they look nothing alike, I'm nearly appalled to think they did – and the panic has receded as quickly as it came. He moves to the record player set up in a corner so he can hear it if he sits on the balcony. It's big and looks very old, with a wide brown base and a clear plastic covering. His records are all over the place – piled up in stacks beside the player, shelved in the bookcase between old DVDs and books, leaning up against the sofa and coffee table. He pulls one from on top of the table, sliding it out of

Layla AlAmmar

its sleeve and turning back to the player. The cover is mustard and brown and sepia-toned and the record is by a band who all have the floppy hair and sleepy eyes of the 70s.

Adam has Vietnam War posters over his sofa – a GI in full gear and helmet strumming a guitar, a poster of protesters in America, another of a bloodied child that says 'Know Your Enemy'. The twin Jims, Morrison and Hendrix, take up space on the opposite wall – the one pouting at me while the other has a twist to his lips like he's keeping a secret. A scan of Adam's shelves shows a lot of books about Martin Luther King Jr and the civil rights movement and other things that I suppose make up the sum total of what he thinks people ought to know about that decade. There's a record peeking out from under the coffee table with the same helmeted GI on its cover and a label that says 'Vietnam War Protest Songs', and I wonder how it is even something like that they've managed to commercialize.

'So this thing in the Middle East. I reckon it's a lot of smoke and mirrors, you know?' he says, taking a seat on the floor by the record player and popping open his own can of cider.

I take sips from mine. I don't have a high tolerance for alcohol, and the only times I've had it – in dark, cold town squares in Germany or by railway tracks in Austria – the results have been unpleasant. I don't remember much of those nights, but waking up, I would be sore with a taste like sewage in my mouth and a few euros in my pocket or stuffed down my shirt.

'It's all about money, you know? The Americans never started a war but they were getting something out of it. All this bollocks about freedom and the rights of people to govern themselves and be rid of dictators is all just that: a fat fucking load of bollocks. They don't care about any of that. It's all about where they can get their money and their oil and sell their tear gas canisters and guns and tanks and medication that you need because they fucking invented the disease!

112

If you went by manufacturer alone, you'd see them wars were just being fought by America. America vs America in a global fight for God-knows-what.'

No-Lights-Man might be crazy. He's not entirely wrong, but with all that frantic energy and manic speech and fast eyes, he might be insane. I desperately want to know what's under his bed. I want to peel apart his layers, like an onion, and lay bare all his bright, brazen whiteness.

'And now instead of it just being Vietnam, we've got loads of little Vietnams scattered all over the place – Iraq and Syria and Afghanistan and Yemen and all the others. The Americans are ruining the world, I swear. If they'd just fuck off and mind their own business, everyone'd be a lot better off.'

As though Western meddling began with Vietnam, I think, but I just sip my cider while the lead singer of the band growls about living on a farm or in cotton fields or something called a bayou. Things I don't need to know about because I will never see them. It all seems far from Adam's experiences as well, but he's into it, bopping his head and humming along every now and then.

'People aren't standing for it any longer. We're going to rise up and bring it all down.' It takes everything in me not to snort at that, and for the first time, I wonder how old he is. Although it all sounds incredibly naïve, and I don't remember using those kinds of words, I imagine it was the same sentiment that stirred us to draw posters and banners and shake our fists as we marched up and down the streets of Aleppo. 'I've been working with this group of organizers, and we're planning a bunch of big marches – here and in London and Manchester and other cities. These big marches to show them that we have a voice and this war stuff is not on. It has to stop. They need to get out of the Middle East and out of Africa and leave people alone to deal with their own shit.'

Yes, I think, leave the man alone to kill everyone until there's nothing but an empty country to run. I grab a pen and a ripped-open envelope from the table and scribble on it.

Vote?

'Yeah, I vote. We all vote. All me mates do. But it's not enough. Voting will only get you so far, especially when it's a choice between bad and worse. All politicians are gutless crooks. Everyone knows that. The system is corrupt. You can't play within it. You have to look outside it, wreck it from the outside. Dismantle and topple it.' He's getting worked up now. He turns the record over, replaces the needle, then reaches for a brown wooden box on the table, pulling it towards him. From within he pulls out a little square of paper and his baggy of green fluff. 'The status quo stopped working ages ago. Voting numbers are down. Kids don't care about voting; they want to make their voices heard in other ways – music and books and films and protesting in the street and sit-ins and the like. That's where the truth is. That's where real life is. Not in the Houses of fucking Parliament.'

He rolls the joint in brisk, practised movements, sealing and pinching at it until he's satisfied. Hooking his foot into the cracked opening of his door, he pushes it open further before lighting the cigarette. 'It's bullshit,' he says on his first drag before passing it to me. 'It's all bullshit, but we have to do something.'

The way he says 'something', it sounds like 'summat', reminding me of that first northern city they sent me to while they processed my papers. They don't want refugees clogging up London – that's how the lady at the centre phrased it, as though we were clumps of dirt or hair stopping up a drain – so they send us north, to Cambridge and Doncaster and Loughborough, spreading us out so as not to frighten the country with an unmanageable horde of displaced persons.

I've heard pleasant stories of men and women and young families who were placed with loving, supportive sponsors. Sponsors who treated them like kin and begged them not to leave when their six months were up. I know of some, younger ones, who remained with their sponsors, like unofficial adoptees or foster children who were actually adults. I've heard of them being shown around the country, taken down to Brighton to see the Pavilion or Stratford-upon-Avon to see where Shakespeare lived and Anne Hathaway's cottage or even to Grasmere to see Wordsworth country or up into Scotland. Their happy faces, arms thrown around their sponsors, smile out from newspaper articles and the pages of magazines and social media sites.

It wasn't my experience. There were no sponsors for me, no warm English cottage or Sunday roast traditions to be invited to take part in.

I wasn't stable enough for that.

21

Spectrums

What would later be called the Battle of Aleppo had begun. Advancing closer and closer, the fighting tightened around us like a noose – Zahraa to the northwest, the airport to the east, army tanks rolling into the streets of Salaheddine down below. Every day brought news of incursions, of neighbourhoods taken, of heritage smashed and lost forever. And for what? It crept closer, a black cloud, an evil roiling with thunder – the sound of rockets in a distance that wasn't very distant at all, the horrible buzz of helicopters – until we were confined to a ten-block radius.

And outside, in our neighbourhoods, *jinn*, themselves sometimes haunted, dangled from street lamps. They swayed from long tails or furry arms or thin trails of smoke, and occasionally they would plunge into the heart of a passing baker on his way to open a shop he couldn't afford to close no matter what dropped from the sky. They unman him, those *jinn*, striking icy daggers of terror into his breast. They silence children, excising the tongues of boys who follow where the men go and girls who scurry across rubble and ash clutching chickens to their chests.

Most days our mothers kept us huddled in our homes. Another kind of womb, I suppose. Baba and Little Ahmed would venture out for necessities, usually together but occasionally he snuck out on his own – something Mama, with terror in her eyes, beat him for when and if she ever found out. Invisible lines had sprung up across the city, and they would cross them to stand in line at the baker's shop while around them there was shelling and gunfire and *malak almawt* cackling as he lifted more and more of us away. His eyes are number-less; there's no escaping them. Nada's husband had already taken them to safety, and so it was just Mama and I and the radio. She would cook whatever she could find in the cupboard and I would read or watch the baby and hold my breath for the sounds of death.

The Friday of Grasping for Normalcy. I was allowed to visit my cousins on that day; Amer would walk the six blocks to our flat, come in for a cup of tea and to relay messages from his mother to mine, then we would walk the six blocks back to his home. Ossama was usually there, already sketching or colouring in previous illustra-tions. From the back room there would be the sounds of the Quran and the sighs and lamentations of Amer's father. He refused to emerge, and Donya would take in bowls of rice and stew and cups of tea, only to bring them out, untouched, hours later.

Behind Khalid's back Amer had taken to calling them Friday of the Interminable Lecture. While he and Ossama worked on poster and graffiti ideas, while Donya re-watched videos of protests and chants she had saved to her phone, while I scribbled in a notebook or in the margins of books I was reading, Khalid would lecture us on passivity and how none of our efforts made any difference whatsoever and that, perhaps, in retrospect they would have a kind of meaning, but not now. He said we were play-acting at resistance, that we were little more than children while out there – his long arm gesturing towards the window and the dim pregnant skies beyond – there were warriors. He would rail, tirelessly, for hours, lit up with a zeal I'd never seen in him and which frightened me more than any of the stories we were hearing or the things we were seeing. Amer and Ossama ignored him, putting their heads together in artistic congress, arguing over pigment and lines. Donya would put her earphones in, short chestnut hair swinging as she bobbed along with whatever she was watching, and I would alternate between weak arguments about lack of sustained willpower and the sort of acquiescent hums I'd heard Mama give Baba at various points in my life.

One Friday, though, deep into the other side of September when the ancient *souq* had burned and the first barrels had fallen and there were no more good guys in this fight, he didn't greet us with his customary scowl of impatience. Instead, he moved to the centre of the room, eyes finding mine, and announced, 'I've joined the volunteers.'

'The volunteers?' I said, flicking the paper edges of the notebook in my lap. Donya touched my arm to still my hand.

He nodded, eyes bright, smile wide. 'The Defence.'

Amer looked up, marker suspended over crisp white paper, and studied Khalid for a long moment. 'You're serious.'

'Very.' He gestured to the guys. 'You should join as well.'

Ossama snorted, shaking his head down at the sketchpad. 'If you actually thought we'd join, you'd have told us *before* you signed up.'

I stood, gripping the notebook so hard my knuckles flared in pain. 'It's not true.' I shook my head. 'Your mother would never allow it.'

Khalid tipped his head to one side, smiling in the way he did that made something fragile bloom in my chest, and I had to look away from it. 'It's not for her to decide what I should and shouldn't do any longer. I'm not a child.'

'Back to that again.' Ossama sighed, pinching the bridge of his nose.

'Yes, that again,' Khalid barked, turning on him. 'Look at you, drawing your little pictures. You think that's going to do anything? You think anyone gets taken away for doodles?'

'Is that your goal?' My voice came out shrill, like a bird screeching past a window.

He faced me again, hands up in supplication. 'What I'm saying is you get taken away for doing something, and my aim is to do something. Something! Something more than pretty little posters!'

Ossama made a rude gesture, then attacked his sketchpad with the thickest, blackest marker he had. He was good now. Fast. He made the barest of outlines, rapid fire, one after another – disembowelled children at school desks, men with machine guns for genitals, inflated heads and popping eyeballs with fiery veins peering into houses and hearts and minds. Skeletal hands and arms emerging from piles of decay, tanks and boots rolling across monuments and citadels and a culture that was older than the world. Khalid watched, mouth pressed into a thin line.

'It's dangerous,' I said. His eyes flicked back to mine, and if he could, I thought, he would have walked over and pulled a bit of hair from under my veil to wind around his finger, tugging at it to tell me how silly he thought I was being.

'They're mad men,' Donya added with a shake of her head, 'running *towards* explosions, chasing warplanes and helicopters—'

'*Saving people*,' he said, clenching his fists. 'Saving lives. Diving into rubble to pull them out. Men, women, babies. Who's going to help them? Look outside! There are no ambulances any more. No one is coming for them.'

I took a step towards him. 'Khalid—'

'None of us is going back to school next year. Perhaps not ever. The war is here. The fighting will come closer. It'll get worse. People will die and when the day of judgment comes, we will all have to answer for what we did here, what we did here now!' He spread his arms wide and shook his head at me, desperation burning in his eyes. 'What would you have me do, write us a revolution?' he scoffed.

'Shall I write some haunting protest ballad? Some beautiful verses for a glossy magazine? Or maybe a novel where the corpses come crawling out of bomb craters, jasmines blooming in eye sockets, vocal cords snapping in the air about how hell is here?'

Later, when the shouting was over and Amer and Ossama had gone back to ignoring him, and Donya drifted to the kitchen to avoid it all, Khalid found me in the stairwell, knees folded to my chest, leaning against the wall, swiping under my eyes and nose with my sleeves.

'You say you love me, but you hide yourself to cry,' he said with a sigh as he sat at my side.

I sniffed and shook my head. 'I don't want you to think I'm weak.'

He was quiet for so long I thought perhaps he agreed with me, and I considered storming back up to the flat to ask Amer to walk me home where I could cry and wallow in peace, but Khalid eventually opened his palms, held them apart, and said, 'I don't think anyone is ever just one thing and then that's it, forever, you know? Like strong or weak or good or bad or whatever. It's a spectrum. It's always a spectrum.' He moved one hand back and forth through the air, his shoulder tapping mine when he came my way. 'And we move along it. Sometimes we move steadily from one side to the other. And sometimes we swing violently from one end to another in a matter of hours.' His hands flopped to his knees, and he looked at me with a shrug. 'None of us is condemned to just be one thing, forever and always.' Watching me carefully, he lifted a finger, catching the tear sliding down my cheek before it reached my mouth.

I laid my head on his shoulder, and his arm came around me. His hand drew circles on my back and we sat in silence, listening to the odd car tooting its horn for pedestrians to get out of the way, the faint strain of Abdel Halim drifting up from a flat below us, battling

120

with the Quranic verses that slipped out from under the door of another, a mother yelling at her children to quiet down and their laughing, screaming responses.

'What about love and hate?'

He chuckled and pressed his lips to my forehead. 'The only exception.'

22

The Others

. . . What happens to you will always be more real than what happened to an Other in some distant or not-so-distant past, across a continent or an ocean away. It's to be expected. At the end of the day, you can only really see the world through your own eyes.

It's easy to scapegoat them, those *undesirable* others, when things get rough. Crime rates up? Must be all those black people moving into the neighbourhood. Tourism down? It's those pesky Middle Easterners with their animosity towards bacon and Christmas. No jobs? It's because of all those Others swooping in to steal them. It happens in every society and has happened throughout history. Catholics in America in the 20s or further back in the time of Maria and her Awful Disclosures, Palestinians in the Holy Land, and the Jews in . . . well, the Jews haven't really been welcome anywhere.

It's our turn now. And there are those who are overly optimistic, who say this will pass, and that we'll eventually be as integral to the fabric of insert-country-here as Catholics or Mormons or insert-previously-persecuted-minority-here. Presumably, there will then be somebody else to pick on.

There is a difference though, this time around.

This time there's a conflation, in the minds of a disturbing majority, of Muslim Refugee and Muslim Terrorist. They are seen as one and the same, and the nuances of the situation are largely ignored. Xenophobic rhetoric turns into propaganda, which becomes legitimized into political platforms, which then justifies acts of violence and hate, which brings about retribution, which is then recycled into more anti-Muslim rhetoric. It's a self-perpetuating cycle, into the cogs of which no one has managed to shove a wrench.

Never mind that refugees are not committing acts of terror on Western soil (or *any* soil for that matter), never mind that refugees are fleeing the terror; any time an attack occurs, there comes this blanket condemnation of an entire faith – as though the problem were one of religion rather than interpretation. The majority have no time for such subtleties of thought. Muslim Refugee = Muslim Terrorist is so much simpler.

I suppose that's the point of me, the point of what I'm doing. They – and by 'they', I mean my editor and the people at the magazine you're currently reading and some of you who have left comments in the empty spaces below – want me to reveal myself as some microcosm of refugee society. They want to see, in me, all the hopes and ills and frustrations and struggles and singular stories of some five million plus people. They want me to speak for the chaos of the world, to weave the abstracts of cultural convulsions and scapegoats and simple apathy into my story, so that by seeing 'me', by knowing 'me', you might know them all, and I suppose – by extension – might feel some degree of empathy for them all.

Humanize. That's what they say, when they're fawning over certain books and documentaries and films. A word uttered easily and without too much thought. A well-intentioned word that nevertheless concedes the argument that some people are not people and so require some art form to render them human.

It's the game of fiction, this duping of the public into caring about things and Others they might not otherwise care about. But I suppose it is a sound enough strategy; fiction does make migrants of us after all.

The Voiceless, *The New Press*, 14 June 2017

The hallway outside the Juicer's flat smells of spice – turmeric and garlic and onions and curry powder. Through the door I hear him chop chop chopping away, and unbidden, an image comes to mind of him in those low-waisted shorts with that cut of muscle showing, his arms flexing as he grips and slices the vegetables. I consider turning back, leaving it be, but my curiosity keeps me rooted there and brings my fist up to rap twice on his door.

He opens it, caramel-coloured eyes going wide. We haven't seen each other since that night, weeks ago now. I've seen him through the window and perhaps he's seen me, but we've not been in each other's presence, and he looks me over as though comparing me to his memory. There's a tea towel thrown over his bare shoulder. His chest is also bare, glinting with moisture from the cooking or maybe he was exercising beforehand. He's not wearing the shorts, just a pair of long sweatpants, but they ride low on his hips.

'Well, if it isn't my little wailer,' he says with a smirk.

I'm not his little anything, and my own lip curls in distaste as I thrust my note at him. Still smiling, he shuffles a bit, letting the door fall open to take it. As he reads, I peer around his shoulder, taking in the pot bubbling on the stove and the vegetables laid out in perfect order on the countertop – spinach then carrots then sweet potatoes then broccoli then beetroots. I see no proteins on the counter, no chicken or beef or even salmon, and I wonder if that documentary he was watching has turned him vegan. The dining table is set for one – a dark green placemat, heavy plate and bowl combo, silverware and a cloth napkin. I can't fathom setting a space for only yourself at a dining-room table; why not just eat in front of the telly or computer screen like the rest of us? But no, apparently he's going to eat there, at the head of the dining-room table that as far as I know, he primarily uses for fucking.

'Now how would I know you can speak?' he asks, looking over the note at me. 'Screaming isn't really talking, is it?'

It occurs to me that I could not have phrased the note in a more asinine manner. If he didn't tell Adam I can hear and speak, then I've just confirmed it. Scowling, at him and myself, I point at the question he hasn't answered yet. Tilting his head, he asks, 'Do you really not speak? Only sounds?' I remain quiet, glaring at him. He props an arm on the door jamb and leans forward, blasting me with what feels like waves of testosterone, and I wonder how we can be attracted to the worst sorts of people. 'Look, I don't know Adam from . . . well, Adam, so I'd have no reason to be talking to him about you. But why don't you come in and we'll discuss it?'

My mind flashes again to that night, to me sitting out in the courtyard because Ruth's banging of pots had become unbearable. It had felt like there was electricity in my veins, jolts of it at the back of my head, my mind suddenly too heavy for my skull. My tongue thickened, growing heavier and heavier, stitching itself more firmly to the bottom of my mouth, down into my throat. Choking me. It had felt like I was dying, like I was just going to keel over right then and there.

My panic attacks are strange things. A part of me is certain I'm going to die, but at the same time my brain tells me how absurd such an occurrence would be. I've survived overcrowded rafts on freezing waters, impatient smugglers, trigger-happy border patrols, frustrated and hungry men, police officers who say they won't fingerprint me if I just let them do that one thing they've always wanted to do, months of scorching heat and bitter cold and rain, disease and bleeding blisters and infections that never get a chance to heal. I survived all that, so the thought of dropping dead now, due to nothing but the betrayal of my own nervous system, seems highly unlikely. It doesn't stop the sense of impending doom though, and when it gets bad – like it did that night – I go outside, to sit in public where, if my lungs or heart or something decides to stop, passers-by might be there to call for help.

It was the Juicer who came up to me that night, smiling and chatting like we were the best of friends, not caring a whit that I didn't talk back, that I shook my head and pointed to my ear and shook my head some more. Then, he was stepping in closer, reaching out to push a lock of hair behind my ear, ignoring my flinch at the contact. Smiling and tilting his head and appraising me. He pointed to his flat, lifting up his bag of groceries – an invitation to dinner. The nerves bubbled up and boiled over inside of me. No one had touched me in months. The need for contact is a human weakness. Go too long without it, and your skin begins to itch and crawl, the desire for it settling hard and sour in your gut. I followed him up to his flat, knowing perfectly well that there would be no dinner.

If I step into his flat now, there won't be any dinner tonight either. He's still smirking as I turn and walk away.

Dear Voiceless,

I waited until after I'd published your last article to send you this because I didn't want you to think I expected you to alter your opinion based on what I'm about to say. I wanted you to understand that you are entitled to your views and I value them enough that I want to publish them without attempting to change them or make them, in some way, align more closely to my own. So I have published your last piece, and we've been monitoring the response to it, and so far it hasn't come across as being as inflammatory as the previous one, which I imagine you are pleased about. Although this could also be because of recent events overshadowing it.

What I want to say is that I'm concerned you might be glossing over the very real, unequivocal violence that has been occurring in Great Britain over the last few months. In making your statements about Islamophobia and refugees, etc, I'm afraid you might be downplaying the horrific violence that is happening on our streets. There is a sense here among some of my colleagues at the magazine that you might be trivializing, or splitting hairs even, when talking about this issue.

Real people have died in these attacks. Real people with families and lives and jobs and friends. People who were here last week and are now suddenly not. And now they're saying that one of the attackers might have been an asylum seeker at one point. So, I think that maybe you need to be careful of making sweeping statements about how we shouldn't fear Muslim refugees because they don't have the capacity for violence or something.

These are just some things to keep in mind as you compose future articles.

Best,

Josie

Splitting hairs. I blink, over and over, as I try to process her words. *Splitting hairs.* I click over to a search engine and input the idiom to check that my understanding of it is correct. The very fact she would use such a term indicates to me that she, Josie, my *editor*, has no understanding of what I have been trying to put across. And if she cannot grasp the nuances of the situation, how can I ever expect anyone else to?

Violence that has been occurring in *Great Britain*. Surely this must be a mistake, something she typed out subconsciously and didn't notice when rereading her email prior to sending. Or perhaps she didn't reread it. Either way, she cannot be so obtuse.

Real people are dying. What does she mean by that? What people is she talking about? The twenty-two at Manchester Arena? The five on Westminster Bridge? The twelve people in Berlin? The forty in Paris and the ninety at the Bataclan?

Or is she talking about this latest one? On the bridge? I click over to the magazine's main page and see the headline, large and dominant at the top.

Terror on London Bridge
At least 8 dead, scores injured,
in brutal van and knife attack

Are those eight people the 'real' ones she's talking about? The market there is close to where the magazine's office is. Did she know someone who was injured or killed in the attack? Was she in the vicinity when it happened? Is that why 'it' and they are so very real to her?

I had ignored the headline when it was splashed across the news a few days ago. Seven or eight dead in a city hours away hardly seemed worthy of media attention – even if they were 'real' people. Perhaps I am guilty of the same apathy I accuse others of; perhaps my experiences have rendered me unable to devote emotional energy to an attack on so small a scale; perhaps I've seen it too much and too often.

I find it ironic that this incident is what breaks Josie. Seven or eight dead. In the war at home, some five hundred thousand have died. But I suppose there is a critical threshold after which numbers cease to have any meaning and people stop being 'real'.

23

One and Two

The bombs fell all day, falling against an impossibly blue sky. There were no clouds, only plumes of blackness and ash, throwing insolent shapes, stark and heavy against pockets of azure. A sound like thunder, like warring gods in your mind, like worlds collapsing. One bomb. People rush out of their homes and make their way to the site of impact. First responders, those flashes of almost white, move through the crowds. They dive into the rubble to pull out men and women and children and grandmothers and grandfathers and aunts and uncles. Then, the second bomb falls, taking out more than the first one had. Buildings and rescue vehicles and rescuers and neighbours shouting out the names of neighbours. Children explode into red mist. The air is full of wails that taste of blood. Metallic. Electric. We pick up body parts until more rescuers arrive. We pick them up with our bare hands – a foot, an arm, fingers, laying them on blankets and sheets because we can't stomach the idea of bin bags.

Is there some predator in the wild that does this, that punishes his prey once, with a nip or the swipe of a sharp claw, and then finishes him off with a second pounce? Like a game of cat and mouse. It never seemed cruel when I saw street cats chase their quarry down the alley, but maybe that's just because I never thought about it from the mouse's perspective.

We are mice, scurrying out of buildings, pink noses twitching as we sniff out where Death will land next.

The bombs fell all day, but now, in the dark of another night, it's quiet. Here, in the back of this borrowed car, there is a bubble of peace. I lie here, veil open around my head so Khalid can kiss the secret skin beneath my ear. His too-thin body is stretched out over mine, cradled between my legs. We are fully clothed; we haven't crossed that boundary. Khalid won't allow it, says we have to wait until we're married, but there is no certainty to time any more, and I can't comprehend the things he chooses to care about.

'Just a little. Please. It's all right,' I whisper, pushing up against him.

Cat and mouse, he lifts his pelvis away even as he presses his cracked lips more firmly into my neck.

No matter how many times I ask, he never accuses me of having done it, never makes me feel like a whore for wanting it with him.

'He will fall, like the others have fallen, and then we will be together,' he murmurs, arms snaking around me like a vine.

He can be so stupid sometimes.

'This will never end,' I gasp when he presses against me again.

'My sad, sweet love.'

Later, we rest, side by side, on the too-narrow back seat. It's dark and cold and the silence breeds foreboding, but still I want to stay here forever. I want to leave for the border tonight, for somewhere safe. I want to crawl back to my childhood, to days that carried within them no pasts and no future. Bubbles of honey-coated peace. I am full to bursting with want. The roof of the car is worn and torn, scored with scratches that could be from keys or knives or desperate fingers, and I can't help but think of it as another thing that could kill us.

A nighttime bombing, the car explodes in a burst of molten steel and shrapnel. The *jinn* shriek with laughter, but *malak almawt* sighs because even he must be weary of this by now. The explosion lights up the sky with pain coming too fast to feel, a blissful annihilation. One minute we are here and the next we're gone, as though we'd never been. In the aftermath, when the people rush out of their homes and the first responders arrive, will they even be able to identify us? I hope not – at least it will save my parents the shame of knowing who I was with and what we might have been doing.

The things we choose to care about.

'Anas says we shouldn't go straight to the bomb sites any more.' One arm is thrown over Khalid's face, and he taps the back of the front seat in a tuneless beat. 'He says we should wait until the second one falls.'

Anas is smart, I think, but all I do is lean over and kiss the dry skin of his bicep.

'They always fall in twos,' he says, 'except for the times they don't.'

24

Blut und Boden

It has always struck me as odd, to take such fervent pride in something you had no part in claiming. You don't choose where you're born. You don't choose the nation or the religion or the caste or sect or class. You choose none of it, and yet you're expected to fight for and be proud of this label ~~above all~~ to the exclusion of all others. It becomes entangled in your identity. I am Syrian. I am Iranian. I am American. I am French. I am Muslim, or Jewish, or Hindu.

I am all these things that I did not choose to be.

At borders all across Europe they asked who we were. The Alis from Homs and the Husseins from Iraq who pretended they were from Aleppo and the AlKhalafs from Raqqa, they would all shout, 'Syrian!' before even saying their name. Finally nationality came before ancestry or ethnicity or religion, just as Sykes and Picot intended a century ago when they sat around a table, twirled their moustaches, and carved up the region into nice neat plots – some for the French and some for the British. No longer was it so anathema, so very unnatural, to proclaim oneself Syrian rather than Kurd or Turkmen or Assyrian or Arab or Armenian. I would bite my tongue, and back when I was sometimes talking, I'd say my name first and the border officer would look at me like I was stupid and bark, 'Where home?' When I could no longer speak, I'd just thrust my papers in his face.

Einstein called nationalism 'an infantile thing', the 'measles of mankind'. He's not wrong. It is a most infantile thing. ~~Very much like~~ Akin to children in a schoolyard saying, ha ha, my daddy is stronger than yours. A nationalist may crow about freedom and prosperity, or values and piety, or modernity and skyscrapers, but at the end of the day, the bedrock of why his country is better than yours is simply that he was born into it. There is, on a fundamental level, no other reason.

Schopenhauer said it was 'the cheapest kind of pride', devaluing the human in favour of the horde. ~~Just like~~ Like religion, it's a way of relating to something greater than the self. A nationalist subsumes (subordinates?) ~~himself~~ his ~~individuality~~ personhood to the masses. They call it unity, but in effect it is little more than self-deception in a state of mass delusion. In reaching for one common ideal, one shared belief in what is right and true, they are grasping for homogeneity, and in doing so, make themselves no better than automatons, waving their signs and torches and lengths of useless fabric. They call themselves patriots, but they're not. A patriot is one who loves, a nationalist is one who hates.

It is fundamentalism, as abhorrent and destructive as any jihad.

I look over what I've scrawled on the notepad, uncertain how Josie will take it. We've never corresponded about this topic, but from her online activity I think she may have voted to leave. It makes me question our entire involvement. Is this nothing but a job to her? Does she believe me? Does she agree with me? Does it matter? I wonder if she'll give me any pushback for my views on the nightmare of nationalism that's sweeping the world, that has managed with very little effort to cross so many borders. I wonder if she really thinks Britain was greater back when *they* were the ones flitting around the world in search of fortunes – things and places to call theirs.

She still asks for memories. I never responded to her email about my splitting of hairs and 'real' people, and she has chosen to ignore my ignoring of it, returning instead to a gentle prodding for more personal narratives. She wants stories about home, about family, about the journey and the camps. The whys and hows of it all. And yet, here I am, swallowing the personal in favour of the political. Again. Why? Is it easier? Safer? After all, if no one knows your personal story, they can't use it against you.

She wants me to write of borders, simple pieces with titles like, My Border Memories, My Memories of Borders, All the Borders I've Gone Through.

We are not people first, or perhaps at all, we are citizens first.

What does your country owe you? Power? Control? Preference over those who are not of it? ~~Just like religious bigotry or homophobia or racism, it is ALL ABOUT FEAR. Fear of the other, fear of what they might be taking from you, fear of losing status.~~

There is so much fear, it seems the world is blanketed in it.

There's a knock at the door, and I flinch and drop my pen, hands covering the papers. I stare in disbelief, as though the door has sprouted a head or tentacles with which the outside world is creeping into my home. Why is there knocking? No one knocks.

Chloe wouldn't knock; she doesn't think I can hear. Unless it's some peculiarity of adolescence, an inability to think of things not concerning the self. Besides, I haven't seen her in days, so she might have already gone north with her mother. It wouldn't be Ruth or Tom. They never bother me. Not the Juicer or Adam, and if it is Adam, well, what if there's someone else in the hall?

There's a flashing light, like a mobile app, sweeping back and forth in the tiny gap between the door and the floor.

Adam is still crouched when I open the door. He looks up at me with a cheeky grin, his resemblance to Ahmed hitting me again so hard that I sway with the force of it and immediately avert my eyes.

'Hey,' he says, rising with a short wave.

He lets himself in, shutting the door, and turns to where I stand, at the counter, squeezing honey into my open mouth. It is one of many tricks I have for when the panic flares, when it climbs up my throat like acid, or lava, or burning bile, to clamp down under my tongue for the rest of the day. 'Are you all right?' I nod but squeeze a bit more in for good measure. I imagine it coating the panic, encasing it in cooling amber. I imagine frozen little bubbles of panic floating around inside me. Insulated. Neutralized. When I replace the bottle of honey in the cupboard and turn to him, there is concern in his eyes.

'So you know how we were talking politics the other day?' This pulls a frown from me, as I did no talking beyond a few sentences and questions jotted down on scrap paper. 'Well, things are moving along quicker than I thought they would.' His eyes are bright and a buzzing energy surrounds him. 'I've joined up with a student organizing group out of Manchester, and we want to organize these synchronized marches all across the country, from Brighton to Glasgow, at every major city and even some smaller ones. Can you imagine? One day where all these marches go on at the same time? The entire country marching for what's right?'

Marching for what *you* think is right, my mind supplies, but my mouth obliges with what I hope is an encouraging smile.

'You ought to join,' he says, holding out his hand. In it are printed papers filled with information and what look like fliers with large pictures and bold print. I am shaking my head before he finishes the sentence. 'Look, I know you don't like people, and that's fine. I know you have a problem speaking, and that's also fine. What we need is more bodies. That's all. Just stand on a street and pass out some information – you don't have to say anything. Come to the march and walk with us.'

There is panic again as he talks, and I snatch up my notepad and scribble furious words on it, trying to get the sentences down to stop him speaking.

You don't know what I believe

You don't know me

He looks at it, eyes flicking across the paper then back at me. A slight wince of his mouth and he says, 'You can't believe this. Everything that's happening. You're . . . you're Arab, the imam told me so, which means you're probably a Muslim. You can't think all this is okay.'

I look down at my feet, ashamed for the first time in so long that I am startled by it. I have forgotten what it feels like to have someone expect something of me. But still I shake my head. It is impossible. This thing he asks so easily, like I'm just another millennial fervent with zeal, acknowledging the zeitgeist, wanting desperately to be a part of something.

I am a part of it. More than he will ever know.

He puffs out a sigh, and I glance back up, surprised at his easy concession. He drops the papers on the desk but keeps his fliers. 'In that case, do you have anything you can donate? It doesn't have to be money,' he rushes to add. 'We're taking books, films, music, anything really. We want to educate people, so we're having these salon-type things where we talk about how art responds to the times or how it commented on like the sixties and stuff. I mean, that's where our main focus is.' He shakes his head, eyes drifting. 'I'm convinced of it. History has repeated itself. This is the new sixties.'

The sixties, the sixties. How groovy. Morrison sings about throwing horses off boats while his dad bombs Vietnam. I move past Adam to my wall of books. My flat may be a mess, but my books are as organized as it is possible for books to be, and it only takes a second to pull out the one I want. A vintage edition of Seymour Hersh's report on the My Lai Massacre from 1970; it's got a black, white and yellow cover, cracks on the front and back and spine, sand-coloured pages, and it smells of musty bookshop, of time, of oil from other people's hands. It is an important book, and if Adam is convinced that this is the sixties again, then he needs to know how bad it can get, how bad it has already got. Running my finger over the cover, flicking its edge, I can't help but think, who will write about Darayya, or Homs, or Shu'aytat, or Ghouta, or, or, or? Look them up and you'll see approximations and best guesses. About 700 died here, 500 plus there, 100 plus here. Like you're counting out change or livestock or something. Not people. They aren't people, not to you. They're numbers, guesstimates. And those dots on maps and images on the news, they're just another war zone. To me, that's home. It's my neighbourhood. It's where I went to school. That boy, dead and muddy, is my brother. That man bleeding from the wound in his head is my father. People, all 700 plus of them.

How long can a silence last before it, like the human body, like the human psyche, cracks? The waterwheels have stopped, but will someone finally speak of all those griefs we hoard so diligently?

The silence has cracked, and Syria, now, is all noise. Every death and every blast blots out more of the sun, blinding the world with distorted images and blackness. Until there is nothing left but souls wailing in the dark.

In Queiq, where the river flows into the southside of Aleppo, it was 110 – though some counted 147 and others insist it was closer to 250. Precision, in this respect, is hard to come by. Not such a large number, in any case. Certainly not large enough to warrant much media attention and scrutiny. One hundred and ten men and boys between the ages of eleven and forty. Men and boys who would cross over for supplies and goods. Men and boys who would make the crossing every day, who would be spat on and insulted and shoved until one day, instead, their hands were bound behind their backs, mouths sealed tight with tape, bullets in their heads. Boys who swore they wouldn't cross over, who swore to Mama and who swore to me, but who crossed over anyway. And then a new year, a spring of pulling bodies from a river in the middle of the city, so many bodies that the water levels were reduced so it would no longer carry them downstream.

I turn and thrust the book Adam's way, and he grabs at it before it falls. He glances at the cover, turns it over to read the back, then thumbs through a bit, no doubt noticing my annotations and under-lines and circles. He looks like he wants to say something more but thinks better of it. His eyes drift to the window and he tilts his head like a bird.

Across the way, in South Tower A, second floor, flat three, Matt is fucking Anime Girl on the floor by the sofa. He moves over her, the bones in his spine visible through transparent skin, the small muscles in his backside flexing, thin hips pumping. Her head is thrown back, the heavy fringe clinging to her forehead, bubblegum lips and big eyes open to the ceiling, sweat glistening in the papyrus tones of her neck and arms and the pale, pale folds of her legs.

They are fucking in the spot where Matt's dad tried to choke the life out of his mother.

Adam clears his throat and I look back at him. There's a different sort of light in his eyes now. 'Cheers,' he says, touching the book to his head like a prayer as he turns away. 'Let me know if you change your mind.'

Shaking myself, I sink back to the floor and pick up my pad and pen before he's even shut the door behind him.

25

A Petty Crime

The mosque was vandalized. There was a crowd outside the court-yard this morning, tossing around rumours and speculation like kids with balls in a playground. In the shop Hasan was shaking his head, recounting the series of events for anyone coming up to the till to pay for their tea or oil or onions or just to hear what happened.

He tells us how the faithful who came for the dawn prayers were the first to see it. 'Fuck you!' and 'Filthy Pakis!' and other lazy slurs spray-painted on the walls in red, the paint dripping down so it looked like blood. More spray paint across the iron bars – penises and pigs and men in turbans with tongues wagging after crude little stick-figure girls with pigtails. And around the big chain that the imam had only just begun to lock at night, someone had wrapped the entrails of what no one suspects to be anything other than a pig.

'They think we will see a pig and die,' Hasan says with a snort.

'Like it's your kryptonite,' a student in a university sweatshirt adds, relieved that we might find this all amusing.

Hasan holds his hands a metre apart, explaining again and again how long the intestines were, and how maybe it was from more than one animal, and the student launches into a whole spiel about the length of various animal innards. Hasan stops him with a pale palm and a scowl. He speaks about the dripping blood and the smell that wafted up and down the pavement and how there were tears in the imam's eyes as he went to get a bucket of water and brush to start cleaning up, but then the young men stopped him and called for the police and told him not to touch anything.

When I emerge onto the street, the police are still there. No sirens blazing like when they came for Helen, just a lone squad car with a couple of officers on the pavement taking statements. The imam is shaking his head. 'No, no problems here. No one bothers us and we bother no one.' He looks tired, much older somehow since I last saw him.

'That's not entirely true though, is it?' the police officer says, flipping through his notepad. 'We got called out here just a couple of weeks ago on account of neighbour complaints.'

'We cook enough food for the whole community!' Imam Abdulrahman exclaims. 'Why should they complain of that?'

'I don't reckon it was the food so much as the noise,' the officer replies, jotting down some notes, perhaps about the imam's gesticulations. Maybe he's writing him up as 'unnecessarily aggressive'; 'combative', even.

One of the young men comes forward, gently pushes the imam behind him, and begins to tell the officer all about the man who came with his friends looking for trouble. He's impressive, like a barrister, recalling dates and time of day and what the man had been wearing and how many friends he'd brought along with him. He recounts identifying marks and tattoos and hairstyles. 'He called us all these things,' he says, sweeping a hand at the graffiti. 'It can only have been him. We have trouble with no one.'

I step closer to the gate, reach out to touch one of the spray-painted pigs. It's still wet and my finger comes away bright red. I rub it against my thumb, heart pounding, and then wipe it frantically down my jeans. My mind goes to that day, to seeing Matt through the window, him fiddling with the bag and the cans it held. Petty crime. Is his mother back? Has she returned with Chloe? The flat's been quieter with them gone. I thought perhaps Matt and his father were getting along fine. I had thought Matt would use the cans to paint on the walls down by the railway tracks. Petty crime. Maybe he and his friends would paint some big-breasted pin-up girls on their school or goggle-eyed monsters on old buildings down by the waterfront. Not this. I never imagined this.

This is not petty.

'Did you see anything?'

I turn. The other officer is at my side. He looks bored, chewing on his bottom lip, pen poised on his notepad as he waits for my answer, thinking maybe of fish and chips for lunch. When he finally looks at me, I shake my head. 'Do you know anything?'

I shake my head to that too.

Josie wants memories, so I'll give her memories. I will give her all of them, whether they are completely chronologically factual or not. I'll write about Queiq in that spring when Mama gave up on life and Baba finally resigned himself to the fact that we couldn't stay there, about the bombs that fell and the snipers on the roofs and how every day felt like a giant game of Russian roulette: would today be your turn? Would it be your house they stormed? Your father they took? I'll write about the cousins and aunts and uncles and brothers and neighbours and best friends who were tortured or killed or scattered to the wind like doves that would never again find a place to nest. I will write about the twelve-year-old boy working in a hospital in Aleppo, giving injections and cleaning bedpans, and about Khalid of the White Helmets before they were the White Helmets who told me we would, TOGETHER, leave that circle of hell.

I'll tell her about the crossing of Europe and how I walked a continent. About the weighted-down raft and the people who drowned and the bigger boat and all the camps where people immediately tried to impose some order and structure on their lives. About little handwritten signs saying SCHOOL or PLAYGROUND or LIBRARY and the enterprising minds that set up shop selling whatever they could and dustbin fires that burned all night because there was no other way to find heat. About spray paint on the walls of newly erected huts in broken English or beautiful Arabic. I'll write about being locked in freezing lorries and being chased and shot at and beaten by border guards and smugglers who fleece you and use you because they know your only other option is death.

I write two, three, four articles that I fire off throughout the day and night and another day until she has a fucking timeline of how I got here.

From Aleppo to England

I can count, on the fingers of one hand, the things I have from home.

1. A picture of my mother from when she was my age, married with one child and another on the way.
2. A picture of the whole family taken the last time we were all together. Though we didn't know it at the time. You can never foresee such things.
3. My documents.
4. A dictionary I pilfered from Baba's study.
5. My name.

That's it. That's the sum total of my belongings. I did have some money from home and some clothes and jewellery (handed down from Mama and her mama before), but these are long gone. The jewels were sold and money was spent on food and water and smugglers who said they could get me wherever I needed to go. *I promise. I swear*, they would say, hand on their hearts then palms up to Allah.

I heard those words a lot on my journey here. And they were never worth a damn.

The route I took to England is not unlike that of others in my situation, although many chose to stay in various countries on the mainland rather than try to cross the Channel. Turkey on an overnight bus, then a raft skirting the Greek Isles that gave up somewhere around Siros, then a bigger boat further up the coast, then more buses to cross into Macedonia, then walking and walking and walking until my shoes filled with blood and the word 'pain' lost all meaning.

You cannot imagine the amount of walking that was involved. I could say eight hours or five or twelve at a stretch. I could say it was 300 kilometres or 150, but these are just numbers. They have no meaning. Your minds, your bodies, have no frame of reference from which to bring forth empathy.

So shall I tell you instead how the topography of her, of Europe, is encoded in my body now? She's in the limestone of my skin, dry and easily split. Her salt is in the dark seaweed of my hair, the tang of my sweat. My breasts, the hills of Serbia. The rolls of fat on my belly, my back and hips, like the creases and trenches of Macedonia. Her marshes and fens lie in the shadows of my armpits, the morass of my mound. Walking across Europe, I hung myself from the sky. I swung from star to star and curled up in every crescent moon.

Or perhaps that's too lyrical, and I should be more grounded.

So, instead I'll say that most of the camps are bad. The sort of place you wouldn't want a family pet living in. There is disease and filth and the violence of the desperate. The policemen that patrol are hideous men, capable of more than you would think a human is capable of. When there are moments of light – a child learning to read at his grandfather's knee, an aid package over-flowing with unexpected delights, a beautiful day where the sunlight plays in the trees – they are fleeting and have a dreamlike quality.

Most of the time, it's an endless stream of shit.

Sometimes, quite literally.

Can you imagine what the conditions of home must be to render such an ordeal not only tolerable, but *desirable*?

When I got to England, I'll admit, I thought things would be easier. I thought the country would be more helpful. I thought they would do more for us. For so long, I had felt it to be a kind of utopia, a place of endlessly rolling hills and lilting accents, a place I dreamed of coming to under very different circumstances. But it's not. I was mocked on arrival, pushed around, poked and prodded, assumed to be some stupid sheep herder begging for scraps off Her Majesty's table.

I try to fit in. Americans call it *assimilation*. This is the process of taking in and fully understanding information and ideas. It can also mean the process of becoming similar to something.

This is what I'm doing. I already have the understanding. Freedom, work ethic, independence, I believe in these things. I am also attempting to be similar to you. In many ways I feel I already am. I left the *hijab* in Syria. I wear the same clothes you do, I watch the same panel shows on Channel 4 and the BBC, I listen to the Beatles and the Rolling Stones and Bowie and all the other music you take such pride in. I read your books and your news, and I use my money to attend one of your universities and buy food and more clothing that you wear from your shops. I am becoming, not similar to you, but you.

I'm not a freeloader. I was at university when the war broke out. My father was a teacher, my brothers and sisters were teachers and engineers. We had a comfortable life. We were productive. I don't want handouts from this country. Refugees are not coming to suck up what's yours. We want to work, we want to go to school, we want to be full and active members of society. We are not leeches, or parasites, or vermin.

We just need a little help. That's all.

She publishes the first one almost immediately, within a few hours, without returning to me with edits, without comment. All I get is what has become her standard email with a link, and I wonder if she's tired of me.

Throughout the day, responses trickle in. Most are positive. People tell me I'm welcome here and that they're glad I made it and they wish me a good life. There are those who say they cried while reading it, and they can't imagine having the fortitude to make such a journey (I never imagined it either, but you would be surprised what the human body can endure). People chuckle at the music and TV references, astounded that I would find humour and entertainment in the same places they do. It is mostly positive, though I wonder if it is just another echo chamber at work. Does empathy translate to action?

Some attack me, naturally. Mustafa from Birmingham says it's wrong for me to try to be English, that I ought to hold on to my heritage and culture and religion and that my family would surely be ashamed to read such things from me. Amina from south London tells me it's ignorant to think I need to take off my *hijab* to be a part of this country, and that she was born here and she wears hers with pride. It is a fair point.

Unity in diversity. That's what they're always telling us, despite how empty the word has become.

And then there's this:

BeccaDent says: I'm as touched by the Voiceless's story as the next person, but there are a couple of things about it that bother me. To start, why won't this person use their name? What's the point in hiding that? What else are they hiding? It almost makes me think this isn't a real person, but that it's some journalist or someone pushing an agenda and deciding to masquerade as a refugee to gain credibility. Another thing is if this person is who they say they are, I kind of wish they would just tell their story without adding all of the politics into it. I know it says the Voiceless is studying political science, but that hardly makes them an expert. We all took a poli sci course at uni. I don't know. It's a good story, but something about it just didn't sit right.

For many long minutes, perhaps hours, I'm unable to process this comment. I just sit there, in front of the laptop, blinking over and over while I try to understand it. A series of furious urges come over me: to throw the computer out of the window, let it sail over the balcony and crash to the courtyard below; to open up loads of fake social media accounts with which to attack her and all the others; to lock myself in the shower and slice into the skin of my arms or legs until this hideous pressure goes away.

Or maybe I should return to that state of absolute silence, like my time at the hospital where I spent my first six months in the UK. Instead of home-cooked meals and trips up the coast, I was subjected to psychological testing, writing out answers to whatever questions or ink blots or cards with weeping women Dr Thompson sent my way. And what did I get for it? Involuntary admission. Reason: Patient is a suicide risk. My asylum officer joked and said it was a good thing since they were low on sponsors at the moment anyway. It was fine by me too. At least it was warm and I had a bed and food and use of a shower.

The doctor pulled out a laminated poster to show me something called Freud's Topography of the Mind. She said to look at it like an iceberg; that was how it was illustrated, this vaguely diamond-shaped thing bobbing in calm water under a perfect yellow sun and a pale blue sky. Why was the sun there? It wasn't relevant to the theory as she explained it. It distracted me, that yellow circle with crude rays spiking out of it, like a child's drawing. She spoke of the ego and the id and the superego that sometimes intrudes, that sometimes attacks. Life instincts and death instincts. Instincts that make you more (less?) human. She gestured to the tip of the iceberg, *That's the conscious part. It's where your thoughts and perceptions live. All the things you're aware of.* Below it was the subconscious, where she said my memories were stored. She skipped over that section pretty quickly, but it was the smallest slice of the iceberg so maybe it was unimportant. Below that, deeper into the darker blue, was the largest segment, the unconscious. *Here's where your fear goes*, she said, tracing a bright red fingernail over the area. *This is where the trauma is.* There was a word cloud in that part of the diagram, crowded with terms she didn't read out for me but which caught my eye. Irrational wishes. Immoral urges. Selfish needs. Who made those determinations? Who decided whether something was irrational or immoral or selfish? Who were the gatekeepers?

I didn't understand any of it. Was the goal of my time with her to eventually flip the iceberg over? Did she want that dark mass to be on the surface? The very idea of it struck me with a paralysing horror. She was so wrong about the fears; they weren't all the way down there, in that dismal blue. They were on my skin, crawling all over me, all the time, biting, like electric sparks.

She spoke to me of trauma. She spoke of events, exceptional moments in time, how they shatter identity and fragment the self so that there's a clear distinction between who you were before and who you are now. A past and a present, and (maybe?) a possible future. She spoke of identifying the traumatic event, talking it out, and integrating it into the present, that this was how one moved forward and found a new way of being. A clear before and after, split with an unwavering line you can label 'traumatic event'. How they love their dichotomies. Such pretty little black and white worlds, just like Khalid said. They're so used to categories and plots that make sense. As though the world were not chaos and void.

What if there is no before or after? What if you live your life *within* the long pause of trauma, perpetually astride that line? What if the trauma is a place that time cannot penetrate?

She spoke of *a* rape, *a* mugging or assault, *a* period of war. All of them singular moments, stand-alone events, bounded in time. What of occupations that have lasted half a century? What of detainment? What of surveillance apparatuses and institutionalized oppression and indefinite states of emergency? Could she trace the form identity took in such cases? Could she integrate cloudy and heavy and cutting shards into some kind of whole? It was clear that she lived, that all of them here lived, outside the kind of reality of which I would need to speak. To make her see it, I would have to find new words, new definitions with which to confront her.

Impossible. I didn't know those words.

You have to step outside something, for a little while at least, in order to name it.

I showed the doctor what silence was then. It was a silence so extreme, it seemed, at times, that I was the only person left in the whole world, so complete was my dissociation from everything around me. In Allende's *The House of the Spirits*, Clara goes mute and feels she is filled with the silence of the whole world. I too felt myself filled completely with silence, but it was not that of the world. You can say many things, but you cannot say that the world is silent. It is noise and chaos. A relentless assault on the senses. It is bombs and gunfire and babies crying in trees and mothers wailing and fathers shouting and rushing rivers and howling winds and crunching tyres and and and. It is the furthest possible thing from silence. And it seemed to me that the only way to counter this cacophony was to go quiet, to express nothing. The only reasonable response was to fill myself up with silence.

So I did. One night in that sterile room on that small hard bed. It was dim, and down the white walls came dark streaky tricklings of freezing cold water. It dripped harder and harder until they became rills and streams flowing down the wall to the floor below me. More and more water, icy and loud, it rose higher and higher. Reaching the bed, drenching the mattress, seeping into me so that my skin soaked it up, and I, too, was freezing, blood going hard and sharp like broken glass in my veins. Higher still until I felt the waters cradle my head, an icy numbness, and for the first time in a long time, I was at peace. I pressed my head into the pillow harder, urging the waters to take more and more of me, until it poured into my ears, up my nose, and down my throat. Until it filled me completely.

Perhaps I should have tossed myself from that raft after all.

Perhaps a relapse is coming. I don't know. Instead of silence, I now feel filled with a screaming rage that burns along my nerves like wildfire and threatens to burst.

The hallway outside the Juicer's flat smells of nothing tonight. There are no sounds beyond the door, no chop chop chopping of vegetables or counting out of exercise reps in breathless grunts, but I know he's here. I saw his light on, saw him walking around the flat in his black shorts with his chest bare.

I'm not here for a meal.

26

The Eye

The room is darker today. Outside, the world is flat and angry and the colour of sand. Black paper birds roll about the sky, agitated and confused, tossed about by some capricious god. There's no sun, just a muted haze like caked mud. The buildings across the way are silent; no one moves there. There is black-speckled grime on all the windows. Not a cloud in the sky, just a whirling of dust and wretchedness.

We were puppets, moving back and forth across this cell like what we did mattered.

Nubby fabric for skin, comically large heads on undernourished figures, exaggerated caricature-like features. Puppets bobbing along in this room that was a sound stage: the aluminium desks were made of matchstick boxes, frayed on the edge; the room is the inside of a cardboard box with 'windows' cut into its side; the red plastic cup is a scrap of red paper and, when we walk, we don't kick so much as shuffle it across the floor.

High in the corner of the ceiling, where the lid of the box seals us in, is an eyeball. A golf ball or ping-pong ball perhaps. Large and white with red veins and a bright iris inked into it. Scanning back and forth, back and forth, from one wall to the other, from window to door, it misses nothing.

Our limbs flail when we move, as though they're disconnected from us. Our eyes are wide black buttons and our mouths are flat ovals that look permanently shocked. At the table, Amer is alone, bent over the fabric, a thick marker gripped in his fingerless fist. Pink felt tongue clamped between the seam of his lips, he concentrates as he moves the black colour across the white banner. *Where's Ossama?* appears over and over across the length and breadth of the fabric. Amer writes it in Arabic, in English, in French, in languages none of us know. His handwriting is blocky, inelegant, disjointed, and he grunts with the effort of each letter. *Where's Ossama? Where's Ossama? Where's Ossama?*

Every movement is an uncoordinated jerk, my hand whipping the window even though there's no glass to wipe, and the bit of tissue stuck to my palm flutters ineffectually. Khalid is against the wall, a wide and stocky shape with a large thumb of a head, like the person who made him had never even seen him, hadn't been informed of his wiriness, of the shadows that play in the sinew of his muscles. A crude *keffiyeh* is wrapped around his head, and there's no expression on his face.

Outside there's laughter and chatter. I glance out of the window that isn't a window and see a large crowd gathered below us. It's not a street – no pavement or charred remains of cars or bent streetlights. Instead I look down at a dark pit with rows and rows of red velvet seats. The people are people, not puppets like us, and they sit there, chatting and passing popcorn and chocolate bars and cans of soft drinks back and forth while they wait.

'It's done,' Amer says, flopping back and forth a few times, the marker flying out of his fist to sail through the window. The crowd roars with laughter and applauds, a harsh rhythmic clapping, like an Egyptian *kaff*, like a protest about to kick off. I turn to the table, my movements difficult and stiff, as though I were moving through sludge. My hands don't work well, fingers sewn together with just an awkward thumb hanging off the side, but between us Amer and I are able to roll the fabric up into a scroll and move towards the window.

We release the banner, and it unfurls in lumpy drops down the side of the box. At once, the black words bleed down the whiteness, as though Amer used paint instead of markers. Letters and words become unintelligible, the *noon* sagging at the bottom and the *meem* growing distorted, until it looks like there was no one named Ossama at all.

The crowd takes it in silently, heads tilting this way and that, eyes flicking between the fabric of the banner and the fabric of our faces as we lean out of the window. Even the paper birds pause in the sky, peering at the words as though they could read them. The pause blankets the world, or at least the only world that matters. Then, there is indignation and angry shouting and popcorn thrown at the banner and drink cans and sandals aimed at our heads.

Amer and I pull back and turn to Khalid, but he and the Eye are looking at a forgotten corner of the room. Ossama hangs there. A tight black rope secures him to the lid, and he swings back and forth. Eyes wide and white, his mouth gapes, pink felt tongue lolling out at a comical angle. His arms are bound, and a redness, like ink from a disapproving teacher's pen, oozes from his skin.

Outside, the crowd begins, again, to applaud.

27

This Is My Truth

In the morning there's another knock at the door, another flash of light sweeping the floorboards. I barely hear it, barely see it, for the summer storm raging outside. The sky is nearly black, despite the early hour, flashes of lightning break through, cracks of thunder that pull at my nerves. I am dazed and tired and sore and filled again with silence.

Adam pushes past me into the flat, agitated and twitchy, flinging raindrops everywhere. His pupils are so dilated his eyes look blacker than usual, like twin black holes, like black stones, like coal or onyx or . . .

'You hear what happened at the mosque?'

I nod, leaning against the wall.

'I passed by yesterday, and the imam was out there still cleaning off all the paint.' Adam paces back and forth in my living room, running a hand through his hair, words spilling out of his mouth like someone's after him. 'He told me what happened, and I helped out for a bit until the other men and women took over the cleaning. Now it looks like nothing happened. But then, later, I went down to the station to help out a friend. The cops picked him up on some stupid drug thing, thinking he was selling when he wasn't. Anyway, I was down at the station, right? And I seen this big man there, in the waiting area with a cop on either side, face like a blob of ketchup it's so red, shouting about how he had nothing to do with it, and I'm thinking to meself, he looks familiar. Do you remember weeks ago, those guys who was making trouble in the mosque, when they were having that party over there?'

I nod again, moving slowly to the kitchen, looking through the cabinets for the honey.

'It was him! That same guy. They think he done the spray-paint job on the mosque, probably with his mates. Everyone knows he's a racist, so it doesn't surprise me. That's how these things happen, you know? This shit escalates. They're not content with just shouting about it for long. Shouting turns to vandalism and then to outright violence. I told one of the cops that, at the station; pulled him aside and told him all that.'

I grab a notepad and scribble on it, turning it to him.

Are they going to arrest him?

'If they have enough evidence to, yeah, I reckon they will.'

They can't arrest him for being a racist

He snorts. 'If only they could. There's probably stuff at his place, more paint or receipts or maybe his mates will turn on him, I don't know. The police are going to give him a hard time though, that's for sure. The city doesn't want to get a reputation for tolerating this sort of thing.'

When Adam leaves, I watch from the window. I count how long it takes him to emerge from the building – three minutes and fifty-four seconds. Then I count the one hundred and eighty-seven steps he takes, head down and collar turned up against the pounding rain, back to the East Tower.

I scowl at the sky, hating the overt symbolism of this raging storm. If this were a story, any editor worthy of the name would reject it. There would be an underline in red or a big circle around the paragraph and a comment in the margin saying, *this is too on the nose*. The juxtaposition of a perfect day would be infinitely preferable. That's what Josie did, with one of the memories I sent her. She asked if I could tone down the descriptions of the weather, saying it matched up too well with the emotional undertones of the memory, that the reader didn't need the symbolism of the weather. And here I thought I'd just been painting a picture. Europe in the dead of winter is no picnic, Josie; you ought to know that. She wanted me to alter the memory, so as to show a contrast, some symbolism over reality. Maybe a bright and sunny day after the night of hiding in the woods, something to hint at optimism and hope, as if the reality wasn't that I was, every day, terrified that running and hiding and being smuggled was going to be the rest of my life.

It's like I said. People aren't interested in the truth so much as the narrative.

Here's another narrative, I think, my eyes drifting over to South Tower A, second floor, flat three.

Helen is there, on the sofa. I guess she and Chloe didn't leave after all. The flat is empty. I know because Helen is weeping openly. She's never so free when her family is there. She's quiet and stoic with the children, weak and bowed with her husband. She is not herself when they are there; she's the person they've made her. A woman so weighed down, it's a wonder she can walk upright. A woman who is beaten and torn and stretched and alone in a flat with three other people.

What was she like before? Does she even remember a time before she was married to a brute, anchored to him with kids? What dreams did she have for herself, what plans? Was she taller then?

I wonder who she was before the Dad found her.

What would they do to Matt, if I told the police what I'd seen through the window? He is only a kid after all – though, back home, they would be merciless, even with a child. That's not how it's supposed to work here. A civilized country like Britain would put him in counselling or anger management or give him a social worker, surely. Could he go to jail for this? Helen would weep herself dry and then find a way to weep some more, the Dad would rage at her and the world, Chloe would drift further and further away, maybe to drugs, maybe to drink, maybe to men like her father. That home, through the window, would shatter into a million pieces.

Helen jolts upright, startled, and turns her body towards the window while she swipes at her face with the sleeve of her jumper. Her mouth moves, forming words I can't make out, and she plasters her fake smile there before facing whoever has entered the flat. More words and half-hearted gestures, and then her son comes into view. He doesn't embrace her, doesn't pat her back or put an arm around her shoulder, but his expression shifts to something like concern or maybe helplessness. She shakes her head, brings her hair forward to hide her face, and he huffs before moving out of sight. A few minutes later, he returns with a mug of something that he places on the low table before her – tea or coffee, or maybe hot chocolate. Helen looks like she could use some chocolate. He moves out of view again, and then he's back, presenting two closed fists to her. She smiles. Just a tiny quirk of her lips, but it is a smile. She points at his right fist, and he opens it to reveal a shortbread biscuit. His mum takes it and gestures at the other hand. It holds a piece of chocolate, and Matt grins before popping it in his mouth.

The Big Man is a Bad Man. Full of bad thoughts and ill intentions. He didn't spray-paint those heinous things on the mosque, didn't hold his breath while handling pig entrails, but I would bet anything he applauded it, maybe wished *he* had thought of it.

I draw invisible letters on the glass, write out stories there that no one will ever read.

Maybe they *can* arrest someone for being a racist.

The storm is over. But for the great puddles in the road, it's as if it never happened. The sun is busy drying it all up, wet patches of grass glinting like jewels as I cross the park because I just need to move, move, move. Droplets shake themselves from the leaves above me, but my hoodie is up and I feel nothing. The air is fresh and sweet and calm. Here is your juxtaposition, Josie. I chuckle to myself – that's what I should call her in my next email. *Dear Juxtaposition Josie.* I've always loved a good bit of alliteration.

There are people in the park, now that the weather has cleared. They're throwing mucky tennis balls for their dogs to chase and shouting at one another across the greens. Women in leggings and tank tops run laps despite the breeze. There's a group of students throwing a frisbee, and down they go tumbling laughing to this empty muddy earth whenever they miss a catch. There are young mothers with sturdy buggies, jogging their babies around the park, and children zipping down wet slides and swinging in shiny swings and screaming because children are unable to modulate their volume. Matt is there, with his boys, standing in a hostile group, swigging from cans and shouting out their fun, oblivious to me and everyone else in the park. Adam is at the opposite corner, handing out fliers with his friends. Our eyes meet as I pass, but he doesn't try to stop me.

On my third lap, I veer away, threading through the alleys and side streets, past the Ginger Giant's bookshop, ignoring the offerings he's setting out in boxes and on tables now that the rain is gone. He looks up and nods as I move behind him. I hug the shopfronts to avoid the walls of water that cars and buses send up when they pass.

There's the fancy organic shop none of us go to, with farmers' market produce arranged in pretty stacks out on the pavement. Inside it's all bamboo decor and greenery and hemp bags and natural products. On one side is a small bar area selling fresh juices and organic, artisan coffee. It's manned by a girl who looks like she should be teaching yoga, long and lithe in a vest top and cardigan and loose trousers, with blonde waves tumbling around her shoulders and no makeup on her pretty face.

The Juicer is there, at the bar, with a basket full of leafy greens and fruit and lemon and coconut water. He's managing to flirt with Yoga Girl behind the counter while also sending his testosterone-laden pheromones to the one at his side.

It's Anime Girl. She turns to scowl at Yoga Girl, snidely asking for a smoothie in her heavily accented English. She's in another one of her school uniform-type things: black skirt that barely hits her thighs, button-up shirt she hasn't managed to fully button, Mary Janes and white ankle socks. She looks all of twelve. Little Lolita. The Juicer likes it, smiling and offering to pay for her drink while standing just far enough away that it doesn't look like he's doing any more than indulging her. She lets out a peal of giggles like he's the funniest thing she's ever encountered.

I walk on, thinking she's so tiny he'll tear her in half if he fucks her.

28

The Ceremony of Innocence Is Drowned

My mind folds in on itself, like origami, and Khalid comes to me. Khalid in the white helmet that gave him such purpose, his face blanched in debris, his hair snowy with it. He comes to me as a fevered poet, as a diviner in holy vestments, as a crowned king, as a cackling god. Recitations from long ago, in a language that might die with me. He fills the silence with silence – or as many synonyms for it as he can find. He sings to me of the quiet, the mute, the thousand houses and all the dead words residing in their dumb walls. The hush, the eloquence of our silence, and how we must, nevertheless, one day puncture it with screams.

In dark alleys, beneath the yellow lights of the citadel, behind the great park, too near the mosque, I asked him to stop because I wanted him safe, and he snorted and tugged a lock of hair from under my veil and said, *Safe, huh?* and I would pull myself out of reach (why do you pull away when you don't know which reaching for might be the last?) because he wasn't taking me seriously.

At university, in the capital, there are all sorts of Others. People from all corners of the known world, all carrying their own particular foreignness, their prejudices and vices and virtues. People from home who are still so Other. Seeking education, seeking work, seeking a life. All those simple wants that everyone shares. People for whom history is not past but premonition. People like Khalid, with a call

160

to action in their veins, with a wild optimism, with a loftiness of thought that is wholly Other.

People for whom words have power and who seduce you with each utterance.

He took lessons from them all – the Green Movement and their attempted trade of Guevara for Gandhi (*Guevara maat*, Khalid would sing, loud and mournful), Bouazizi's fire (I trembled and for days wouldn't speak when he talked of it), Egypt (oh, Egypt), Sana'a's Day of Rage and Tripoli's Green Square. He crawled further back into the well of time: to '67 and the realization that we were, all of us, entirely alone; to the literature of political commitment (the literature that so terrified Mama); to Kanafani and Mahfouz and how al-Himsi founded modern literary criticism, and imagined nights in those late-nineteenth-century salons of Maryana Marrash.

In whispered phone calls, in quiet stairwells, in the back seats of borrowed cars in dark, empty lots, he recited them all in tones lucid and clear, all those prophets and prophecies of revolution, history that moves like a wheel, rotations that go nowhere and yield nothing. He chided me for not knowing the work of my people, for countering his verses of Negm with those of Yeats, *As though he had anything at all to protest.*

So much pride in what he did not choose to be.

Do I tell Josie about that pride? Do I include Khalid in the things I share with her and the world? Must I give them everything? My own voice, my own story, stutters and falters in its way. All this time I've spent shifting and shaping myself into an entity that can function here, and now my memories too need to be moulded into something easy to digest? I don't know what such a story would even look like, what shape it would take. The structure of narrative has collapsed; imprecise in my own mind, with jagged pieces it takes so much to screw together. What could a story like that accomplish? Do I risk turning us – me, Khalid, Amer and Ossama, Mama and Baba and the others and the little ones – into nothing more than characters, to be followed and felt for but ultimately supplanted with newer, fresher takes? What do all these stories do?

I wonder if Khalid would want this, or if he would see it as just another kind of treason.

It is not enough to survive, he said. *It is not enough for anyone to survive, moving through the world like dumb animals.* A hand against my scalp, so gentle, under my hair, lips beneath my ear, a voice that encompasses all of human experience. *Imagine, in the West, there are those who will not eat cheese, who will not drink milk, out of consideration to animals. So much dignity they give them. And us?* A breath of a chuckle, warm lips pressing into skin. *We've been this way for so long*, I said, pressing into him, trying as hard as I could to fuse us together. *No one is truly voiceless*, he whispered, *either they silence you, or you silence yourself.*

White doves flit from rooftop to rooftop. Empty buildings.

29

As Though We Were No One

. . . We are here, but not. A case number, invisible, and yet a burden all the same.

I read testimonies from detainees and asylum seekers and refugees like me. They tell their stories to writers who have no concept of the sort of reality they're being exposed to, writers who are then charged with taking that raw story and transforming it into a tale for the public. These well-meaning writers invariably make an inward turn, where they take bottom-of-the-pyramid needs of shelter and a stable food source and warm clothing and streets that lie outside the path of bombs and turn it all into a soliloquy on how time is what ultimately kills you or the hypocrisy of Western ideals of justice and democracy or how the limbo of the asylum seeker is worse than what they left behind.

Barrel bombs kill you. Those bombardments of hell that lay waste to your home, your corner shop, your school, and scatter to the wind thousands of people into a hundred thousand infinite parts. Snipers on the roof of your mother or father's workplace. Prison guards with iron rods that they use to beat submission into your wet skin. Smugglers and traffickers and desperate men. These are the things that kill you.

When you are a citizen of a nation that values you, even if only a little, where you don't need to fear it turning on you in some predatory manner, you have the liberty to explore high and existential themes in your writing. For you, a wounded animal can be a metaphor for a wounded psyche and biblical stories can act as a salve binding us to some sacred history that teaches us how we are meant to be with one another.

But when you become an enemy of your country, the art of fiction is turned on its head. And so you find, in the literature of defeat, a reversal, where the wounded psyche itself becomes a metaphor for very mortal wounds inflicted on a people. You find literature that speaks of migrating birds and crashing waves and women who are drops of water in a cloud because the truths cannot be revealed, or they are so terrible that we must hide them in the spaces between our words.

I want to tell these writers to look beneath and around the lines of the tales given to them, pay attention to the gaps, to the lacunae, to the silence, to what is not being said. Could they turn their minds to the questions no one is asking and the answers that remain buried in the caverns of a person's chest or embroidered on their tongue?

That's where the story is.

The Voiceless, *The New Press*, 5 July 2017

First Josie wanted memories. All the memories, for weeks it's all she asked about, but now she says they are too much to be believed, and I wonder if she's playing with me. She's read the other pieces I sent, where I talked about the hot and overcrowded bus through Turkey and the camps in Greece and the little toe that became so infected I thought it would fall off like a rotten piece of fruit. I wrote about guns to my head in front of the open backs of freezing trucks and that afternoon when we swallowed tear gas and dodged rubber bullets on the Macedonian border.

I still have not, cannot, will not, tell her about Syria. The bombs pulverized our home and that door has caved in, perhaps forever.

Only it's a bit overwhelming, she says. *I thought that the first article was enough, in how it detailed your journey from home to here.* Those were not details, Josie. It was not even the beginning of 'detailing'. *People will have a hard time believing it all happened to you.* Has she read the comment by that woman? Becca with her suspicious mind? They think I'm some magpie flitting across Europe, collecting other people's tales and passing them off as my own. *I believe you, but others will suspect.*

As if it matters to them whose story it is. What matters is that it happened, that it *is* happening, in so many places and to so many people. My memories have fractured, and I don't entirely trust the pieces. Words and numbers don't mean much. Pictures, even less. What do I do with the things I've seen – the arguments, the blood, the bodies, the special kind of silence that follows when loved ones leave? How much of it is mine? How much is theirs? All our sorrows leaving a scorched trail across Europe.

Not satisfied with sterile facts, she wants a story, a narrative arc and maybe some character development. She wants a tearjerker, emotive and affecting, something to rev the idle engine of empathy. It's not how we've been trained to speak of what we've been through. At borders and centres and clinics all they wanted was the information – dates, names, places, frequency. Don't get too emotional. They need to believe you. It's journalists and authors and poets who have the luxury, the enormous well of credibility, to then take those facts and spin them into something moving.

A part of me is terrified that a story will diminish the real, that it will cheapen the experience beyond what I can bear.

I do want to publish these. Don't get me wrong. But maybe we could lighten them a bit, or just focus on one episode and unpack it for the readers.

Shutting the laptop with a loud *thwack*, I return to my unmade bed and bury myself beneath the thick duvet. Maybe I'm done with Josie. Maybe I'm done with all of them. Maybe it's time, again, for silence.

———

Mama wilts with the spring. Ahmed emerged from the river, jasmine blossoms for eyes, and tucked up into a ground heavy with grief and vile acts. She'd crawl in there with him if she could. My father searches, frantically now, for a way out. Do we risk the drive to Damascus, where the airport remains open? Or would it be safer to head to Latakia and fly from there? Or, worst case (ha!), a boat to Alexandria? How long would it take? What would it cost? Nada is there already, with her husband and children, waiting for us. But Baba has many to think of still, many who depend on him: a mother and a wife, a baby girl. Not to mention brothers and cousins, some who have left already while others remain and must also be considered. We aren't, any of us, consulted; he directs his questions to the ceiling or the amber prayer beads he rubs all day or the money he withdrew long ago from the bank to keep wadded up in boxes under the bed and which he obsessively counts as though the bills were some guarantee of safety.

Malak almawt no longer hovers outside to converse with the *jinn* who dangle from streetlights and swat at pedestrians. They dwell in the house now, here with us. Crouched in corners where they sharpen their teeth, or curled on our chests at night when sleep is elusive. Hungry. Vicious. They hiss and lick at our hearts. They pluck at the strings. We flinch and pace and kneel. And Death,

166

that horrid deliverance, perches on Mama's shoulders, bending her low and whispering in her ear all the things she'll never be able to unsee, to unhear, to un-know.

There's no air here, no expanse for the lungs, no repose, no refuge for the mind. And our souls flutter, aimless, like birds in a cage.

Gripping the handle to the front door, two hours before the dawn call to prayer, I hear her behind me. The shuffle of wrinkled kaftan and restless feet. The sigh. The wet tut of her tongue. *Mama.* Her eyes are vacant, empty wells. There's no expression on her face because there's nothing left to feel.

She presses a cloth bag into my hands – a bag within which I will later find dried dates and loose pumpkin seeds, random coins from summer holidays past, soft banknotes trapped in rubber bands, and the solid gold necklace and bangles she wore when she married Baba all those years ago. But then and there, in the darkness before another dawn, with the *jinn* whispering in the corner, I hear the slight clinks of metal on metal and shake my head. *Khuthee!* A harsh whisper, a command to take these final things she has to give. Is it the last word I'll ever hear from her? She says nothing else, and her eyes have said nothing for weeks. Does she understand my need to leave? Is the bag a sign of approval or a heavy white flag of surrender?

Mama is a flower and, one by one, she is losing her petals.

30

The People in the Windows

The old man and Matt are in sync tonight. South Tower A, fourth floor, flat three and South Tower A, second floor, flat three are like parallel worlds, moving in perfect harmony, obeying some unseen cosmic conductor.

The old man and Matt rise from their sofas at the same time, and though Matt gets to the kitchen first, he dawdles so much that the old man catches up with him, and a couple of minutes later they are both filling the kettles in their respective flats. Same movements too, standing there holding them under the running water while the other palm hovers over the tap, ready to close it when enough water has streamed in. Plopping the kettles on, they stand there, leaning against the countertop for a minute, like they're resting or gathering their thoughts, before moving on to find mugs and tea bags and whatever else they need. They differ here: Matt goes for a heavy mug while the old man gets out his box of Twinings; then, Matt is pulling out the tea while the old man retrieves his white teacup and saucer from the sink. One chooses to splash milk into his tea when it's done, the other will go for honey and lemon. One takes his mug deeper into the flat, the other sits in the armchair waiting for the delivery man to bring his stew.

Matt seems at ease, utterly unperturbed or perhaps even unaware of what his actions have brought about. Does he know what happened with Mr Big Man? Has he heard about it from those useless wastes of oxygen he calls friends who definitely have spent time down at the station? Does he feel any remorse for what he's done?

Or is it entirely justified in his head, mere retribution for our invasion of his homeland?

Lies, distortion, violence, retribution, lies . . .

Movement catches my eye. Anime Girl is dancing again. Black lace bra cupping breasts she doesn't really have, hot pink knickers with the word CHERRY stamped across the bottom. Her dancing is manic today, not the hypnotic swaying and turning of before. Today she's jumping around the room, long ropes of hair flinging around her head, arms swinging and legs kicking. I have a strange sense that the music isn't turned on in her room, that she's dancing to things she hears in her head. In the living room, her parents sit in an unnatural stillness on the beige sofa watching television. He has a soft drink bottle in hand and she's sipping a hot drink. There is a half-empty bowl of crisps on the table in front of them, and every so often one or the other will turn from the television to say something. The father switches the channel, and they both break into huge grins. Anime Girl twirls around and around in her room, faster and faster until she's a blur of black and white and pink. Faster and faster until I can no longer pick apart her limbs, her face, where back ends and front begins. She twirls so long and so fast I begin to worry she'll fall into something and knock herself unconscious.

I squeeze my hands around the railing of my balcony.

Anime Girl flings herself onto the bed, knees drawn up, arms spread wide, chest heaving and heaving. Sweat glistens at her hairline and in the dip of her collarbone. Her eyes stay closed for a long time.

31

Sweet Dew

Mahmoud had reservations about the lorry. It would have been foolish not to, and two years on his own had wiped the foolish clear out of him. The air was cold and wet and dark, and the wind at his face was harsh and stinging. There were eight of them there – a husband and wife and grandmother and child of four perhaps who took very deep and measured breaths, and who stared around them with wide, unblinking eyes; two men who might have been brothers or cousins or merely friends; a young woman wrapped up tight in many layers of clothing as though it might protect her from something; and Mahmoud.

'Inside, everyone,' the smuggler said, looking around the dark, empty car park as he opened the back of the truck.

It was dark in there too, like a cavern or a hole dug deep into the earth. A long, pitch-black space with rows upon rows of fruit. Melon, Mahmoud thought as the scent hit him and he began to salivate. How long had it been since he'd sunk his teeth into a ripe melon, so that the sweet juice trickled down his face and he had to wipe it away with sticky hands? Melon drizzled with honey, drizzled with lemon juice, chopped up with other fruit and tossed into a bowl of yoghurt or

170

sliced to be eaten on its own. *Ya Allah*, the sweet dew of melons.

Fruit meant the lorry was refrigerated, which meant it would be even colder in there. Mahmoud could not see enough space for them and turned to the smuggler – best not to give them names, even in one's own mind – just as the father of the little girl began questioning him on the very same issue. The crates of fruit were stacked up, one on top of the other, barely any empty places between the rows and none on the sides by the walls of the truck.

'You will lie down,' said the smuggler in a perfectly reasonable tone, 'on the fruit in the baskets. On your back is best.'

The grandmother was compliant, already hitching up her robes and moving to climb into the lorry. The mother of the little girl pulled her back to her side, palm remaining on the girl's chest, eyes wide and white and shiny with horror.

'There is no way,' the man said, shaking his head and pulling the little girl to him instead, as though that would make her safer. She stood gaping up at them all with huge, saucer eyes, dirt on her face and in her hair, a thumb stuck in her mouth. She had not made a sound in the three hours it had taken them to walk to this car park. 'We will not breathe in there.'

The smuggler shrugged as though to say this was not his problem, which, of course, it wasn't.

The man was right. They couldn't breathe. None of them could. They lay down on the rows of fruit as instructed, the hard curves of melon digging into their backs and necks and heads and legs. On their backs was the only, rather than best, option. Mahmoud was one of the last to climb in, slipping between two bottom rows of fruit near the door. Further up by his head was one of the two men; the other one was in the row above them. Directly above Mahmoud was the grandmother and husband and wife and little girl. By Mahmoud's side was the young woman, who trembled nonstop, whether from cold or fear or exhaustion or some combination of it all, he couldn't tell.

When Mahmoud breathed, it rebounded off the wood above him, wood he could touch with his nose if he just craned his head up a bit. His breath was likely at its most acrid, but they had all long since lost the ability to notice such things. He could not move or shift position or reach for anything in his pockets. All he could do was lie there and hope not to run out of air as the cold enveloped him like a vice.

The young woman beside him – he could just make out her outline in the dark as his eyes adjusted – had managed to bring her hands up to her chest. They were folded across her heart as though she meant to hold it in, as though she were about to be wrapped in a shroud and buried. She was trembling violently, breathing too fast and hard, using up the oxygen. Palms out, she pressed against the wood on top of her, her shoe scraping, as though for comfort, against the metal of the truck door.

'It's the only way,' Mahmoud murmured.

She nodded, blowing a stream of cold air past her lips.

'Stop breathing so much,' the man at Mahmoud's head barked.

The engine roared to life, wheels moving them forward, crunching over gravel and dust.

For the first hour or two, the people in the lorry murmured to each other. In hushed tones, they shared news from home, recounted horrors they'd met with along the way, and traded stories of the old days – as though they were clansmen and not strangers whispering in the dark. It seems they spoke, if nothing else, to generate some heat with which to slice the frigidity around them. The man above Mahmoud's head spoke about his woodworking shop in Daraa and how he was a master, and that if he could just get someplace safe, he would find a use for his skills.

'I can make a table, so easy, in two or three hours maximum,' he said, jerking his foot with conviction, so that his boot skimmed the top of Mahmoud's head. 'Tell them, Miran.'

'Excellent skills,' Miran concurred from the row above. 'But nothing like me with soccer. I want to join a league in Germany. I could play in the World Cup even.'

The first man scoffed. 'In your dreams perhaps.'

'I have to piss,' the grandmother mumbled. The husband hissed that he'd told her to go before they arrived at the truck and why couldn't she act like an adult.

If Mahmoud closed his eyes, he could almost imagine he was at home, where he was never cold, in his bright room on his comfortable bed with its thick, furry blanket. He could hear the low sounds of Fairuz on Mama's radio, her softly humming along while she made tea. He could see his friends, cross-legged on the floor around the *narghile*, taking turns, Adnan laughing as he dealt out the cards. But then the lorry would bounce over a speed bump or dip into a portion of ruined road, and Mahmoud would be jerked back to reality.

He spent the third and fourth hours, when his teeth were chattering and the cold was like a million ants under his skin, imagining open space. He thought of the wide, green fields of Macedonia and Serbia and the big, blue sky hanging above them. He thought about the desert land straddling Turkey and Syria and how there seemed no end to the horizon, no vanishing point for him to reach. He thought about fresh air and stretching out under the stars and nights camping in Wadi Rum when they were children. Every year Baba would take them there; they would drive down, playing Dabke music and dancing so hard the car shook and Mama would yell at them to quiet down. He and his siblings would laugh and play stupid games and fight and eat fruit kebab or potato chips dipped in yoghurt all the way down through Jordan. When they reached the valley, it would be night already, and they'd pile out of the car and set everything up – the tents, the rugs unfurled by the fire pit Baba was digging, the food, the sleeping mats. His older brother or sister would fight over who got to start the fire, and then they'd roast skewers of meat fresh from the coolbox and heat up bread and wrap it all up with cool tahini sauce and drink it down with tamarind and liquorice juice until they were full and happy and sleepy. His mother and father would take the tent, but Mahmoud and his siblings would just roll their mats out by the fire and sleep under the stars.

There were nights so big, it seemed like they'd floated up off the earth and into clear space.

He thought about the narrow, rocky beaches of Latakia and summer holidays splashing in the blue waters. Mahmoud had never been a strong swimmer, preferring the tough earth beneath his feet rather than the nothingness of the sea. If he could have, he'd have walked all the way into Greece instead of facing those choppy waters.

'I would kill someone for water,' the father of the little girl said, startling Mahmoud and making him wonder if he'd spoken his memories aloud. The people in the lorry murmured in agreement, dry gums smacking in the dark.

Mahmoud had stood on the pier, a pier that hardly warranted the name, with fourteen others who had paid their £800 to a thief. They'd stood and stared at the raft and the thirty or so people it held. Thirty or so men and women and children, all as desperate as he was, bobbing in the Aegean. Clutching each other, men on the outside, women and children in the centre. It was sagging already.

'No way,' said the young man next to him. Syrian also, but from southeast Damascus. He shook his head, gripping his waterproof bag of documents. 'No way it can hold us all.' He turned to his friends, palm open towards the smuggler as if to say 'Can you believe this guy?'

'This is what you pay for,' the man replied, shrugging as though to say he didn't give a shit. He was, like all smugglers, vicious and insane.

'No,' the young man said, shaking his head and pointing a finger in the man's face. Around Mahmoud the others were already trying to load themselves into the raft while he was trying very hard not to fall to the ground in some semi-liquid, boneless heap. 'No, you said maximum twenty people. This is not maximum!'

'You don't like it?' the smuggler asked, pulling a gun from his waistband and cocking it at the young man's head. The women and children screamed, so synchronized that it seemed rehearsed, like they were all actors in some horrid film. The men yelled at the smuggler to show mercy, to fear Allah, but it was a pointless supplication and, in any case, the young man did not seem at all afraid.

What must a young man have seen to not fear a gun at his forehead.

He was not afraid. If anything, he seemed to burn with ire, with dignity, with a fierce unyielding pride. Backing away from the barrel, he secured the document bag around his neck, tucking it deep into his shirt, turned and dived into the water.

He and his friends swam to Greece. *Majaneen.* Mahmoud saw him at a camp in Elefsina, and he said they swam the whole way there, and that even for August, the water was fucking cold.

Was he braver than Mahmoud? For swimming instead of clinging to a raft in open seas? If there had been a gun to Mahmoud's head, would he have risked it as well? Baba had always said that the only two choices anyone had in life were to die or fight.

Would a day come when Mahmoud could stop fighting?

The smuggler had mentioned three checkpoints: *Make it past all three, and poof! Germany.* The first time the truck stopped, when the wheels ground to a halt, so did all whispered conversation, and Mahmoud's heart – a heart he thought had lost the ability to pump in fear – began beating out a tattoo that sounded unbearably loud. He feared the officers or patrolmen or whoever was outside was bound to hear it.

'Ya Allah, ihfithna min al'shar. Innaka raheemun 'atheem,' the grandmother began to pray, before the husband shushed her.

There was quiet conversation outside, a language they could not pick out, some laughter, but the door to the back of the truck did not open, and when the wheels began to turn again, there were sighs of relief all around.

Limbs went numb and then burned with pain like iron pokes; breathing became an increasing challenge; time was no longer a construct they had any use for. There was only this. This being trapped between wooden crates of melons in a cold, cold truck. A cold that language could not reach. No one had spoken for some time. There was nothing to say.

'*Yil'an abook*,' the man at Mahmoud's head swore as Miran, in the crate above him, could no longer hold his bladder.

Either they would make it to Germany, or they'd be caught and beaten and jailed and thrown back across the border to start all over again.

Right before the truck stopped a second time, when they were all breathing as little as possible and still saying nothing at all, the wife let out a squeak of terror.

'She's not, she's not breathing, 'Alaa,' she cried, hissing when her husband shushed her. 'Stop the truck!'

Mahmoud heard a slap in the dark, the wife weeping with a muffled sound. There was another slap, some kicking of feet, increased sobs of distress from the wife and grandmother, ineffectual female sounds, pleas to a god Mahmoud wasn't sure was listening, more weak slaps and kicks, and then the little girl gasped and cried out too, and now all three – the wife, the child and the grandmother – were weeping while the husband, in a rough and terrified whisper, shushed them all in turn.

Beside Mahmoud, the young woman began, again, to tremble.

Sometime after the second, equally uneventful stop, she lost control of her bladder. She let out a small sound – the first he'd heard from her – and he sensed the warmth and felt the wetness against his fingers.

'It's all right,' he whispered, sighing as he released his own.

He had gone blind. So dark was the back of the lorry that Mahmoud began to think he would never again see the light. *Die or fight*, Baba had said, but it seemed like Mahmoud was about to accomplish both. His head lolled from side to side, images flashing in his mind, synapses going off like fireworks, like gunfire outside the market he'd gone to every day since before he could walk. Sami filming girls in the park with his new phone, on a day with a bright blue and blessedly empty sky, running away with a cackle, white teeth gleaming, when they yelled at him to stop. At the baths with his father and brothers and uncles and cousins because someone was getting married. Mama's Friday chicken kebabs and the rice that was so fiery his tongue would go numb and he'd have to down glass after glass of icy buttermilk to dull the flames.

'Stop hogging the *liban*, Zain,' Mahmoud murmured, running a dry tongue over chapped and parched lips. '*Ya kelb!* I said, give it to me!'

'Shhh,' the young woman beside him said.

'We're going to die.' He flung his face from side to side. His brain was on fire, his chest threatening to burst clean open. He could see it, blood spouting out from his neck like a geyser, like Amer's had on that street outside the university.

'*Iskut ya haiwan!*' the man at his head hissed at him to shut up, kicking with the heel of his shoe.

178

Guts spilling out like that man at the mosque who'd been hit with shrapnel and had lain there, clutching his insides as though there was anything anyone could do to help. 'We're going to die!'

'Allah forgive you, please be quiet,' the husband whispered above him.

'Shh,' said the young woman again, and then he felt her fingers touch his. Pinkie and ring and middle finger curling around his own. They were slivers of ice, wet and unsteady.

Mahmoud squeezed his eyes shut and tried very hard to swallow his panic.

Die or fight, Baba.

The truck stopped a final time. The door opened. A driver's face, swearing in Spanish or some dialect Mahmoud hadn't encountered on his journey. The word 'Germany' spoken into a mobile. And then, the door was closed again. Mahmoud could not breathe. His head was swimming and voices he hadn't heard in months were moving between his ears. Mama telling him to put his head over a pot of boiling water and mint leaves to open up his lungs when he had a cold, Baba yelling at his brother that he would beat the gay out of him, his grandmother giving him sips of her tea when he was a toddler and cackling when he couldn't handle its strength.

A lighter clicked up over his head, the man lying there managing to bring it to the cigarillo clamped between his teeth.

'*Kess emak!* Are you insane?!' came the shouts from the crate above them. The husband or maybe the brother-friend-cousin Miran.

'What? I can't celebrate? We're in Germany, people!' he replied. Above his head, they shouted at Mahmoud to do something, to pinch the man's ankles, but Mahmoud had nothing left to give anyone.

'You can't wait, *ya kelb*?' the grandmother wailed.

Mahmoud listened to him smoke, the sucking in of precious air, air that really was no more, and then the exhale of smoke that stank of earth and cloves, and thought, *Yes, this, this is how I'll die.* Among the melons and strangers, on German soil, he would die.

The door to the truck burst open again. Officers barking in their harsh language, a language that always came out sounding angry. One set of hands gripped Mahmoud's ankles and pulled him out, his bones bumping and jarring over the melons. It rang out in his head with a xylophone sound, like from cartoons when he was a child. The man stood him up, telling him not to move, but nothing worked, and there was suddenly far too much air. The last thing Mahmoud saw before blacking out was the young woman shrinking away from the grip of the officer that pulled her out.

Die or fight.

———

Dear Voiceless,

I love this. It's one thing to be able to write opinion pieces on the issues of the day and how they affect you; it's quite another to be able to construct a piece of fiction that is as tight and moving as 'Sweet Dew'. I feel like fiction is such a liberating medium for you. You can say what you like and embellish as much as you want without fear of reprisal.

The magazine runs a prize, the Short Fiction Award. We open for submissions in another month or so and I think you should submit. *As a regular contributor to the magazine, you might be barred from participating, but I'll check with the team here and let you know. If you are allowed, you should definitely try. If you are unable to submit to our award, I strongly urge you to submit it somewhere else. I'll make up a list of popular and well-regarded writing prizes and send that over.*

You need to consider using your real name, though. I think it's time to let people know who you are. There's nothing to be afraid of. You're safe now. And more than that, don't you think maybe your life was spared for a reason? I mean, I know that sounds like a cliché, but maybe it's because you're meant to do something with it, use it to increase awareness about what your people are going through in different ways, not just through articles?

Best,

Josie

Yes, Josie, fiction is very liberating.

32

Dreamers and Sunshine

The next morning there's shouting in the courtyard as I exit the building, one lone voice hitting me in the face as I step into the sunshine. There's Ruth, wrapped up in her dirty dishwater cardigan, hair pulled back tight, features contorted into acute anger. I've never seen her so red in the face, not even when she was calling the police because the Dad was trying to kill Helen. In front of her is Holiday-Goer Mum, cowering in her lavender windcheater, glancing up repeatedly as though hoping her husband will think to look out of the window and come and rescue her.

'You watch that daughter of yours! She's terrible! Terrible, I say to you!'

Holiday-Goer Mum mumbles something, nodding her head like one of those little bobblehead dolls you find in souvenir shops.

'She dances in that window. Right there! For everyone to see,' Ruth shouts, pointing up at the flat with its bright orange suitcase propped against the glass. 'In her underthings like some little loosey, dancing and swaying. Who does she dance for? Who? Do you think it is fine for her to do this?'

More mumbling, nodding her understanding while also shaking her head that, no, her daughter should not behave this way.

They're drawing a crowd: Chloe and Helen lean out of their

respective windows to watch, Chloe from her room, her mother from the living room; the single father from my building pauses in the courtyard, weighed down with the bags of junk food he always buys ahead of his children's visits; Adam exits his building, pausing with a smile to watch the show; the old man stands at his window, trembling hands gripping the ledge, little eyes squinting; Tom is shuffling out of our building, brushing past with a thickly knuckled hand on my arm, whether to support his wife or implore her to let it go, I can't tell.

'And she's outside in the street and the park. I see her! Skipping like a little girl in those nothing skirts, wanting men to watch her, smiling when they do. It's not right! She is asking for it, and you should be careful before she is ruined.'

Holiday-Goer Mum fishes a mobile out of the many pockets of her jacket, holding up a finger and putting it to her ear as she makes a call. Her face is full of a confused humiliation, one that says, *If only I understood you, I could defend myself.*

Up in the East Tower, the Juicer is at his window. He winks at me and pulls the curtain closed.

Walking towards the park, Adam falls into step at my side. 'Old Ruthie on another crusade,' he says with a chuckle. It's a fine day for a walk, sun bright in a cotton blue sky, air still and sweet. On the way is an old telephone booth that's been repurposed into a tiny coffee window. We stop there, and Adam treats me to a cup as though we're friends or something. I watch him closely, knowing my face is full of suspicion, as he chats with the coffee man and hands over his coins and dumps too much sugar into his already-sugary drink and laughs and laughs.

Friendship is predicated on a kind of relatability, the idea that you and another person share some commonalities. Whether it's liking the same books or films or going to the same school or working at the same company or having grown up together in the same small town or perhaps even hating the same things, there is something that binds you to that other person. Adam and I share nothing apart from the fact that we live on the same estate. What is it that makes him treat me as a friend? What commonality does he find here? Or is this just his nature?

Friends are tricky; I have grown wary of them – as I have of so many things. They are the family you choose, lives you decide to share, and in a way that can make them more important than flesh and blood kin. You are not obliged to overlook their less admirable qualities, the way they interrupt your stories or neglect to reply to your messages or occasionally dismiss the things you care about, you *elect* to.

And when friends are taken from you, it can be devastating. More than that, even. I don't quite have the words for it.

We take our coffees and walk through the park, and Adam tells me about the student group he's joined up with even though he isn't a student any more. He tells me about the marches and how they're arguing over which weekend to hold it on. 'I keep telling Neil that it rains, nearly everywhere, on average, that weekend, but he says I'm crazy.' He tells me about the university kids who have joined up, and how he doesn't think it's due to any real commitment to the cause on their part but just because they feel like they should *do something*, or maybe they're trying to pull Neil or this other girl, Andrea, who Adam says is entirely out of fucks to give at this point.

I pull a pen from my pocket and write on the side of my coffee cup, *What's the cause?*

'It's what it always is, I suppose,' he says with a shrug of his thin shoulders. 'Equality. Humanity. Showing the world that we aren't all racist dicks.'

I nod and take another swig of coffee. How easy it is for them:

some bureaucracy to get a permit, a few weeks of hassle to organize everyone and get the word out, messages whipping back and forth, and then a series of nice little protests. Protests where they can say what they like, shout what they like, insult whomever they want – the PM, the government, the Queen, any of the many powers that be. Then they can go home and take a shower and have a nice meal and wrap themselves around their girlfriend or husband or partner and fall asleep, content in the knowledge that they added to humanity in some positive way that day.

These are not the protests I'm accustomed to.

In the beginning, we didn't use social media to organize anything. It was pure word of mouth that sent hundreds and thousands streaming into the streets, whispered phone calls and typo-riddled texts. It was spontaneous, natural, a human response to the inhumane. There were no men with megaphones shouting out pre-arranged chants. It was just a mass of people, unifying, solidifying, growing many heads and many tongues, all of which learned to say the same words: *Now it's your turn! We want the fall! Freedom! Dignity!* For protesters like that, there is no inviting home to return to, no proud father to welcome a daughter home, no warm woman for a self-satisfied man to bury himself in.

For us, there is detention. Military basements. Hanging naked from the ceiling like lamb at a butcher's shop. Blood. Electric cables and iron rods on wet skin because it hurts worse that way. Anything to drive out revolutionary thoughts. Shit and piss. Holes in the head. Whatever is worse than monsters. Strange voices screaming for help, for mercy, for Allah. Desperation. Darkness. Whatever goes beyond terror.

For us, a protest isn't a measured expression of discontent. It's a reckless flinging of ourselves headlong into a future whose dimensions we just can't get to stick.

'I finished that book you gave me,' Adam says, throwing his empty coffee cup into a bin we pass. 'It's really interesting, and I think it could be really useful for us, you know, for people to realize what this is all about. I lent it to Neil and he's going to pass it on to Andrea, and then we might do an evening talk about it, for the kids who've joined up with us. They don't learn these things in school. At all. They learn the most useless, colonial shite in school. It's not worth it to even go, but Neil says the university is his most fertile hunting ground, and I can't say things like that to the kids.'

'*ISIS,*' comes a vicious hiss to my right. Matt and his friends are there, by the steel fence that separates the park from the children's playground. They're standing in their baggy jeans and hoods, hands thrust into pockets, scowls on their faces like they have anything in the world to be mad about. Matt sneers at me, and hisses again, 'ISIS bitch.'

'Oi!' Adam barks, coming to a stop. 'Shut it.' I pull on his sleeve, trying to get him to keep moving.

'It's what she is,' Matt says, jerking his chin up, just like the Dad does when he sees me through the window. 'I seen her. At the mosque and the raghead's shop. She's one of them.'

'What if she is? What's it got to do with you?' Adam replies, squaring off against him now, widening his stance and standing up straight. It's like he's trying to take up more space. My nerves shiver and I pull harder on the back of his shirt.

'They don't belong here. Coming here to take what's ours.'

Adam chuckles, the sound loud and mocking to my ears. 'Oh, is that what your daddy's been feeding you? How about you think for yourself, instead of being a fucking parrot for some brainless sheep?'

Matt's friends come up behind him. There's four of them and only one of Adam because I will be less than useless if this escalates. Matt puffs himself up as well. 'Aw, she your little bitch, then? Is that why you're defendin' her?'

Adam lunges, his fist connecting with that jerking chin. Matt's head snaps back with a pop, and Adam takes advantage of the moment, pushing him to the ground and punching two or three more times. If Matt's friends are surprised, they quickly overcome it, all of them piling on, pulling Adam off and pummelling him in the face and stomach and ribs.

Such easy violence. Why is it so easy?

I look around, but there's hardly anyone in the park, and those who are there seem disinclined to help: a mother with her buggy changes direction as though she hasn't seen anything; a jogger runs past, shaking his head, air puffing from his lips; a dog rushes up and starts barking around the pile of men while his owner calls him from across the park.

Adam is making painful grunting noises, trying not to cry out for help, a desire to maybe retain some dignity despite the circumstances. Dancing around the boys, I try to find a way to grab Adam and pull him out. I can barely see him now, through the flash of punching arms and kicking legs and angry faces, so I just start pulling at whoever I can. I yank on hoodies and belts and hair, pulling and shoving and trying to make a space for Adam to get out from. I pour my still-hot coffee on one of Matt's friends, and he howls in pain, backing off and swiping at his hair and face. I push through the others, pulling on Adam's arm until he's out from under them, and then we're running, running, running as fast as we can. They chase us halfway through the park, trainers slapping on the path, before falling back, letting their *shits* and *fucks* follow us the rest of the way instead.

In Adam's flat, we assess the damage. There's a purple bruise darkening around his right eye, his lip is split, and he favours his left ribs.

Moving through the flat, he flops onto the sofa with a long sigh, breath vibrating or trembling towards the end. His eyes are wet, and he turns his face to the side, looking out of the window, so I can't see.

I rummage in his fridge and freezer, but men are generally useless for this sort of thing, and he doesn't have much that could be of help here. I find a cold can of cider and rush over to hold it against his eye, but he takes it from me and pops it open instead, taking a long swallow. Going back to the kitchen, I find another can and some frozen sweetcorn. I hold the former up to his eye and lay the latter against his ribs. He winces and hisses at the cold but says nothing.

Taking his free hand and pressing it to the bag of sweetcorn, I let go and move to his record player. Opening it, I see one already loaded up, the sleeve propped up against the wall. Dennis Wilson's *Pacific Ocean Blue*. Apeman on the cover, sad eyes, hard mouth, tinkling piano on the opening number. Returning to Adam, I sit at his side, holding the cold can to his eye while the other one looks out of the window.

How do you say I'm sorry and thank you when you can't speak? Is this enough?

He jumps up, leaning closer to the window for a moment, then turning towards the door. I catch a glimpse of the Dad stalking his way across the courtyard. Adam is halfway out of the door before I catch him. Gripping his sleeve, I shake my head, trying to say with my eyes what my tongue is unable to manage – that it's not worth it, that people cannot be other than what they are.

None of it gets through, or if it does, he chooses to ignore it, shaking me loose and running out of the door, letting it slam shut behind him.

I can't watch this altercation, already the panic is frothing at the base of my skull, and my mind searches for distraction. The apeman is singing about dreamers and sunshine and rock 'n' roll, but it isn't enough to dull the pop and fizzle under my skin. Turning in place, I scan the flat. My book is on the coffee table, cracked open with bits of tissue marking various places in it. Records are strewn about and papers and fliers. There's a large map of the UK tacked to the wall, red stars surrounding various cities and a big calendar with dates circled in blue and red and pencilled in with information.

Through an open doorway, I see his bed. The narrow double bed, with its lumpy duvet and pillows. Grey and white sheets. And under it, I know, is the box.

The lid squeaks when I open it. Loud and eerie, like stairs in an abandoned home leading down to a dark basement. I flinch, shake myself, and listen for the door, but these buildings are well oiled, and, in any case, I'm still alone.

It's a vintage box, creased leather and rusty metal hinges, with hard sides and a lock for a key that hangs open. It's the kind of box they sell at second-hand markets, trying to convince tourists that it's a hundred years old or something. It smells of nothing, though. It seems to be the height of ordinary, and I begin to sense I might be disappointed by what it contains.

There are loose papers at the top – printouts of articles and cut-outs from newspapers, pages of hastily scrawled notes, soft and worn leaflets about war that look decades old nestled into plastic sleeves. Beneath that I find old magazines, some dirty, most political with pictures of dead presidents and headlines about whatever war was on at the time. There are military ID tags, dog tags, spelling out names and etched with numbers. I run the shiny little ball chains through my fingers, pulling apart clasps and shoving them back together, wondering who they belong to and how Adam got hold of them.

Then, I find the sketches.

Pushing everything else aside, I pull out more and more sketches: there are small ones scribbled on regular notebook paper in a ballpoint pen; there are napkins marked up in pencil; there are large ones, on professional grade paper, done in charcoal; there are sketches of buildings and trees and flowers and squirrels and swans and the bridge at night with the river flowing and shimmering and empty beneath it and caricatures of political figures and actors and singers.

And then there are the people in the windows. Us. I am not the only one watching, it seems.

There's one of Ruth and Tom, shuffling down the pavement outside Hasan's. He's in his Sunday suit, with the plaid jacket and crisp checked shirt. She has her hand at his elbow to steady him. There's Helen, with a load of laundry, manic eyes looking up, mouth pressed into a tight line. The Juicer, muscles exaggerated to comic proportions, flexing in the park – something I've never seen him do. Matt and his friends in their angry huddle, only Matt looks less like Matt and more like the Dad. There's a beautiful rendering of the mosque, all clean lines and dignified curves, the imam a tiny figure in the doorway. Faith is larger than any one man, it seems to say.

Then there's one of me. Standing at my window, not on the balcony, palms pressed to the glass, eyes open in terror, mouth covered with a wide, white strip of tape. Hair wild around my head, like Medusa. The sketch is surrounded by blackness, as though the paper had been black and the drawing erased out of it. As though a bolt of lightning had illuminated this one fragment of time before plunging us all back into darkness.

Beneath it, I find one of Anime Girl. She's reclining on a sofa, legs bent and propped up on the back. One arm is hooked over her head. Fringe thick over closed eyes, the other hand cradles a glass of dark liquid over ice. The vest is bunched up under her nothing-breasts, and there is a thin table placed in such a way that you cannot tell if she's wearing anything on her bottom half. There are inviting folds and shadows and a bare hip and the illusion that there is nothing there.

Her face holds secrets. Many secrets, I think.

Was she like this in the holiday flat? Was she actually on her bed and Adam drew her on a sofa? Or did she pose for him here, on that sofa in that living room where I just held a can of cider to his eye? Did he fuck her like I'm sure the Juicer did?

Dumping everything back in the box, I shut the lid with a squeaking slam and leave.

33

All of Us, Fools

. . . Do not speak to me of blood and soil, of natural citizenship, of cemetery lineage and a claim that goes back a certain number of generations and no less. This land is not yours or mine to claim. No Land is. We are custodians of the earth and the oil fields and the mountains and the lakes and the farmland. Custodians only. None of it is yours to plant a flag in or stamp with your imperme-able brand of curiously Judeo-Christian Frenchness or Dutchness or or or.

What is a nation? What are the borders that contain it? Invisible lines in the sand, slicing through forests and plains, bisecting moun-tains, and dividing villages. As though the person just on the other side of the line were so very different from you.

What does it mean to be American? A red-blooded one, as they're so fond of saying, and I wonder what colour they imagine the rest of the world bleeds. Every year they celebrate the brutal taking of a land that, by any definition of blood and soil, was not theirs, a systematic replacing of the native population.

Is that why you fear refugees and immigrants so much? Because you know that with determination, and no small amount of violence, complete and total dominion can be achieved?

Speak to me then, not of *blut und boden*, but of economic strain, of the loss of tourism and the ghettoization of your quaint, cobble-stone villages, of pensioners removed from their homes to build more camps. These are conversations we can have. But do not come at me with blood and soil. The soil of my homeland is drenched in the blood of its people, the rivers run red with it.

And we can claim nothing.

The Voiceless, *The New Press*, 12 July 2017

My shoulder hurts, where the tattoo is, where he pressed his thumb so hard like he wanted to rub it off. He was rougher than he usually is, rougher than I needed him to be, but I can't say anything, and it did manage to empty my mind.

It is late evening, but the sun will linger for another hour or more. The wind has a bite to it, an indication that autumn might be on its way sooner than expected. The courtyard is quiet as I leave the East Tower. I should go to Hasan's, stock up on essentials, but I've been avoiding that whole street since the thing at the mosque, and I am in no condition to face it now.

Not as quiet as I'd thought as I hear sniffling to my left. There, huddled by the hedges, is Chloe. There's a holdall at her feet. She squats beside it, face in her palms, crying. Pausing, I glance up at their flat. It's dark. I turn to my building, glance up at my own dark flat, and think I ought to just walk on by. When did I become so entangled in the lives of these people? Why? It was easier before, when I just watched from the window, when I knew nothing and no one saw me. *Some of them saw you*, my mind whispers, thinking of Adam and his sketches and all of what he must have seen.

It was all so much easier before.

I put my hand on her head, and Chloe flinches. My blood boils with the knowledge now, the certainty, that the Dad hits her too.

Seeing it's me, she relaxes back onto her heels, wiping a filthy jumper sleeve under her eyes. I crouch down in front of her, tapping her arm for her attention and gesturing to the holdall. She looks at it, shakes her head, sighs, appears on the verge of weeping again, but then she sucks in a breath and pulls herself together.

Meeting my eye, she says, 'I want to run away.'

I am familiar with the urge, so I nod encouragingly.

She shakes her head again, eyes looking towards the edge of the courtyard, where her father, if he returns, will come from. 'He came home in a rage. Lost it at Mum. I couldn't tell what it was about. They've gone to hospital again. I can't. I can't.' She starts to cry, rocking herself forwards and back on her tiny feet.

I give her a moment and look up at their flat, wishing I could smash it to pieces, thinking that no matter where you are, danger can find you. We are not safe anywhere. Not really. From the moment you're born, the moment they slap your bottom and you draw breath, the vigil begins. God breathes life into you, and then it's Good Luck and Try Not To Get Dead. Whether it's bombs falling or strapped to heaving chests, or bullets from the tops of buildings or in cinemas or a father's fists or electrical wires or a man telling you to just relax and it won't be that bad, there is peril everywhere. Peril for men. Peril for women. For children and fighters and lovers. Peril everywhere, for everyone.

'I can't leave her. I can't leave her here,' Chloe whispers into her arms, head still shaking.

I tap her again, and when she looks up I regain my feet, hoisting her holdall onto my aching shoulder and indicating for her to follow.

Ruth is banging her pots, the booming voice of a game-show host slicing through the wall and into my head with its false cheer. The sun is an hour or two down.

Chloe sleeps in my room, in my bed. Her holdall is on the floor beside her, in case she does decide to flee after all. I cannot think it would be the worst decision. But the rain has started up again, a furious battering against the window, and I don't think she'll leave before morning. It is human nature to put these things – the wrenching apart of families, the killings of selves, the changing forever of realities – off for as long as possible.

There's a blanket under me, a pillow at my side, but I doubt I'll sleep much tonight.

My laptop sits, battery dead, on the wobbly desk. Around me are notes for pieces I'm working on, drafts of 'Sweet Dew', printouts of articles that have been published, so I can ensure I'm not repeating myself too much and without adequate reason. I push a hand through the papers nearest me, swirling them in an endless loop of words and crossed-out lines. There are pens and pencils scattered around and research and the open maw of the black suitcase with its notebooks and journals and medical reports and memories and awful dreams.

My mind is curiously blank, but swimming in there is the question of what to do about Josie. Do I stop writing for the magazine? Focus more on fiction, where, according to her, you can bring all the drama you need, no matter how unlikely? Is there any point to what I write? Or are we all just screaming into the void?

I can't remember what it was for, why I sent her that first piece even. What was I seeking? There was no shortage, even all those months ago, of refugee voices in the news. Even then, there was enough coverage. Was it an effort to tell it my way, without intermediation and interpretation from a journalist? I felt I had something to say, and a right to say it, but for the life of me, I cannot recall what that something is. Hiding behind an alias, hoarding specific memories, so that family members scattered around (you'd be surprised where you can get a wifi signal) couldn't recognize me. And even if they did, if Baba in Alexandria (have they ended up there, as planned?)

logged on, with his big glasses and index fingers carefully punching out letters, or cousin Mahmoud in Belfast, or Brother Firas (if he lives still) in wherever he is, so what? Josie publishes my articles from her little office in some little part of London. Even if they went there, or contacted her, they'd never find me.

Maybe, at the end of the day, I just wanted to be able to say something.

There's a knock at the door. He doesn't bother with the flashing light. Just a knock, and then another.

His other eye is purple now. The right one, nearly black. Lip still split, there's dried blood on his white T-shirt, mud on the knees of his jeans, and he still has a hand hovering over his injured side. His knuckles are bruised, and there are scrapes on his pale, thin arms, his face, his neck.

'I gave as good as I got,' he murmurs, and though his eyes are dark, there's a twinkle in them. I shake my head, the question clear on my face. 'Let's just say I know where Matt learned his dirty tricks now.'

It feels like a snowball. A giant snowball rolling down the hill. Am I the one who gave it a kick? By not telling the police about Matt and the spray paint? It's rolling and rolling, and I can't stop it. I turn around, frantic, and grab a notepad from the kitchen counter.

Hospital?

He shakes his head, still standing in the doorway. 'I don't want to make things worse.'

For who

'They'll ask questions,' he replies, leaning his head against the door jamb. 'They'll ask if I want to press charges. No one needs that.'

By no one I think he must mean Helen and Chloe because it seems Matt and the Dad might need exactly that. I press the pen into the pad, darkening a black spot, wanting to tell Adam about

196

the spray paint, about everything I know, but I don't. Perhaps he's right, perhaps my first instinct was right, and everything will be fine. Perhaps we are, all of us, fools.

Putting the pen and pad down, I pull out a pack of ice from the fridge and hand it to him. He presses it to the fresh bruise, eyes not leaving mine, and says, 'I don't want to be alone.'

What might this bring? Where will it end? He didn't sleep with Anime Girl. I can't imagine he did. Why would I care if he did? He is a hundred times more substantial than the Juicer. He wouldn't do that. The illustration must be his imagining, like the one of the Juicer in the park in that ridiculous pose. He might lust after her. She's a young girl who dances naked in a window, a provocateur. It would be natural for him to lust after that. But lusting is not doing. He would not DO.

I let him in, closing and locking the door. I gesture to the blanket and pillow on the floor, and he gives me a quizzical look, but I just shake my head. His mouth twitches into a smile, then a wince when the cut in his lip stretches. Kicking off his boots and leaving them by the door, he walks past me and eases himself to the floor with a few groans and intakes of breath.

He's filthy and bloodied and bruised and smells like sweat and rain, but when he holds out a hand to me, I go to him. He tucks me into his chest, one hand patting the same three-finger span of space on my back until I fall asleep.

34

Nothing to Win

In the morning, many things wake me: the bright sun streaming through the windows, bouncing off the hardwood floors and against my eyelids; the unlocking, opening and closing of my front door; Adam knocking a pencil off the desk. It washes over me, the knowledge that I slept through the night with not one but two strangers in my flat – the one place in the world where I feel halfway safe.

Adam has papers in his hands, and he's looking through them – notes on an article tentatively titled 'A Job-ian Acceptance' and other bits and pieces he must have picked up off the floor. I cannot muster the energy to be upset about this. Fair's fair, after all.

I push myself up to a sitting position and rub my palms into my eyes. He says good morning, then, 'Chloe left, said to say thanks,' and then he's focused on one article in particular, and even from this distance, I can tell it's one of mine. '*Blut und boden,*' he murmurs to himself, swollen eyes scanning the page.

If it is at all possible, he looks worse this morning. Both eyes are nearly shut, so much so that he has to hold the paper practically to his nose in order to read it. His bottom lip is twice its size, and there is a purple/red bruise beneath the stubble of his jaw. I hope the Dad looks just as bad, but I expect he doesn't. He's a Big Man too, and I think he kicked Adam's arse.

'You're the one who's been writing those pieces,' he says, turning to me now. 'The Voiceless. Of course you are. Neil started showing them to me weeks ago, said he was desperate to get in touch with the writer, but that the magazine wouldn't give out any information.'

I shake my head, because Josie never said anything about anyone contacting her about me, and because I do not want him divulging my identity to this Neil person.

'You're brilliant.'

I blush, looking down, fingering the blanket that covered us the night before. I have a sudden feeling of unreality, that this is a fragment of a dream, a reality in which I am normal with a normal life and a normal partner and everything is . . . normal.

He crouches down in front of me, eyes bright despite the swelling. He has rallied overnight. 'You have to join us. You have to join the marches. Can't you see how important this is? You could write about it even. For us to have someone write a piece about this, in our voice, not some wanker journalist, but one of us, it would be unbelievable. It would do so much for us, for the cause. You have to do it.'

Us. Us. Us.

I shake my head, over and over, the entire time he talks, until he runs out of words and just looks confused. I cannot, I will not, join another protest, not even their polite, candy floss kind. What *is* his cause? What is it they want?

'Why not?'

I shake my head again and grab a pencil and notebook.

You say I'm 'one of us' but who is 'us'? Do you even know? What exactly are you fighting for? How can you even call these ridiculous gestures fighting? You yourself told me that it was mostly just a bunch of idiot university twats who want to feel like they're doing <u>something</u>.

'I didn't call them "twats",' he interrupts, leaning over the paper to follow my writing.

Your protests do nothing. They are pointless. You're chasing a high you will never reach. It's exciting and you feel important and like you get it but you don't win in the end. THERE IS NOTHING TO WIN. Moving from issue to issue 'cause' to 'cause' until it's no longer about freedom or equality or human dignity or any other bullshit idea you've convinced yourself of. It becomes about the protest about delusions of anarchy and civil disobedience. It doesn't work. You don't win because there's nothing to win, no endgame, no goal. YOU DON'T EVEN HAVE A GOAL

I rip the paper at the end of the sentence, a full stop where the pencil pierces the paper and slashes it into an angry dash. He looks up from the paper, mouth twisted into a grimace. His chest is moving rapidly, knuckles pale where they grip his knees. We stare at each other for long, long moments.

Finally he blows out a puff of air and rises to his feet, turning to leave. 'Well, at least I'm doing something, not hiding behind easy words on the internet.'

They're only words. They shouldn't feel like a blow. But they do.

By noon, the Holiday-Goers are leaving. Sitting on the balcony, I watch Mum and Dad struggle to get their luggage down and out of the door, the latter with a large navy suitcase, the former with two backpacks. He confers with the taxi driver as he loads the things into the boot of the car. The parents keep their heads down the entire time, as though there might be people with pitchforks in the court-yard.

I tell myself I'm not watching Adam's window, but it is a lie, and his flat is where my eye goes most of the time. But the lights are off and the curtains are drawn and I can't see in.

Things are quiet across the way, in South Tower A, second floor, flat three. Helen is asleep in Chloe's bed, Chloe squished up beside her with headphones on, watching the computer screen. Helen doesn't look any worse than usual; there's a bandage on her wrist and what looks to be a bruise on her cheek. The holdall is pressed up against the window, hidden behind the curtain. Matt and the Dad do not appear to be in the flat.

Anime Girl finally exits the tower. She looks chastened and down. In loose sweatpants and a large T-shirt, no makeup, hair pulled back in a lazy ponytail, she is nothing like herself. Or perhaps this version is the real her, and the Lolita she plays is the show. Who knows? What is a girl at fourteen or fifteen or however old she is? She's like clay, loose and malleable, constantly shifting into what she thinks she needs to be, what people might want her to be.

'They're leaving,' Ruth exclaims, leaning over the balcony with the phone pressed to her ear. 'I said to Tom they would leave. Looks like they gave hell to the little one, too. She looks normal now, nice loose clothing. It amazes me, you know? They're supposed to be so polite and kind. How do you suppose they got a daughter like that? Hmm? Yes, I expect travelling would do it. I doubt she will do these things in her own country.'

———

Dear Josie,

Thank you for your kind words and the list you sent. I do appreciate everything you've done for me, and I will consider submitting the story as you suggest.

I know I'm safe here, although the meaning of that word has a habit of slipping through my hands like water. I can't explain, even to myself, my hesitation, my continued sense that I'm still living in some indefinite holding room.

There is a theory, Freudian perhaps, of compartmentalization. It says that memories can be hidden in different parts of the mind, where the waking consciousness can't reach them. It is a way of containing contradictory components of the mind, a way to avoid cognitive dissonance, if you will. I imagine it as a kind of grand estate, and the flats all have people in them, and the ones in flat A are unaware of what's happening in flat B.

Of course, there are obvious issues with that analogy.

You know how it's wrong to go snooping in other people's rooms? That's kind of how my memories feel. It's how I feel about my past. I've already brought more of it out than I thought I would. If I give more, if I use my name and all of my story . . . who knows what all that rooting around will dig up?

35

The Eye

The cell is limned in red. Hazy, a fine metallic mist hangs in the air, latching itself to the tongue and sliding down a clenched throat. A blood-drop sun pulses in the sky. Its rays burn like acid, like gas, like the chemicals he swears he isn't using. Look around, everything is red. The aluminium desks, the white tiled floor, the yellow sponge spilling out of the cracks in the leather chairs, it is all bathed in a heavy maroon glow. No matter how hard I scrub, the windowpane will not let in anything but red red rays.

This cell is bordered in oxblood, in burning embers, like a smouldering fire pit. The cell – the word, the concept – looms large in our imagination: room, house, prison, country, all of them cells. All these places where you are watched and heard and monitored. The only safe space is the one between your ears or in the grave.

Ossama and Amer have blood on their faces, and they labour over a fabric that matches. They move their markers over the cotton in silence, nothing to hear but the scratch as the tip traverses the surface, painting it in heavy-helmeted thugs with stern mouths and tanks crushed by flowers and birds soaring over waterwheels. *Death before humiliation, death before humiliation, death before humiliation* is repeated a hundred million times, in a hundred million ways.

We are trying to tell you that there are worse things than dying.

High in the corner, the Eye watches us. Like every other time and in every other place, it watches us. The veins are more prominent today, bulging red veins that beat to a soundless rhythm. Back and forth, back and forth, no brain behind to interpret what it sees.

The huddle is gone this time. It's only Ossama and Amer bent over the desks, me by the windows, and Khalid against the wall, his gaze moving between the Eye, the painting of the fabric and the dead world outside. He's in a beige jumpsuit, a white helmet dangling from his fingertips, and he looks more tired than there are words for.

Do you know they call you a liar now, my love? A propagandist? A terrorist even?

Terror. Terror is no longer the one-two explosion of barrel bombs or the pop of gunfire or the knock on the door. No, we have re-defined it. Terror is the silence between explosions, the quiet before the knock on the door, before the bullet hits its target and you can breathe again because this time, it wasn't you.

We are breathing because outside the bombs have not stopped falling. We inhale one and exhale the other. It's like thunder behind the eyes, like a thousand drums beating in your chest, like the walls of existence are collapsing all around you, all at once. It is like no sound you've heard before.

'It's done,' says Amer, straightening up and cracking his back. Ossama concurs with a nod and answering crack of his neck, '*Yella.*' We, the three of us, roll up the fabric until it's a thick scroll. We carry it to the open windows. I turn to ask Khalid to join us, but he's under the Eye now, inspecting it, reaching up with hesitant hands to poke at it, as though it might bite, and my breath catches in my lungs.

'*Yella,*' Ossama says again, prodding me to release my end of the fabric.

We let go, and the cotton unfurls down the side of the building.

It's met with silence, a silence so complete it seems to have swallowed the world. The banner flaps and slaps against the wall, dripping red and black onto the empty street below. The wind catches it, ripping the fabric from our hands and sending it flying over the buildings. The heavy thugs and tanks detach. Inky blobs fall to the pavement without a sound. The flowers burst forth into colour and the waterwheels and birds go spinning and screaming into the sky.

Behind us there is a crash. Khalid is attacking the Eye with his helmet. My heart stops as he hammers at it. Furious. Desperate. It drowns out any and all other sounds. Bashing and bashing, he lets out short grunts and yips and what sound like whimpers, until the Eye cracks and splinters and is ripped from the ceiling to lie in a broken heap at his feet. He's sweaty, jaw locked in a grimace, panting, like a feral animal, like the wolf they've turned him into.

Is this victory? Or just another kind of death?

36

Missing Pieces

My dreams are darker, harsher, than usual. The things I see there are clearly not my own imaginings but real events that have seeped out of the boxes I put them in.

I dream of neighbours taken in the middle of the night, sharp wails and useless pleas. They never return. I dream of friends shot on their way to work – because, of course, they need to work – their lives ending in a pool of blood on streets they've walked down their entire lives. I dream of babies going to school and bombs falling from the sky, and they really shouldn't have been going to school at that point. I dream of rubble and people trapped for days and hospitals that can no longer help and a world that DOES NOT CARE. Desperate voices in dark basements. Confined spaces. A river that is more blood than water. So thin, your body begins to eat itself. Ahmed, tiny hands bound, eyes and mouth taped shut, a bullet in the head. Ahmed in the Queiq, Qashoush in Orontes – that rebel river – his brave and terrible chant ripped from his throat to take flight, finally free, like a bird, across Syria. Cold, hungry, always thirsty – when was the last time the shower worked, Baba?

At times my mind feels like a refugee all on its own, left to wander harsh and hostile landscapes.

Even when I dream of pleasant things, they are no longer pleasant.

The citadel lit up at night on the hill, men smoking watermelon-flavoured hookahs and sipping *mate* beneath its glory. The mosque with its cool marble floor and quiet arches. The bustling corridors of the *souq* with the smiling men in the stalls hawking spices and fabric and rugs and shiny prayer beads, where Khalid and I would agree to see each other. We couldn't talk openly there, not like in Damascus, but we could brush our fingers together as we moved through the crowds, he could put a hand low on my back, and I could press my shoulder against his. I dream of the *hammam*, older than the world, where Mama held us between her knees and scrubbed us down. The park where the family met for lunch on Friday, spreading out across the grass, eating chicken kebabs and laughing while the children chased each other and screamed. These things come to my mind, bright moments in between the darkness and gore, but then they too are subsumed by it: great big rocks roll down the hill, crushing the men and their pipes; the Mosque is a heap of rubble hiding dead souls; the *souq* is a charred ghost town and Khalid doesn't come when I call. Even the steam in the baths is a bloody vapour.

There is no glory there, no home, and my mind cannot bring it back. I cannot, even in my own mind, make it whole again.

It's late and Hasan's is quiet. The street is dark and still. It's a deep night, heavy clouds, no stars. I haven't been here since the vandalism at the mosque, opting to do my shopping at the big chain down the street.

When I walk in, Hasan raises a hand in greeting but makes no comment on my absence. He is the perfect shop owner, I think, thoroughly uninterested in the lives of his patrons. He doesn't try to get to know them or hear their life story. He doesn't ask after children or sick parents back home. He stands at the till and rings up your items, and that is the extent of his interest.

I move with purpose through the shop, not wanting to spend more time here than necessary. Is it right that I should reject it all? The mosque with its hip imam? This shop with its food from home? How much farther do I have to walk for this feeling to leave me?

I grab a jar of cheese, the biggest they have, so I don't have to come back for a good couple of weeks. Scanning the shelf of sugary, fizzy drinks, I pick up a couple of bottles of the orange. Then I stop and stare at the new juice he's brought in. Imported, for sure. Brown-red tamarind and black-red liquorice.

Can Mama and Baba and the little ones find tamarind and liquorice juice in Alexandria? I imagine they ought to be able to, what with that shared heritage and culture Baba so values.

For a time, at the hospital, when I realized my obstinate refusal to interact wasn't going to get me anywhere, I adopted a new identity for myself. I told them, or rather wrote to them, that it was all a mistake. I was not a refugee seeking asylum. I'd never been to Syria, let alone grown up there. I told them my name was Mary Lennox, and I was from the north of England – somewhere with rolling green hills and valleys and sheep and a secret garden and God's own sky – and that I was brought to them by mistake. I spun out this whole story about a beloved uncle waiting for me, a cousin named Colin, and a pet bird called Craven. I told them we were farmers, cheesemongers, milkers of various livestock. I told them my dream was to one day run a bookshop in town and that I had a childhood sweetheart called Dickon who was waiting for me.

It was a good story, and for a while I felt like I could believe it, that I *did* believe it. And when Dr Thompson showed me the book, I cried for the first time in months. I wanted to remain Mary Lennox, I wasn't hurting anyone with it, but she said you can't live your life in a delusion.

It's easy to be someone else. It's even easier to be no one at all.

The door bangs open, a loud clang that shoots through me, so that I jump and grip the bottles and jars in my hands tighter. Mr Big Man and two friends come into the shop, throwing sneering glances at Hasan. My heart kicks up, mind sinking into an old and familiar panic. Hasan's fingers curl around the edge of the counter in front of him, but he doesn't avert his gaze, staring at Mr Big Man with dark, serious eyes as the men move past the register and down the front aisles.

'Let's see what they have then,' one of Mr Big Man's friends says with a snort, pushing a couple of packets of instant soup off a shelf. He is a Big Man too, with a thick face and heavy arms and legs, his small mouth twisted into an ugly sneer.

I back away from the drinks section, moving deeper into the shop, my heart feeling liable to escape. It beats so fast and so hard, I am dizzy with it. If Mr Big Man sees me, he'll know. He'll know, somehow, that I knew about Matt and what he'd done, that I'm the one who got him in trouble with the cops because I didn't say anything. He'll know. He'll see it on me, the way people here see things in me that I don't want them to see. He'll see it, and he and his friends will hold me down. Sticky, metallic taste in my mouth, blurring my eyes, and pain everywhere.

'You leave now, please,' Hasan calls out, but it sounds weak. His voice trembles.

They move across the front aisles, dipping a few paces into one then out again and to the other. They kick at cabinets, sweep items off shelves, and say awful things. Hasan threatens to phone the police, reaches for his mobile a couple of times, and I wish he wouldn't threaten it, that he would just do it. My insides are going cold, the blood in my veins turning to sharp ice.

'Nothin' but shit,' another of Big Man's friends says. This one is smaller but with a wiry strength and a face like a fox. He knocks a bottle of olive oil off the shelf, and it hits the floor with a mighty crash. I drop down by the huge bags of rice and flour, clutching the jar of cheese and bottles of cold tamarind juice to my chest.

Mr Big Man chuckles and between the stacks and aisles I see him bend down and swipe up a shard of glass, pale green liquid dripping and glinting from its jagged edges. 'Everything about them is shit. Bloody Muslim fucks.'

37

Peril, Everywhere

I was supposed to be safe here. I was supposed to be safe here. I was supposed to be safe here. I was supposed to be safe here. Safe here. I was supposed to be safe here. I was supposed to be safe here. I was supposed to be safe here. I was supposed to be safe here. I was supposed to be safe here. I was supposed to be safe here. I was supposed to be safe here. I was supposed to be safe here. I was supposed to be safe here. I was supposed to be safe here. I was supposed to be safe here. Safe here.

A hand on my head. These people won't stop touching me. I jerk, a shock blanket crackles. Shiny. Wet with rain. Soaking. Wish my heart would just stop, just drop out of me like a stone. Noise. Sirens. Yelling. Men barking. Glass shattering. Barrel bombs falling, hanging in fluffy white clouds and a bright blue sky. They always come in twos – the first to injure, the second to kill. A hand stroking wet hair, pressing down on my shoulders. A voice. I can't hear. I can't speak. Fill me up with silence.

'It's all right. I'm here.' Adam. Looks like Ahmed. Little Ahmed knew better than to cross over like that. I put my face in my hands. I can't see either. Fill me up with silence. An arm around my shoulder, pulling me into a wet chest. Murmurs and whispers, nonsense words that don't help anyone or anything.

IT IS ALL USELESS.

His hands pull at the blanket, at my hands, prying me open, picking me apart, so his dark eyes can scan me. Right one still huge and swollen. Big hands, artist's hands, cradle my face, make me meet his eyes. He is forcing me to tug my sanity back down from the cloud it's floated up to. I resent him for it, try to pull away, but he holds me tighter, thumbs stroking the skin beside my eyes, like I'm some wild animal he's found injured by the side of the road.

On the pavement, on the street, by the huge, black dumpsters next to Hasan's shop. The rain is coming down hard, but no one seems to notice. The rain is air in England. We don't make special accommodations for it.

'It's going to be all right.'

No, it's not. It was supposed to be safe here. His arm is still around me, the pair of us rocking back and forth now with the force of my motion.

The cop drops to her heels before us, eyes appraising me then flicking towards Adam. 'We need her to tell us what she saw.'

Shaking my head, I rock harder, pushing my face into my knees again. I can't breathe here. I can't breathe anywhere.

'She can't speak.'

'Can't speak?'

'No. Could she write it down instead?'

I'm shaking my head, but it's all so useless.

'They need to know what happened,' Adam says against my ear, one hand moving up and down my back so that the blanket crinkles and crackles, and I have to pull away to make it stop. I need silence. Why can't Adam understand this?

Shooting to my feet, I let the blanket drop and move to cross the street.

'Woah, woah, hold on,' Adam says, hand gripping my elbow. I jerk my arm away.

There are patrol cars parked outside the shop, lights flashing and bouncing off wet tarmac, blocking off the street so that no other cars can get in. An ambulance has its back open at the door to the shop. The lights are all on, everywhere. Imam Abdulrahman is there, hand clapped over his mouth as he talks to an officer. His beard is soaked. The rain comes down harder, like bullets or debris. A world coming to an end. There's a crowd swelling. A news van. A blood trail coming out of the shop. Adam holds me in place, arms locked around mine, like a lover.

The cop is back, shaking her head at Adam. She won't bother talking to me now. 'The detective says to take her to hospital for an evaluation.'

Shaking my head harder, I turn in Adam's arms, looking up at him, the panic so overwhelming it must be spilling from my eyes, seeping out of my pores. He nods over my head at the officer, saying he'll take me to the car. My body trembles. I can't go back to that place. To those tests and the pills and injections that make everything even fuzzier and the white walls and small, small rooms and all the things they want me to remember, the things they want me to put on display for them. I can't. Adam turns me back around. The cop is moving towards the crowd near the shop, her back to us, speaking into a device at her shoulder.

'Run,' he says, breath puffing against my ear.

I slip on the way home, feet sliding on wet pavement. I fall once, twice, hear someone calling me, but I just get up and keep running. *At the station, the asylum officer pronounced my name 'runner' and then laughed and laughed before saying, 'Well, I s'pose that's what you are.'* I run and run, flying over road and grass and rubbish. Around parked cars and dumpsters and homeless men huddled on street corners. At Dunkirk, there were big metal bins, and the men never let the fires in them go out, and when the children caught rabbits, the men would cook them, and the children would wail.

Adam catches up with me in the courtyard between the towers. He grabs my arm, pulling me to a stop and turning me around. I push him away, slapping and shoving. 'Easy, easy. It's all right. No one's going to take you anywhere. It's only me.'

He drags me, kicking and slapping, to the East Tower, pulling me into the little vestibule, and then into the waiting lift. I press myself back against the wall, arms folded across my stomach, bent at the waist, a pool of water forming on the floor at my feet. Trembling and soaked. It is all so useless.

In his flat, he ushers me into the bathroom, stripping off my wet jumper and jeans and shoes and socks with almost clinical efficiency. In my bra and knickers, he pushes me into the shower, blasting me with water that scalds though it is probably lukewarm at best. My legs will not support me, and I buckle to my knees, but Adam just lowers the showerhead.

Minutes pass before he turns off the water. I haven't stopped trembling (I'll never stop trembling), but he seems to have given up on this as a goal. Pulling me from the shower, he wraps a huge towel around me, rubbing hard and fast like he's drying off a child. He puts another one over my head, rubbing like Mama used to when we were kids and she had no more patience for us. Is she still doing that with the little ones, with Nada's children? Did they all make it? Do they know I think of them even though I don't want to? Do they think of me?

Adam dresses me in a dry woolly jumper that scratches my skin and a pair of sweatpants that are at least a size too small. He leads me to the sofa, pushes a mug of tea into my hands, but they don't work either and the tea dribbles over the edge, so that he has to take the mug back and hold it up to my lips for me.

I can't. I can't manage to do anything but sit there while my body shivers and my heart tries to climb out of my throat and launch itself across the room, out of the window, off the balcony, and up into the heavens. I don't want to be here any more. A shard of glass, sharp and thick, slashing into flesh, blood spurting like a punctured water pipe. A body draped in white, stretched out, loaded into the back of a truck, bound for the earth. Back home, Khalid was pulling babies from rubble. Death is the only peace. It is the only safety.

Adam puts whisky to my lips now. Three fingers in a heavy glass. It burns going down. I cough and splutter, but he shushes me and urges me to drink more. Says it'll make it better. 'Just trust me,' he says, and I laugh, a loud cackle that shocks him, the whites of his eyes gleaming in the dark flat.

I crawl away, off the sofa, to the floor, on hands and knees to the balcony door. 'Please. Don't be afraid.' *There is only fear, Adam. There's nothing else in life.* I press my face to the cool glass, watch the stuttering rain outside, and turn away from the booze he tries to pour down my throat. *It was supposed to be safe here.* My knees bounce and jiggle, and I push my hands into the floorboards and shake my head so my forehead hits the window over and over. Giving up, he drains the glass in one swallow, moves to the record player, and puts on something low and hard, clanging guitars and growling voices and heavy drums. He pulls out his bag of green fluff, rolls a joint and lights it, taking several long drags to get it going. He blows the smoke my way, like he hopes it will do what the alcohol hasn't.

I was supposed to be safe here. How much blood have I seen? How much blood is it possible to see? Blood from a bullet to the head, from concrete and dust and rocks falling on faces and chests, from hands split open by sharp, rusty metal, from a shard of glass to the neck, from gaping midsections ripped open by gunfire, from blisters bubbling on feet, from torn genitals, from punched noses and split lips, from slashed wrists and razors to arms and legs. How much blood is it possible for one person to see?

When the record is finished, he puts on another one. He sits at my side, blowing smoke at me, eyes darting to my face every few minutes as though to check I'm still here.

The dead are the only ones who know peace.

Adam sleeps on the floor at my side, curled up like a baby, knees tucked into his chest, hands pillowing his head. The third or fourth record has long since played itself out. The room reeks of weed, a putrid, fungal smell that I can taste in the back of my mouth. The wall at my back has given way to cradle me, like a cave or a grave or a big spoon to the little one Adam is positioned as.

The opposite wall vibrates, has been vibrating for untold hours now, a movement that I imagine I have caused. Water streaks line it, dark and thin. Shadows move in syncopated waves, from window to door, window to door, like they're trying to escape. A humming sound is falling into my chest – Poe's 'Silence' and saffron waters and rain that falls like blood. I press my hand there, fingers climb up to grip my throat, but I don't know where it's coming from. There are eyes everywhere. The people in the windows. They all see me. All those eyes picking me apart like vultures. The humming and humming in my chest is what will drive me mad. After all this time, after everything that's happened, this will be the thing to kill me. This humming in the caverns of my heart.

I turn my face to the ceiling, open my mouth, moving tongue and lips and throat, pushing the air out; maybe if I push hard enough, my heart will come out.

There are bodies in the ceiling, bodies under water. White faces, blue veins, wide-open eyes, hands bound, mouths gaping around strips of tape. Screams that no one can hear. Boys and girls and men and women and grandmothers. Ice-water trickles down the wall and into my mouth, into my spine, pooling around me. Hands bound, but more arms emerge from their sides, arms thin and wiry as tentacles. Ahmed's little arms, thin as tree branches. Khalid, white helmet cracked, with long arms that never brought pain. Icicle fingers scrape at my head, twirling the black strands of my hair, dipping into my open mouth. I don't struggle.

Maybe they will pull out my heart or freeze the humming or twist my tongue into something that will make a sound.

The light in the bathroom comes on, Adam silhouetted against the darkness, just a shape until I can focus. 'Jesus,' he breathes, eyes going wide. The floor is wet, streaky with blood, and he steps carefully until he can crouch at the door to the shower. The water beats down, hot water to drive out the ice in my veins. I have shaving razors in my hands. There are slashes, deep ones, on both forearms.

'What'd you do?' he mutters, hands landing on my shoulders, pressing against my biceps, hovering above the bloody trails. He turns off the water and pulls at my hand. 'Come on. It's all right.' I pull away when he reaches for me again. 'I'm not going to hurt you.' I push at him, moving my hand through the air in a writing motion. It takes him a moment to catch on, but when he does, he nods and leaves the room.

He comes back with a pad and pen, trying to coax me out of the shower before handing it over. I follow him, grabbing the pad and pen and sitting on the toilet while I write. The water and blood leave spots and smudges on the paper, water streaming off me onto the cold tiles below.

I saw Matt with the spray paint weeks ago i saw him through the window with spray paint

He reads it. Over and over, and I see the thoughts in his mind. I see him going over the last few weeks, remembering it all. The horror when it finally dawns is terrible, his face contorting and folding in on itself. He backs away until he hits the sink, staring from the paper to me and back to the paper.

'How could you?'

I shake my head, drops of water dripping onto the page, making it soggier and softer until it seems it might disintegrate in my hands. Through the red and black streaks and smudges, I write, *I couldn't.*

'A man died for this.' He doesn't read the pad, just shakes his own head, hands coming up to rub down his face and cup around his mouth. 'How could you not say anything? How could you not tell me? I thought we were friends.'

Friends, I think, bowing my head against his words, *you don't even know my name.*

'You could have told me. If you didn't want to get involved with the police, I would have done it! I would have gone to them! Why didn't you tell me? Why didn't you just fucking think of someone else for a change?'

He's right. I know he's right, and I drop the pad and paper and wrap my arms around my torso and sob. My guts are twisting and wringing themselves out, wrenching my insides. My body is tearing itself apart. The humming in my chest is a howl. A wail. A shriek. A siren. All the noise of the world is inside me. Every blast, every pop pop pop of gunfire, every crying mother and whimpering child, every crashing wave, every grunting and moaning man, every swear word yelled in every language of Europe, every asthmatic child dying in every poorly ventilated truck with huge wheels that crunch over gravel and dirt. They are all in me. I have swallowed them with the silence. I open my mouth, gag, press harder into my stomach, but nothing comes out, not even the bile bulging in my throat.

'Fuck.' He grabs a towel and drops to his heels before me. He continues to swear as he pulls my arms away from my body. Telling me how wrong I was, he presses the towel against the long cuts in my arms. He presses down hard and the coarse fabric stings, but I don't so much as hiss. He tells me how disappointed he is and how he can hardly believe the Voiceless and I are the same person. 'Actions are what matter. Not words. Not beliefs. If you believe in something, you have to act it, *loudly*. There are so many twats out there protesting and shouting about white power and creeping Islam, and they're ready to die for that! If you *don't* think that way, if you think it's bollocks, then you have to be out there too. You have to be protesting and fighting and willing to die for that too. Otherwise, they win just because they're shouting the loudest. Otherwise, people die.'

As if I don't know all the ways in which people can die for what they believe in.

He wets another towel and wipes my arms clean. Then, he presses the dry one against the cuts again. He tears off long strips of loo roll and wraps them around my arms, taping them down with random plasters he finds in drawers and otherwise empty medicine cabinets. And all the while he's talking about protests and fighting ignorance with sheer force if we have to and he can't believe I would stay silent on this, that I would let this happen. He says it's my fault. He says you have to live the things you believe in, you have to *be* those things you choose to be.

The People in the Windows

Ruth is holding court down below. The sun is shining on her, like she's on her own personal stage. She's talking to the people in the windows; they circle her in a silent, enraptured huddle. Tom is at her side, in his Sunday best, wringing his handkerchief as she speaks. I can't hear her – for once she isn't yelling her words. The father whose children visit twice a month stands there with his groceries, too stunned to lower them to the ground. There's the single mother with her tween son; she has an arm wrapped tight around his shoulders. Ruth gestures wildly, arms flinging every which way. Agitated and red-faced, she points in the direction of Hasan's then to my flat, but I'm backed up against the glass, and they can't see me.

The Juicer is returning from a run. He pauses at the edge of the group, listens for a moment, his beautiful features bright in the sun, then continues to the East Tower.

Throughout the day, the tenants absorb this new information, the news of the death of a man, and move on with their lives. The single father's children arrive, and he chases them around the courtyard for a while before loading them onto their bicycles and scooters and riding out of the estate. It's a sunny day, the rain forgotten. Yesterday has been washed away. There's a chill lodged in the wind, but it is a day to be exploited. The tween skateboards in the courtyard until his mum leans out of their window and shouts at him to take it to the park.

They feel safe.

New tenants move into the holiday let in South Tower B, second floor, flat one. Newly-weds by the look of it. He's large with milk chocolate skin and dark hair. She's pale with strawberry curls. The first thing she does is rearrange the furniture in the flat. She cajoles the man into helping her push the sofa away from the window and to the west wall, replacing it with the small beige armchair. She turns the dining-room table so it is parallel, rather than perpendicular, to the window. In the bedroom, she fumes about the direction the bed is facing, gesticulating with long thin arms while he shakes his head over and over again. She tries tugging the bed away herself, but it is too heavy, and besides, the wall she wants it on has a TV mounted to it. She pulls it out, peering behind it, and gestures again to the man, but he just starts laughing, big hand pressed to his belly. She's angered by this, holding her hands out as she yells, but he won't or can't stop. She shoves him in the chest, unable to move him, and finally cracks a smile, which turns into a full-throated laugh that I imagine sounds like a lovely, silver bell. He puts his arms around her, tugging her to the bed, where he lays her down and unwraps her like a Christmas gift.

In that flat, Hasan hasn't died.

Next door, Ruth is agitated all day. She yells at someone on the phone; in her emotional state, she loses her English and slides into that language I don't understand. Pots and pans smash against each other, against counters and burners, against the stainless-steel sink she must also have. At times, I think I hear Tom respond to something she says, but I can't find words in it. It's just the calming noises spouses make around one another, like how Mama used to coo at Baba when, instead of fixing something, he only made it worse. At one point, late in the afternoon, the television comes on, a fiery sermon in what I think is the same language Ruth was shouting in. It sounds full of rage and indignation. Maybe all languages sound angry when you don't understand them.

Adam's flat is dark and quiet. He left me there last night. Bandaged and clean, with another dry towel, he left. I wonder if he's back, if he knows I've gone.

Across the way, the Juicer enters his flat, carting a plastic bag that he drops on the coffee table. He jerks the curtains, but they don't close all the way, a slit visible so that I can see the hard, uninviting sofa. He plops down and tears into the plastic. Pulling out a carton, he opens it and rips off big chunks of roast chicken that he stuffs into his mouth. Over and over his thin, oily fingers dive into the carton and emerge with bright white chicken meat that he pushes past his greasy lips. He tears off the leg and bites into it, his other hand busy getting more white meat off the breast. Over and over he does this, until he's left with nothing but bones to suck on.

————————

```
This statement (consisting of one page signed by
me) is true to the best of my knowledge and I
make the statement knowingly. I understand that,
if it is tendered into evidence, I shall be
liable to prosecution if I have wilfully stated
anything which I know to be false.

Dated the 23rd day of July 2017

Signature
```

At 21.45hrs on Wednesday the 19th of July 2017 I
was in the shop called Maqbool on Forest Road.
There was no one there when I entered apart from
Hasan Siddiqui, the proprietor of the establish-
ment. I was in the left side of the shop, by
the drinks, when the three defendants entered. I
confirm that I did not know their names, but I
have seen at least two of them harassing the
Muslim community before, mainly at the mosque
next door to the shop.

The three defendants moved through the shop,
knocking objects to the floor and kicking cabinets. They made loud, racist remarks about the
proprietor, calling him a 'dirty Paki' and a
member of ISIS. The proprietor asked them to
leave, and then he threatened to phone the
police. The defendants ignored this and continued
to damage the inventory on the shelves. I hid
behind large sacks of flour and rice at the back
of the shop.

Defendant No. 2, whom I have described in the
attached document, knocked a large bottle of olive
oil off the shelf, which crashed to the floor.
Defendant No. 1, whom I have identified from
police photos, then picked up a large shard of
broken glass and approached the proprietor, who
had moved out from behind the till.

A physical confrontation ensued, involving the
three defendants pushing the proprietor to the
ground and beating him repeatedly. They hit him on
the head and kicked him in the stomach. Defendant

```
No. 1 slashed him repeatedly with the glass. I did
not see any other defendant holding a weapon. The
proprietor pleaded with them to stop.
    It was silent for some time. One of the defend-
ants swore at the other, and then all three left.
    I saw the proprietor, bloody and unconscious,
on the floor as I exited the shop. I ran to the
mosque and banged on the door until Imam
Abdulrahman emerged.
```

———————

The weather is in constant flux, summer is never able to get a firm grip on this city. Mornings are bright and sunny, the sky flat and blue, not a cloud or hint of grey. The single dad's kids take advantage of it, screaming through the courtyard by 7 a.m. with their plastic swords and bicycles. Around two or three, big clouds roll in, shrouding the towers in shadows. Flocks of birds roil about in the sky like clothes tumbling in a washing machine. Late in the afternoon, the sky grows pregnant and the breeze acquires teeth. By evening, the rain comes and umbrellas sprout on the walkways like mushrooms.

I don't leave my flat. I move through the rooms like a spirit, wandering into the kitchen to stare at the contents of my cabinets, to the bedroom to convulse beneath the duvet, to the bathroom mirror to check I'm still here, to the balcony to watch the sky and the people in the windows.

The old man across the way sits in his armchair spooning chunks of chicken from a bowl into his mouth. The spoon in his hand trembles so much that most of the broth ends up in his lap and it's just the white meat that makes it to his lips. Over and over, in the slowest motion possible. It takes a long time just to get one spoonful in, and then he chews and chews and chews, heavy jowls working to break down each chunk. I wonder that all that chomping doesn't loosen a few teeth and send them plunking into the bowl or into the back of his mouth to be swallowed down his thin neck.

I can't help watching them. I tell myself that watching these people is what got me into this mess to begin with, that everything was fine before, but the truth is I don't even remember a 'before'. Or rather, there are too many 'befores' to consider.

Two floors below the old man, Chloe sits on the sofa, laptop before her, typing manically. I wonder if she's planning another escape, one she'll actually go through with. I wonder what she thinks about what happened. If she even cares. People can only concern themselves with so much. It's not possible to care about all of it. Not all victims can be 'real people'. There doesn't seem to be anyone else in the flat, but her mum could be in her room curled up with another bandaged arm or something.

I play with the tape holding the bandages to my own arm. We hurt each other, we hurt ourselves. The pain is the same.

The new couple in South Tower B, second floor, flat one work fast. They only arrived yesterday (or was it the day before?) but already they have everything set up the way she wants it, even though they spent most of the time christening every surface of the flat. She seems to have accepted the bed's position, though she scowls at the television in that room whenever she passes it like she thinks the government might be spying on them through the screen.

In my wanderings, from living room to bedroom to balcony, I don't see Adam.

The old man is choking, and at first I have no reaction to it. It seems to me like a film or television show playing out before me. They, the people in the windows, are not real, just slideshows I watch to pass the time. He grips his throat with both hands, eyes bulging

225

in their sockets, white and thick with blood, but I don't move. I sit against my window and wait for the next scene. Mouth open now, head shaking from side to side. This is very good, but that's not how you dislodge food. He starts punching his own stomach with a weak fist, but that's not right either. It calls to mind a diagram I saw once, of how to help someone who's choking. The old man needs to stand up and ram himself into the side cabinet or the bar that separates the kitchen from the living room.

He's going to die too. Right there, right now. Anybody seeing him over there, alone in that flat all the time, knows it. There's no other way for this to go. Ancient man living alone, of course he's going to die there. He will probably be dead for days before anyone discovers him.

It will be the smell that tips them off. It's an odour that demands attention.

I gasp, gripping my own throat, lungs inflating, like I'm coming up from under water. Scrabbling to my feet, I run out of the flat and race down the stairs. I take them two at a time, lunging to each landing, heart pounding, breath whooshing in and out of my lungs.

I burst out of the building and run to South Tower A. I yank on the front door, but it's locked, so I start hitting the buttons for all the flats indiscriminately, but it's the middle of the day, the middle of a beautiful day, and no one is home. Backing up, I look up to the open window on the second floor, flat three.

Opening my mouth, the air comes out in an explosion of sound. 'CHLOE!'

I grip my belly and release the sound again. 'CHLOE!'

The sound of my voice is foreign to my ears, alien on my tongue.

Her head pops out of the window, eyes narrowing then widening when she sees it's me. I gesture frantically at the door. 'Card!'

She doesn't throw it down for me to catch, not the way she and

Matt do for the Dad. Instead she disappears into the flat, and I'm left turning circles on the pavement, looking for anyone with a mobile or access to the building, thinking the old man must be dead by now. I press all the buttons on the door panel again, praying someone will buzz me in without wanting to chat about it.

Chloe emerges from the stairwell and opens the door. I push past, knocking her into the wall, and race up the stairs, panting and using the railing to pull myself up the four flights while Chloe follows. She asks what's wrong and what's happened and what I'm doing, but I can't answer any of her questions and keep enough air in my lungs to manage all these steps at the same time.

We get to the old man's door and it's not locked, opening wide when I turn the doorknob, so that Chloe and I fall into the flat.

'Fucking hell,' she says, slapping a hand to her mouth.

'CALL!' I shout, moving into the room.

The old man is on the floor, face down in front of the telly. He's not moving, and when I turn him onto his back, I see he isn't breathing. His face has a bluish tint, eyes squeezed shut like he doesn't want to see what's next for him. His hands are still wrapped around his throat.

I don't know what to do. I don't know if I should try to prop him up, get behind him and do that manoeuvre from the diagram, or if it's too late for that. Chloe is on the phone, barking out the address and flat number and telling them to hurry and I need to do something other than sit here thinking about what to do.

Fisting one hand over the other on his chest, I start doing compressions, pushing down and letting his chest rise, pushing down and letting it rise. All I have to go on is what I've seen on television, and I don't know if I'm doing more harm than good.

'Shouldn't you do mouth-to-mouth?' Chloe says, peering into his blue and white face.

'Choking.'

She looks things up on her mobile and starts shouting instructions at me – 'You should look if you can see the food in his mouth' and 'it says to hit them on the back, shall we try to lift him?' But all I do is increase the pressure, pushing down hard on his spongy chest, thinking if I can just keep the blood pumping, if my fists can be his heart for just a little bit longer, the experts will show up and fix it. I can feel tears on my face. They blur my vision, but I don't stop to wipe them. My whole body is in each movement, pressing down and releasing, down and releasing, down and releasing.

It takes no time at all for someone to die.

When the paramedics arrive (it feels like hours later), nothing has changed. I haven't stopped, but there's no change in the old man. If anything he looks paler. I am moved out of the way by gentle hands, placed in an armchair by Chloe while they affix a mask to his face and begin pumping air into him and doing all the other things they do that convinces people that everything will be fine.

The bowl of stew lies upside down on the floor, the carpet soaked in broth.

They put him on a stretcher and wheel him away.

39

The Rising Dawn

The sky is the colour of pavement, of dirty water, of Ruth's cardigan and Tom's eyes. It is no colour at all, really.

I have lost another day or so. That much I'm sure of. Days, and I don't know where they go. Like the time in Gaziantep where each day seemed like the last. Like wet tents under wet skies in winters that smelled of despair. Like detention centres – what crime had I committed to warrant those days and nights of cold, of hunger and thirst that would never leave me? Like Dunkirk and that filthy beach and they tell me it was twenty-six nights, but I can only recall six or seven of them with any kind of clarity.

There's been movement in the old man's flat. People come in and out. They look through the mail and pack things in bags and sniff at cheese and milk from the fridge before tossing them into large black bin bags. A man and a woman. I think the man might look like the old man, but I can't be sure. The woman rubs his back a lot. Easy gestures of comfort.

I sit on the floor, back against the wall and watch the sky change colour, or I sit on the balcony in the wind that's getting a touch too cold to sit in, or I lie in bed and writhe with my collections of Poe, or I scribble black, black lines on blank paper. And the time passes. Like always, it passes.

Ruth finds me on the balcony. She comes out onto hers, heaving a big sigh, turning this way and that, and with the 'that' she finds me, in my place, huddled up with the cold window at my back. She makes a noise in the back of her throat, but it's one I can't decipher, and her bird eyes turn to scan the towers and the windows and the people in them. Her gaze lingers on South Tower A.

'Cursed, that place is,' she says, shaking her head over that way as though wishing she could lob her disapproval into the air to sail into any open windows. She chews on her lower lip then smacks it with the upper one before adding, 'There is no use pretending. The girl told me you can hear. Speak as well.'

I don't say anything. Not to try to disabuse her of this notion, but simply because I have nothing to say.

She harrumphs, an annoyed sound like my grandmother used to make when we were underfoot while she stuffed and rolled vine leaves. 'Well, maybe you like to know the old man still lives.' I turn to her, eyes wide and begging for more information. 'His son was leaving the building the other day with some things and I spoke with him. He thanks you.' Her gaze focuses on me, full of questions or judgment or all those things that fill her mind. I lower my eyes to my lap. 'He's in coma, and they will see.'

Coma. A man that old. Death would have been more merciful. I twist my fingers and wonder.

'There is service at the mosque later. For Hasan. You should be with your people.' I glance at her, but she's looking over at the tower again. I have no people. 'This whole block, cursed.'

Wrapped in thick jumpers, like they will protect me from anything or perhaps render me invisible, I make my way across the courtyard. It's quiet; the little shrubs and hedges are beginning to die away. Another march through the end of summer and into autumn and on to another long winter. I pause at the East Tower and look up at the third floor, flat two. No-Lights-Man has No-Lights-On. It's dim and cold from what I can see. I wonder where he is, what he's doing, what all I've lost.

It seems quite impossible that I should still be losing things.

I cross over, through the courtyard and out to the street. Then down the block, away from the park, my feet take me to Hasan's. At various points during the days that I've lost, my mind has tried to convince itself that it wasn't real, that that night didn't happen. It was all a terrible dream that my mind, with its marshes and dark corners, conjured. None of it happened. It was stress and confusion and worry that brought it into being, nothing else.

The shop is closed. The Maqbool sign turned off, door locked. I pause and read the note affixed to the inside of the glass.

We mourn the passing of a great man. Hasan Siddiqui was a beloved member of our community. He was active in mosque activities and was always prepared to help. He treated us like family, and we are very sad to have lost him to this senseless act of violence.

We will have a service, led by Imam Abdulrahman, at the mosque on Wednesday beginning after the Asr prayer (app. 6 p.m). Every friend of the community is welcome to join.

Next door, there are lights strung up in the black iron gates – twinkling blue and white and yellow lights. There is a banner that says 'Welcome', but it is leaning against a far wall rather than hanging up for all to see. People mill about the courtyard, waiting for the prayers inside to end. Standing outside the gate, I hear their whispers and conversation.

'I still can't believe something like this happened here.'

'He never bothered anyone.'

'It's not right.'

'It's all the politicians' fault. They're the ones making us hate each other.'

'This is only the beginning.'

'Aye, seems like it.'

There are members of the community – old mothers and fathers and aunties and uncles and grandmothers and grandfathers in their mourning colours. Children chase each other around the courtyard, screaming with laughter until one of the adults grabs hold of them and starts twisting ears. There are non-members too. Curious university students, mums and dads cradling babies, proprietors of businesses that share the same block and customer base. I see the Ginger Giant from the bookshop. He stands, arms folded over his chest, looking uncomfortable and alone. Everyone mills about the courtyard shaking their heads and casting nervous glances around as though some other calamity is about to strike.

Nowhere is safe.

When the prayers are done, Imam Abdulrahman comes out onto the steps beneath the archway and the larger-than-life block letters that say الله and smiles big and wide. He holds his arms out and says, 'Come in, all, please. You are welcome.'

The rain comes down, hard and unannounced, at his words, and we move forward as one mass. Some community members murmur, '*Allahu Akbar*,' glancing up at the sky, and some non-members drift away. Most of us shuffle in though, quiet and with bowed heads as we cross the threshold.

Inside the mosque is warm and dry, and there is a sudden expansion in my chest, as though something is attempting to break free. Tears pool in my eyes. I can't breathe, and yet I am too full. The floor is covered in blue, white and grey carpets, from wall to wall. Prayer rugs are rolled up against the walls and Qurans lie open on wooden stands. Men and women sit on their knees, hands up, palms turned towards their faces, in the aftermath of their prayers. The walls are unadorned, but the high windows are stained glass. A deep royal blue, like the mosque in Istanbul Baba took us to once when we were very young. Five- and seven-petalled flowers, one in each window, line the perimeter. Their centres are dark blue, the shade lightening and lightening to white tips.

More and more people file in. The white people, the non-Muslims, people coming in off the street, pushing in and filling up the cavernous room. It looks bigger than it ought to be, like the exterior is an optical illusion. It looks like Imam Abdulrahman could hold the whole world here. I move with the crowd, down the lines of prayer rugs, to the opposite wall, letting myself sink to the ground. The imam stands at his pulpit, a small smile on his face. Every so often he nods at someone he knows or puts his hands out in a gesture, inviting everyone to sit. One by one, the people lower themselves to the ground, cross-legged or on their knees or leaning up against the wall or against each other.

There is murmuring and coughing and shuffling of feet and jingling of bag chains and key chains, but eventually everyone settles down, quiet faces turned towards the imam.

'A recitation first, I think,' he says, turning to the man at his left.

I've never seen him before. A young man in grey trousers and a dark blue shirt with a black and white checked *keffiyeh* draped across his shoulders sits before a wooden stand, on which sits a massive Quran. There is a microphone set up before him, but he has no need for it and no one turns it on.

His voice rings out, pure and light and calm. He does *al-fatiha*, and many of the congregation recite along with him under their breath. My recitations happen in my chest. Then he does *al-ikhlas* three times in succession, a blessing for Hasan. Finally, he does *al-falaq*. This last one, he draws out. His pronunciation is perfect. It is an Arab voice speaking Arab words from a native tongue. He could be from Aleppo, so exact are the syllables and accents on his words.

> 'Say, I seek refuge in the Lord of the Dawn,
> From the evil of that which He has created,
> And from the evil of the darkening when it spreads,
> And from the evil of those who blow in knots,
> And from the evil of an envier when he envies.'

I cry – and even here, I make no sound – face in palms, bent at the waist, as words I've not heard in years, in lifetimes, wash over me.

If you believe as Muslims do, the Quran is the word of God, undiluted and uncorrupted. It is the miracle sent to a people who found divinity in language, who marvelled at the potency of oratory, who thought words to be totems of power. Like Moses with his magic and Jesus with his healing hand, a miracle is often needed to bring the people over into belief. To have these verses issue from the mouth of a semi-literate merchant must have seemed quite the marvel, an unequivocal sign of communication with the divine. And despite the ten or so years before anyone bothered to write it down, despite human fallibility, it is believed to be the unadulterated word of God.

I don't believe in much of anything any more, but the verses are beautiful and soothing and the discomfort in my chest eases a little more with each rise and fall of his intonation.

When he finishes, there is silence in the mosque. I lift my head and with blurry vision take in the rapt faces of those around me. White, brown, black, with straight noses and bulbous ones, curly hair and straight, covered and exposed, they all blur into one mass of living, breathing beings. The imam shares a low word with the young man, a large hand on his shoulder, thanking him and bowing his head repeatedly. Ceremony of gratitude done, the young man comes down from the raised area and takes a seat with the rest of us.

Imam Abdulrahman has no need for a microphone either.

'Welcome, everyone,' he says, his booming sermon voice, in that heavily accented English, vaulting over us all. 'Thank you for coming to remember a wonderful man and friend to all of us. Many late nights I spend with Hasan in his shop when he wanted to stay open a little more in case someone was needing milk or bread or sugar or tea. It is a terrible loss for all of us. Some have asked me, and I will tell you that Hasan is on his way home with his family. They ask me to tell you how they are grateful of your thoughts and prayers in this difficult time. We are all shocked by this. We do not support violence in any way, and we do not deserve this aggression.

'These are trouble times, my friends.' The imam's dark and shining eyes pass over us. 'There is too much hate, too much anger, too much ignorance. This is not the way of Allah. It is not the way of Abraham or Moses or Jesus or the Buddha or any of the gods of India. Do you think Jesus will be okay with killing an innocent man? A man whose only crime is selling us too many excellent sweets?'

A gurgle of laughter ripples through the crowd, tentative and quiet, like a breeze or whisper of wind. I look around at all these people, all of them quiet sponges absorbing his words. Adam is standing at the door, arms crossed, brow low. My heart turns over in my chest. I can't read his face. It's quiet too, like the people. Not happy. Not sad. Just present.

'No god you believe in will be okay with this. You must do to others as you want them to do to you. That is it. That is all of it.' His eyes seem to scan us all, one by one. 'There is nothing else which matters. This is what all of the great religions of the world tell us.

The Quran says, many times, *You have received this message before!* Over and over Allah says this is the same truth that was given to all of the prophets before Mohammed, Peace Be Upon Him.' A chorus of 'Peace Be Upon Him' moves through the congregation, the non-members glancing around and murmuring to one another before facing forwards again.

'We are one being. All of us. You are not made any differently than I am. And these religions of ours are nothing but languages. You speak in English, I speak Punjabi, he speaks French, she speaks Japanese or Chinese, but we all say the same thing. These religions, they are words, only a language. Jews, Christians, Hindus, Buddhists, we are all saying the same thing. Your humanity and my humanity are the same. We are of one being, one value. All of us equal, all of us the same.'

When the imam is finished, there is silence, then a small smattering of applause and a chorus of *Ameen* and groans from the elders as they regain their feet. Imam Abdulrahman inclines his head, hand on chest and invites everyone to a buffet of food being served outside under the tents and canopies in the courtyard. Adam turns and heads back out. It would be just like him to stand in the courtyard with the others, commiserating and reassuring and telling them all about his plans to march all over the country, maybe all over the world.

I can't face him, so I stay where I am, against the wall, eyes shut, waiting to be alone again.

I wonder about what the imam said, about religion and language and all of us being the same. And if religions are all the same, then why did they come down in the first place? Why not just come down once and be done with it? Why the reformers and divisions and sects and schisms? I can't conceive of the point of it all. The only reconciliation I can think of is that we were not made in His image, but rather we projected ourselves into the heavens. Seeking assurances, seeking incentives for morality, seeking meaning, we twisted ourselves into all sorts of knots of belief. In our attempts to grasp what cannot be grasped, we spun out all these languages with which to beat each other.

A tap on the wall by my head. And I look up into the benign, sad eyes of the imam. He is in true mourning. Not the mourning of a religious leader for one of his flock, but the mourning of a friend. The lines on his face are deeper than usual. There are dark crescents above his gaunt cheeks and his features are arranged in an expression of concern.

'*Salam*,' he says, inclining his head again.

Yes, you do come in peace, I think, nodding back.

'You are recovered?'

This startles a loud laugh out of me. Is there any such thing as recovery? When life has been nothing but cumulative, recurring trauma – thirst, hunger, cold, poor, weak, hot, ill, battered, bruised, broken limbs, blood, blood, blood – can recovery ever happen in any meaningful way?

'That night was difficult for you,' he says. 'I am sorry for what you have seen, but I thank you for telling the police. Now, perhaps these men will not hurt again.'

I shake my head. I do not deserve thanks.

'We should feel sad for them. We should pray for their souls.' He looks to his small pulpit, as though mentally composing his next sermon. Turning back to me, his black stone eyes meet mine. 'You are afraid.'

I nod, chewing on my bottom lip.

'You came to this country for the same reason I did, I think. For safety, security. This was our big error, you see?' he says with a small smile, like he's sharing a secret. 'There is no safety. It's useless to search for it here or there or anywhere.' His hands reach out to indicate the mosque, the city, the country, the world. 'Your safety will come later. Much later, Allah willing. It will come for you in the afterlife.'

I turn my face away, but he keeps talking, as though he's forgotten that as far as he's concerned I'm deaf, or maybe that it doesn't matter and he's on autopilot and once he begins in this vein, he has no choice but to see it through until the end. An occupational hazard of the religious leader, I think.

'In paradise, you will want nothing. You will have comfort. Your loved ones, all will be there to welcome you. There will be no pain, no terror, no doubt. So our fear here is pointless, you see? You have survived many things. I see it in your eyes. You have continued moving. But still you might be brought down tomorrow by lightning, by a bus,' he shakes his head, 'by sharp glass. The only safety is in paradise.'

I return my eyes to his face, to the blinding certitude there. Where does that certainty come from? Do they teach it to him in imam school? How can he be so hopeful?

'The ground there is firm,' he says. 'It is very firm.'

———————

There's movement in South Tower A, second floor, flat three. Helen moves around the kitchen. Not her mindless scurrying; today she's full of purpose. There's a big box open beside her that she dumps things in – tins of food, utensils, mugs that she wraps in newspaper. In the living room a suitcase is open, full of clothes and shoes and books. In Chloe's room another suitcase is open on the bed, and Chloe rushes around throwing more clothes and shoes and things into it. Makeup palettes, electronics, a curling iron, little beaded necklaces and bracelets, all of it gets dumped indiscriminately into the case. By the door is the holdall, zipped shut and bulging at the seams. She turns in place, Chloe does, and sees me across the way. She freezes, then takes two steps forward, and then her hand comes up in a little wave, a small smile on her face. I raise my own hand even if I can't quite manage a smile. She mouths something, but I'm not as good at reading lips as people seem to think I am, so I shake my head with a shrug. She holds up a finger then turns to her desk. Rummaging through it, she tosses pens and pencils and folders and Sellotape here and there, disembowelling it until she finds what she's looking for. She returns to the window cradling a large notepad and black marker, head down, hair in long strings obscuring her face, as she writes on it.

WE'RE LEAVING! MUM'S LEAVING HIM!

She presses it against the window, bouncing on her feet, a huge smile sweeping her features. I give her a thumbs-up, managing to combine it with a tight grin. She doesn't see though because she's writing more now.

SHE SAYS IT'S TOO DANGEROUS AND WE HAVE TO GO NOW. SHE'S NOT TELLING DAD, NOT EVEN LEAVING HIM A NOTE! MATT'S ALREADY GONE TO MY UNCLES IN MANCHESTER BUT MUM AND I ARE GOING UP TO BERWICK. ITS BRILLIANT THERE.

I nod to show I understand and give her another thumbs-up. She bounces a few more times, looks at the pad like she might have something more to say but decides against it. One more wave, and then she rushes to the other room to help her mum.

I watch them pack everything up, pleased to see Helen isn't leaving him with much; she takes towels and sheets and blankets and books and toiletries from the bathroom and fake flowers and vases in the living room and the photo albums – all the little things that make up a life. Chloe moves things out of the flat, struggling to get them

239

across the courtyard towards the car park. The single dad and his children are back, and they pause their game of tag to help – the boys wanting to show Chloe how strong they are, arguing over who gets to carry the holdall until their father tells them to stop, taking it himself and heading off to the side. Chloe struggles with a big cardboard box, and then Adam is there to help. I sit upright, moving forward to press my face against the cool iron of the balcony railing. He's much taller than she is, and he takes the box, then stoops to listen to what she's telling him. He nods and nods then a big smile lights up his face so that you almost can't see the bruised cheek or lip or still slightly swollen eyes. He lights up with pure joy, laughing at something she says as he hitches the box further up his body and walks with her to the car park. She returns alone, going back up to the flat to get more things.

When it's done, they stand in the courtyard and look up. Helen has an arm around her daughter, Chloe touches her head to her mother's. What was their home is dark and quiet and innocuous. In a few weeks or months maybe, new tenants will move in – maybe a family who will fill the space with happiness, maybe another set of newly-weds who will have sex constantly and in every room, maybe a bachelor who'll host loud parties filled with loud men. They will fill the flat with their experiences and will have no knowledge of what was there before. Rooms do not hold on to the horror that was lived in them. It's silly superstition to think they do. They have no need for lingering terror or the residue of panic or the vapours of resentment.

We carry these things in ourselves, in the rooms and boxes of our hearts and minds.

40

Où Est la Frontière?

Dear all,

Please find attached my short story, titled 'Sweet Dew', that I am submitting for your consideration for the Short Fiction Award. It is complete in just over 3,000 words.

Bio:

I am a twenty-six-year-old Syrian refugee who has been granted asylum in England. I came to this country after a long and arduous journey. 'Sweet Dew' may be a fictionalized account of one portion of this struggle, but it is the reality faced by many of us who have made and are making the journey.

I am studying for a degree in political science. My writing has appeared in The New Press *magazine, under the byline The Voiceless.*

I read the email two, three, four, countless times.

I read it out loud, just to be sure that day with Chloe wasn't a fluke. My voice is raw and much too loud in my small living room. It's a struggle to push out the syllables and air, but I try. I keep trying until words and then whole sentences come out. Massaging my throat, I read the email over and over again. At first, it is my grandmother's voice, tired and rusty from years of hookah use. Then, it is my mother's voice, strong and high like when she was yelling at us children to stay together, to always stay together. On my desk are printouts of my articles, and I read these too, tasting the familiar words on a tongue unfamiliar with producing them. I read 'Silence', shouting lines to the ceiling, and imagine Poe sitting against my wall with a smile on his face.

At my laptop, I delete words from the email and replace them with others, reading these new words out loud too. Along with the document containing the story, which I have looked at and edited until I cannot look at it any longer, I attach the receipt showing that I've paid them to read my story. I end the email with 'Best wishes' then 'Warmest regards' then 'Best' then I add 'wishes' to it again.

I use my name.

And I copy Josie.

Summer is gone, and it feels as though winter is already here. There seems to be no autumn to speak of. We haven't seen the sun for days. Only rain and wind and dark skies, and Hasan's remains closed. I heard people in the courtyard of the mosque that day mention a shop like ours that's a twenty-minute walk away and which is run by a second or third cousin of Hasan's, so some of us have been going there for our bread and milk and orange drink and cheese.

Josie is pleased with me. She sent a long email in which she speaks as though we are only just becoming acquainted with one another, as though we are starting fresh. She says she wants an actual meeting. She invites me to London or offers to come to wherever I am. Her tone is giddy and bubbly and she asks for more pieces and whether or not I'm contemplating writing a book and that I should really consider it and she knows people in publishing who would be interested in such a narrative.

It is overwhelming, and I don't know how to feel about it.

I cannot change what happened to Hasan, the way I failed him.

I cannot go back and tell someone about Matt and the spray paint. I don't know that it would have made any sort of difference. Mr Big Man and his friends were violent. The possibility of this outcome was there from the day they stormed the mosque gate. Does that absolve me? No. It doesn't change anything. Hasan is gone and his family is in mourning and Matt got away with his not-so-petty crime and life is just this thing that breaks apart and that you have to keep trying to put back together.

Neither can I change what's happened to me, what it took to get me here. And if I ever see them again, I know I won't be able to make Baba see that it was the best decision I could have made *for me*, that his protection was unnecessary in a world that is not, in any way, safe. The old rules no longer apply. Perhaps they never did. The systems have been uprooted and we are all now just blowing loose in the wind. On the bigger boat, up the Grecian coast, a man sat beside me, face in hands, fingers rubbing at the prayer mark darkening his forehead, and said, *It's better if you're alone*, and I knew what he meant. Family units of thirty, forty, fifty people – all important, all nucleus – how can you hope to keep them all together? How can you keep them safe? At least on my own, I did not have to worry about other mouths to feed, did not have to worry about Mama's blood pressure and grandfather's propensity for pneumonia and Uncle Sami's diabetes – all of us walking across Europe with nothing but our prayers.

If there is money to be made in these endeavours of mine, I will send some to them – through cousins and family friends scattered across the world whose online presence I follow with anonymous, ghost accounts. If there isn't, I will make my way somehow, in some way.

I find Adam by the buses, three big ones lined up in the car park behind the university's main campus. He'd left fliers all over the estate.

I found them taped in the lifts and on the row of mailboxes. They were scattered around the courtyard and affixed to lamp posts and left on the seat of the uncomfortable chairs in the laundry room down the block. I even saw some on one of the tables outside the mosque on the day of the funeral. They were bold, black and white, calling us all to action. An 'Army of Tolerance' he called it – and even here, there is the language of conquest – one that is ready and willing to show how pluralistic this country is and that racism and bigotry will not be tolerated. On the other side of the flier is a map of England, big red stars showing where each of the marches is taking place. There's a list of times and dates and meeting points and if any of those nationalist crazies want to disrupt the event, they will not need to try very hard to do so.

He has his hood up against the wind. Drowning in a long, military-style coat, he looks thinner than I remember. In big black boots with a fierce scowl on his face, I think he must be strong as a reed. Who is this man, defending people he has no personal connection to, defending them simply because it is the right thing to do?

He gestures here and there, directing people to different buses and crossing things off the list he has pinned to a clipboard. There are signs nailed to wooden sticks and rolled-up posters leaning against the sides of the buses. On some of them I see sketches done in Adam's precise and haunting style, all stark lines and careful strokes. Some people take signs, others have brought their own. Adam was right; there are a lot of university students here. Kids in jumpers with emblems plastered across the front or carting backpacks or wearing caps emblazoned with their university crest, they shout and laugh and shove each other. Jolly good fun. All these people, so excited to be doing something in a world they were told was theirs to inherit but which seems to be slipping further and further out of control.

Our eyes meet, and Adam pauses in the middle of giving an order to some younger man at his side. His eyes scan me, but I never know what he's hoping to see, what any of them are looking to see. Walking towards him, my heart pounds hard against my ribs. I haven't felt it in days, but now it thumps and thumps – as though suddenly remembering its function or simply to remind me it's there. The incessant beating of our hearts. When I stop in front of him, he traps the clipboard under his arm and takes my hands, holding them in one of his while he pushes the sleeves of my four layers of shirts and jumpers up, first one then the other. His cold fingers run over the skin of my arms, feeling the scabs of my healing cuts and searching out new ones. But there's nothing for him to find, and he releases a small sigh before looking me in the eyes again.

I have so much to say to him. In my flat, I had rehearsed our conversations, thought about what my first words ought to be. *Thank you. I'm sorry. Please forgive me. I hope we can still be friends.* Everything sounded trite and unnecessary and I hadn't been able to settle on anything.

Moments pass, and finally, with another sigh, he asks, 'Are you coming with us?'

I nod, a sudden terror filling me at the thought that perhaps I can only speak in the solitude of my own flat, with nothing and no one to hear me. Perhaps the silence is still there. Perhaps this is the new normal for me, and can it in any way be considered an improvement? I try to make some kind of sound, but Adam has turned away.

He grabs a rolled-up poster and hands it to me. 'Go on in that one, then,' he says, nodding towards the bus nearest us. I take the poster and coax my lips into something resembling a smile.

I take a seat near the front, by the window, the poster standing between my knees. In my mind are flashes of other buses, other protests, of posters in Arabic saying that it was his turn. I think of the people lost, too many to count, and whether what we did had any meaning at all. Firas, the hunter, leaving home because Baba could not beat the gay out of him. Khalid pulling people from the rubble when the barrels began to fall. Cousin Tarek organizing protests and getting detained for it, indefinitely. It's worse when you don't know if they're gone or not. Mama wailing that for your children to be interested in politics is a fate worse than death. Massacres, oppression, condemnation; how many years, decades, will pass before it's resolved? Our blood runs everywhere, down the streets of Aleppo, of Damascus, of Homs, of Calais, of Chios, of Bicske. All these people. All these lives. Not numbers and figures and pie charts. People.

Adam boards the bus and speaks with the driver for a moment, nodding and patting him on the shoulder. He turns and does a head count, smiling at the excited protesters. 'Conserve your energy. It's a long way to Manchester,' he says in response to their hooting and yelling.

He takes the seat beside me with a long sigh as the bus rumbles to life, wheels turning and crunching below us. He glances at me, eyes darting away from mine, like we are strangers or lovers who've shared an awkward first night together, and shrugs off his coat. 'You didn't think to bring one?' he asks, draping the thick, dark wool onto my lap.

I watch his movements, wait until he finally meets my eye.

'My name is Rana Halabi. It means "from Aleppo". I think the sun's meant to come out later.'

Acknowledgments

There are many people to thank for making this book a reality. My agent, Melissa Edwards, for championing my writing from day one. The teams at Borough Press and Algonquin Books for all the support they've shown. Ann Bissell, it's been a joy working on this second book with you, and I hope there are many more to come. Special thanks to Amber Burlinson for her thorough and sensitive copyediting. Betsy Gleick, thank you for your belief in this story, for all your insightful notes, and for bringing my writing to an American audience. My gratitude also to Ben Fowler, Jen Harlow, Holly Macdonald, Christopher Moisan, Stephanie Mendoza, and Travis Smith.

As always, thank you to my friends and family for their firm and constant belief in me, particularly my mother for instilling a love of books in me from a very early age and my father for supporting my desire to write and study literature.

Last but not least, I must extend a special thank you to Faraj Alnasser, a young man from Aleppo, who, on a beautiful Sunday in Hampstead Heath, shared his story with an unflinching bravery and honesty. The joy, love, and hope with which you approach the world, despite all you've seen, is as great a testament as any to the resilience of the human spirit.